Also by Claire Boston

<u>The Texan Quartet</u>
What Goes on Tour
All that Sparkles
Under the Covers
Into the Fire

<u>The Flanagan Sisters</u>
Break the Rules
Change of Heart
Blaze a Trail

Change of Heart

The Flanagan Sisters # 2

Claire Boston

BANTILLY
PUBLISHING

DEDICATION

To my sister-in-law, Shelly

Chapter 1

Carly Flanagan really couldn't appreciate what accounted for modern art these days. She stared at the canvas in front of her, keeping her expression blank. There were several splotches of color, as if the artist had flicked his paintbrush at it haphazardly. The price tag was in the four figures. She suppressed a sigh and moved on to the next painting, which was more of the same. She didn't know why she'd agreed to sponsor the exhibition.

That wasn't true. She knew exactly why – her younger sister Zita had asked her to. The problem was, Zita was too kind-hearted and people took advantage of her. As soon as they discovered she was Carly's sister, the requests started coming and Zita could never say no. Carly needed to start vetting some of Zita's requests – if she could find the time.

Taking a glass of sparkling water from a passing waiter, she moved to the next piece. She didn't check her watch, but figured she had about another hour before she could gracefully depart.

"It looks like someone vomited on the canvas." The deep voice was close to her ear and Carly looked up.

He wore a dark brown pinstriped suit that molded to his body, the jacket accentuating his broad shoulders. It was an odd choice for an exhibition opening where most people were wearing tuxedos and evening dresses. Her gaze reached his face. He was around her age – late twenties, early thirties – and his longish black hair had been smoothed back, with the occasional hair resisting the gel. Carly met his eyes – green, clear, and with a definite spark of mischief in them. Her heart stuttered and she refocused to recall what he had said.

"Art is in the eye of the beholder," she replied, losing her fight not to smile at him. She had to be careful. She'd learned early in this business not to trust what people said. He could be a reporter baiting her, or an artist looking to curry favor.

"I'd rather not behold that, especially at that price."

She agreed with him, but kept that to herself. "Then why are you here?"

"I like art," he said, gesturing to a different painting.

Carly followed the direction of his hand and her breath caught. It was a forest scene, with huge trees soaring to the sky, and a tiny cottage nestled below them, a puff of smoke coming from the chimney. She wandered closer and details jumped out at her. The chipmunk on a branch, the mountain lion almost hidden by some bushes, the small white flowers of a creeper twining its way across the porch. She could practically smell the forest.

It was peaceful, secluded, comfortable. It was a home.

The longing swept through her. She wanted it. Not just the painting, but the place. It whispered peace to her. She wanted to reach out and touch it, and had stretched her hand out before she stopped herself.

"What do you see?" the man asked.

Carly shook her head absently, still caught up in the painting. "Not see," she said. "Feel." She blinked and snapped out of her trance. Would he judge her?

The man's eyes were guarded. He raised his eyebrow and nodded for her to continue.

The temptation to tell him was strong. The way he looked at her, his full attention on her, waiting for her next words, made her want to trust him.

Then he smiled, a small, but knowing smile. Her whole body heated, and the shock of her reaction brought reality back into sharp focus.

No. She wouldn't expose herself further. Anything she said could be on the pages of a glossy magazine next week.

"Excuse me." Not waiting for his response, she strode across the room to the gallery owner, trying to get her heart rate under control. It was probably just her reaction to the painting. Men didn't affect her that way, not since Andrew. She shook her head. She'd put him behind her.

"Carolina, thank you for coming tonight and for your support." Stewart Williams was an older man with salt and pepper hair and impeccable posture.

Carly straightened at her full name, remembering who she was supposed to be. "You're welcome," she said, smiling. "It's a wonderful exhibition. In actual fact, I'd like to buy a painting."

Stewart blinked, but quickly recovered his composure, taking her by the elbow and leading her over to his desk. "Which one are you interested in?"

She hadn't noticed the name of the piece, or the price, so she pointed to it, relieved to see that the man she'd been talking with had moved on.

"An excellent choice," Stewart said, and excused himself to go and place a sold sticker below the artwork.

"Are you enjoying yourself, Carly?"

She turned to find Zita, looking gorgeous in a canary yellow evening dress with ruffles down the split like a flamenco dress. Her sister had inherited the height and strawberry blonde hair from their Irish father, whereas Carly was the spitting image of her Salvadoran mother.

"I've bought a painting," she said, not quite believing it.

"Cool. Which one?"

Carly gestured toward it.

"That's one of Evan's," said Zita. "Have you met him yet?"

"Your neighbor?" He was the reason Zita had asked Carly to support the exhibition.

"Yeah." Zita scanned the area. "He's over there."

She took Carly's hand and dragged her across the room before Carly could refuse. She never knew what to say to artistic types, and certainly didn't want to discuss why she'd bought one of his pieces. She was still trying to figure out a way to get out of it when Zita stopped in front of the man in the brown suit.

"Evan Hayes, meet my sister, Carly," Zita said, dropping her hand and beaming at him. "She bought one of your paintings."

He was the artist? This man who had scoffed at other artists' work and asked her what she thought of his? What game was he playing?

"We met, though we didn't exchange names." He smiled a little sardonically at her. "I hope you enjoy the painting."

Carly nodded, not trusting her voice. She had a feeling she'd been played.

"Evan not only paints, but he also draws and does graphic design. I don't think there's a medium yet invented that he can't work with." Zita was clearly oblivious to the tension between them.

"I imagine each medium has its own challenges," Carly said.

Before Evan could answer, Zita said, "Oh, there's Rebecca. I have to catch her." She hurried away.

Carly wanted to throttle her sister for leaving her with this man. She had to extricate herself.

"It's all just putting an image down on canvas," Evan said, and she realized he was responding to her previous comment.

Curious in spite of herself, she asked, "Isn't it easier getting the color you want using paint rather than pencils?"

"Sure, but there are always workarounds."

"Like what?"

"You can layer color, and darken or lighten it using white and graphite. There are heaps of techniques." He shrugged. "It just takes practice and patience."

He didn't speak like a lot of artists she'd met. Most of them liked to wax lyrical about their method and the difficulties of getting the right depth of color so the image came off the page. He made it sound like it was just part of the job. She moved over to another of his paintings on the wall. "What was the hardest thing about this one?"

He gave her a half smile, and then faced the painting. "Getting the idea."

Her heart beat a little faster at his smile. She frowned, ignoring her physical reaction. "The idea?" Didn't he paint what he saw? "Did you make it up?" She'd always assumed landscape artists looked at a setting and then recorded it.

"I wanted to paint something fun, but not frivolous." He stepped next to her, not touching, but close enough for her to be very aware of his body heat.

She crossed her arms and examined the painting. It was a beach scene in the height of summer. People were gathered in groups along the sand; some were young families with children building sand castles, others were teenagers trying to look cool, and there were a few older couples reading books or people watching. At the edge of the water, people waded, a father helped his young daughter to swim, some kids splashed about, and further out, there were surfers waiting for the next wave. Carly could almost smell the salt air, and feel the heat from the sun and the sand beneath her toes. Many people would look at the painting and see fun, but it reminded her too much of El Salvador when her father was still alive, and the time he took the whole family to the beach for a special day out. All she saw were days that would never be again.

"You don't feel it," Evan said. "You feel something else."

She didn't like him being able to read her so well. She had spent years sculpting her public persona. She'd thought she had perfected the confident, polished lie.

"Old memories," she said, and looked for a way to escape.

He took hold of her hand. "Don't run away again."

Carly faced him, the warmth from his hand moving through her body. He was watching her, calmly waiting to see how she was going to react. Part of her wanted to step toward him and draw comfort from his touch, but her sense of self-preservation kicked in, warning her not to trust. He hadn't actually lied earlier, but he also hadn't been upfront.

"I need to keep mingling." She withdrew her hand from his. "I enjoy your work, Evan."

She moved away before he could say anything else, and was promptly approached by a woman wearing a brightly colored dress that was very much like the vomit painting, only on fabric.

"Carolina, let me introduce myself. My name is Isobella Carmichael. I wanted to thank you so much for sponsoring *my* exhibition."

This was the woman who'd done the paintings with all the splotches. Carly grinned, remembering Evan's comments. "Lovely to meet you."

"You bought one of Evan's paintings tonight. It's so very

kind of you to support the arts. Now, let me show you my works and explain the meanings behind them." She led Carly toward the wall of horror.

"I'd dearly love to, Isobella, but I'm afraid there are a few more people I need to talk to before I leave. You know how it is – responsibilities."

Isobella frowned. "But you spent all that time with Evan."

"Yes." Carly had learned not to explain herself. "Excuse me." Spotting someone she knew, she made a beeline for him.

"How are you, David?" Even with her four-inch heels, she had to crane her neck to look him in the eye. He was over six foot with blond hair and blue eyes, and was as stylish as ever in his tuxedo.

"Carolina, so great to see you." He shook her hand and kissed her cheek. "I hear you had something to do with this exhibition?"

"Only a minor part," she said.

Carly had a soft spot for David Randall. He'd shown her the ropes when she'd first started going to charity events, helped her navigate through the deluge of requests that poured in after making her fortune in the IT industry. She could always rely on him to make accurate, if slightly inappropriate observations, which kept her amused. Plus, his family was wealthier than her, so she didn't have to worry about him hitting her up to support some cause or another.

"I hope you didn't choose the artists," he said, glancing toward Isobella's paintings.

Carly swallowed her smile. "Not at all. The artists are all from an arts center near where my sister Zita lives."

"Speaking of sisters, your other sister, Bridget, was the heroine during Dionysus's oil refinery incident last month. I didn't realize you were sisters."

"I never thought to mention it." She could hardly have told the son of the CEO how frustrated Bridget had been with his company.

"So," David said, glancing around, "do you think there are any available ladies here tonight?"

She laughed. "Always on the lookout." Though never one to commit. He always had a different woman on his arm.

He shrugged. "One day I might find someone who isn't interested in my money."

Carly understood completely. "There's probably a few. Zita's around somewhere with her friend."

"You'll have to introduce me later. I might go mingle over there. I'll see you later." He headed for a tall blonde woman in a red dress.

Carly would have found it funny if Isobella hadn't immediately started walking over to her. But someone else arrived first.

"Carolina!" the man declared. "You don't mind if I call you Carolina? Such a beautiful name. I'm not so fortunate – my name is Desmond. Have you had a chance to view my paintings yet?" He gripped her arm.

Carly gave him a pointed look and he relaxed his hold. "I haven't made it all the way around the gallery yet."

"Then let me show you."

She let him lead her over to a wall of abstract paintings, all gray and drab, and struggled not to cringe.

"This is my interpretation of the way industry is ruining the environment," Desmond began.

Isobella moved alongside Carly. "I have a similarly themed piece, if you're interested."

Desmond glared at her. "I'm sure you know, Carolina, that it's difficult for artists to get exposure, and we have such important messages to spread. So few people frequent art galleries these days." He tutted.

"That's why it's so wonderful that you've given local artists this opportunity to show their work to the wider community," Isobella said.

This was getting a little too much. It was definitely time for her to go.

"What we really need is a patron," Desmond added, appearing to have decided they had a better chance working together. "Someone who understands the importance of art."

Carly knew what was coming next. At least Evan hadn't been after anything.

Isobella nodded. "It's so difficult to earn a living from painting. One cannot simply dash out a canvas every other day.

So much thought and emotion must go into it."

"I'm . . . *we're* sure you understand," Desmond said, with a nod to Isobella.

"Indeed," Carly agreed. "When I started my first business I had a second-hand laptop and a big idea. It's a hard road."

"But there are people who can smooth the road," Isobella said. "People like yourself, who want to give back to the community and help others reach those heights."

"The Local Artists Center of Houston has been searching for someone to financially support the hopes and dreams of their members," added Desmond.

"We thought you might be that person," Isobella finished the spiel, as if she was offering Carly the biggest prize in the world.

Carly debated how she was going to respond. "What would be the terms of the agreement?"

Desmond and Isobella exchanged a glance.

"Terms?" Desmond asked.

She nodded. "I imagine you've written a business plan and have calculated how many years you will need a patron before you can sustain yourself? Send it to my office and I'll review it."

The eyes of both artists grew wide and Desmond's mouth moved, but nothing came out. Carly grinned on the inside.

Someone tapped her on the shoulder. As she turned, the smile crept onto her face and she suddenly found herself face to face with Evan. He winked at her and her smile widened. "Zita asked me to tell you it's time for your speech."

Carly was grateful for the excuse to get away from them. "Of course." She turned back to the still stunned couple. "Excuse me, I must go."

Evan fell in step with her as she walked toward Stewart. "I imagine those two were hassling you to be a patron for LACH."

"They made a request. Are you a member?" Was he letting them do the dirty work so he would appear to be the good guy? She acknowledged the naïve hope that he might be interested in her, before pushing it away. She knew better.

"I joined when I first moved to the area. Some of them are a little too pretentious for me, but meetings can be fun."

Carly understood, but it wasn't particularly professional for him to admit it.

They reached Stewart. "Carolina, we're ready to start. Why don't you come with me?"

She nodded to Evan and then followed Stewart to the small stage set up at the back of the gallery. He ran through the short program with her, and then stood on the stage to get everyone's attention.

Carly stepped to the side, forcing a polite, interested expression onto her face while inside, her stomach was churning. Getting up in front of all of these people was her idea of torture. She hated being the center of attention, and always felt she was being judged. She was too small, too rich, her accent was slightly wrong. It didn't matter that she'd lived in Houston for twenty-two years, she'd never lost the hint of her Salvadoran accent.

Regulating her breathing, she ran through her speech in her head.

"None of this would be possible without our generous sponsor, Carolina Flanagan."

Carly smiled and walked up the steps of the stage, nodding at Stewart before facing the crowd. She placed her hands either side of the lectern to stop them from shaking. "Thank you, Stewart," she said. "Many of you have heard the story of how I started my company with a laptop and an idea, which grew into the billion dollar corporation that it is today." She smiled at an older, blonde woman who nodded her head. "What you possibly don't know is that a lot of my success is due to luck."

There was a murmur through the crowd.

"I was sixteen when I wrote my first software program, but I didn't know if anyone would be interested in it, or how to sell it." She'd been happy coding, and so clueless about the industry. "Then I discovered that a huge software convention was going to be in Houston. My tutor bought me a ticket, because I couldn't afford it, and he went along with me." She'd been so desperately shy. There was no way she would have had the courage to talk with anyone there. "At the lunch break, he chatted to a guy who distributed software and he loved the sound of mine. After the event, I sent him the details and, before I knew it, the software had taken off."

Her eyes roamed the room and found Evan. She jolted at the intensity of his gaze and continued. "That's why I try to pay that luck forward. This exhibition displays some of Houston's local artists, who haven't had a chance like this before. There's always a possibility that an art critic or another gallery owner will see their work and it will be their big break. And so I would like to wish the artists the best of luck and thank you all for coming."

At the polite applause, Carly descended the stairs, as she worked to control her breathing. It was over.

"Nice speech, Sis," Zita said, giving her a hug.

"Thanks." Not even her family realized how much she hated public speaking. She'd been doing it since the beginning of her career, but it never got any easier. "Do you think anyone would notice if I slipped out now? I'm getting a bit of a headache." Or she would soon if she didn't get out of there.

"Of course, Carly. I'll give everyone your apologies," Zita said. "Go home, take some painkillers and hop into bed. Do you want me to call you a cab?"

Carly shook her head. "I'll be fine." The gallery wasn't far from where she lived and the walk would help clear her head. "I'll see you tomorrow for lunch." She skirted the crowd, keeping her eyes on the entrance and walking at a pace that showed she had a purpose. People were much less likely to intercept her if it looked like she had somewhere she had to be.

She was almost at the door when someone said, "Going so soon?"

She recognized Evan's voice before she turned to him. She suppressed a sigh. "Yes. Was there something you wanted?"

"I wanted to spend a little more time with you." His smile made her body tingle.

"Why?" The question was out before she could stop herself.

"You're a beautiful woman with great taste in art."

Even knowing his words weren't true, a rush of pleasure went through her. Beautiful she was not. Well-groomed, yes — she'd spent a fortune on a stylist, and the makeup and clothes to match her business persona, but it was all smoke and mirrors. "I'm not going to buy more of your work because you compliment me." Carly moved toward the door again.

He followed her out. "That wasn't my intention." He placed

a hand on her arm to stop her and when she turned, she saw annoyance in his eyes. "Have I offended you?"

He hadn't, but it was an excuse she could use. "You criticized your fellow artists and then showed me your work without admitting it was your own."

"I tease Isobella about her art all the time." He shrugged. "And I wanted your honest reaction to my paintings."

The confession made her pause. "It's hardly professional."

"You're right. My apologies. I should have been up front."

She nodded curtly to him and continued down the street.

"I meant what I said about wanting to get to know you."

More like her money. She wasn't going to be suckered into anything. "I need to get home," she said without looking back.

Carly strode down the sidewalk, tense, ignoring the twinge of disappointment when she realized he wasn't following. She was being ridiculous. Sure, he was handsome, but he only wanted her money. Andrew had taught her that.

"Wait!"

Her heart jumped. Should she wait for him, or keep going?

His footsteps on the pavement solved that decision as he jogged up next to her. "Are you walking?"

Surprised, she said, "Yes. I only live a couple of blocks away."

"At this time of night? I'm sorry, I can't in good conscience let you go alone. Can I walk with you?"

"Shouldn't you be schmoozing with the people at your exhibition?" She couldn't prevent the annoyance from slipping into her tone. She hadn't allowed anyone to stop her from doing what she wanted. She wouldn't have got where she was if she had.

"They'll be there when I get back. Can I walk you home?" It was a simple request, asked without any guile.

She wanted to say no, but she suspected he'd follow her anyway. She sighed. "If you want. But I'm not in any mood for conversation." There was something about him that made her forget her social graces.

His lips quirked in a smile. "Warning noted."

For the first block they were silent. Her footsteps ate up the pavement, eager to be away from him.

"I'm amazed how fast you can walk in those heels," he said as they crossed a road.

"Practice." Carly lived in her heels. Her height was a constant disadvantage, made people treat her like a child, and she'd quickly discovered that the four extra inches went a long way to gaining more respect. Plus, her stylist had forbidden her to ever wear flats for business.

Her apartment block was just up ahead. "This is me," she said as they reached the entrance. "Do you want me to call you a cab?"

"I'll manage."

She stood there for a second, not sure what else to say. "Thank you for walking me."

"Thank you for the company."

She frowned at him, not sure if he was making fun of her.

"Do you prefer Carolina or Carly?" he asked.

She blinked. She was Carolina for all of her business associates and work colleagues. Only close friends and family called her Carly.

"Carly," she found herself saying.

He nodded and smiled. "Goodnight then, Carly. Sweet dreams." He turned and walked back the way they had come.

Carly watched him for a minute. He hadn't tried to kiss her, and hadn't asked for her number. So much for wanting to get to know her. She'd been right to be cautious. Shaking her head, she stepped into her apartment building.

He was a strange man.

Chapter 2

Evan wandered back to the exhibition, the enigma that was Carly Flanagan firmly on his mind. She'd had such a visceral reaction to both of his paintings. She understood they were more than images on a canvas. But she didn't want anyone to know, anyone to see the real her. She'd fled when she'd realized she'd said too much.

Then there was her professional self. He'd seen Isobella and Desmond corner her, had admired how she had remained polite and patient – those two drove him crazy – and had arrived in time to hear Carly talking about business plans. He'd wanted to high-five her for so politely putting them in their place. There was going to be a *lot* of talk about it at the next LACH meeting. Evan grinned just thinking about it.

But she'd really blown his mind when she'd stepped on the stage for her turn to speak. She'd hated every minute of it, but he'd guarantee no one noticed. He'd almost missed it himself, would have if he hadn't been paying close attention to her. There was the tiniest tremor when her hands wrapped around the lectern and there was her measured breathing. Everything else was perfect, but the breathing was too perfect. How did the CEO of a billion dollar company fool everyone that way?

What it came down to was, he needed to know more.

He walked back into the gallery and Zita pounced.

"Where have you been?"

"I walked your sister home."

"She walked?" Zita's eyes narrowed. "I thought she was catching a cab."

"So did I until she strode off down the street. I wanted to make sure she got home safely."

"Thanks." Zita hugged him. "She doesn't always accept help."

"I didn't say she liked it," Evan said and Zita laughed.

"I'm surprised you could tell. Carly is nothing if not exceedingly polite all of the time."

He smiled. He'd obviously gotten under her skin a little, because she'd been annoyed at his offer. He took Zita by the arm and led her away from the door. "She must be busy. Do you see much of her?"

"Yeah, at least every second week for lunch. Both of my sisters come home. It's pretty much law in our house. You do *not* want Mama asking why you weren't there." Zita grinned.

"When's your next get-together?" He hated using Zita's open nature to get information, but he was unlikely to run into Carly at any other time.

"Tomorrow." She squinted at him. "Why all the questions?"

He ran a hand through his hair and shuffled his feet. "Promise you won't laugh, Z?"

"No."

He laughed. "She caught my eye, is all. I want to get to know her, but I don't imagine I'll run into her again."

She assessed him. "What about her caught your eye?"

"Aside from her incredible beauty? She felt something when she looked at my paintings. Not many people really get it." None of his family did. Feeling a little awkward, he added, "I don't think she shows that side of herself to many people."

She nodded. "You should come for lunch."

He blinked. "What?"

"Tomorrow. Lunch. My house, twelve o'clock. Perhaps Carly will catch more than your eye." Zita walked away.

Evan let out a breath. He hadn't quite been expecting that, but the idea thrilled him. It was a chance to see Carly again, and perhaps find out who she was at home. Though he wasn't sure how happy Carly would be.

"Evan!" Stewart called. "Another two of your paintings have sold. Let me introduce you to who bought them." He gestured toward a couple who screamed old money.

Evan went to schmooze.

***

Carly groaned as her alarm sang her awake. Her dreams had been so vivid, she felt as if she hadn't slept. And the worst thing was the leading man in her dreams had been Evan. She hadn't had a sexy dream like that in quite a while. She sighed and climbed out of bed, padding to the bathroom, and firmly pushing the remainder of her dreams from her mind. She wasn't likely to see him again. He might be Zita and her mother's neighbor, but the properties were so far apart she wouldn't even catch a glimpse of him.

She was fine with that.

He was too unsettling.

After making herself a coffee to go, she drove to Bridget's place. Bridget and her partner Jack came out of the house as she pulled in.

As Jack opened the rear car door, he asked, "*Qué pasa?*"

Carly grinned. He'd been practicing his Spanish since he and Bridget had become an official couple. "*Nada.*"

"How was the exhibition opening last night?" Bridget asked as she slid into the passenger seat.

"There was quite a range of styles," she said, checking to see if the road was clear before reversing out.

"I can imagine. Zita was excited about her neighbor's work . . . I can't remember his name."

"Evan Hayes," Carly answered without thinking. "I bought one of his paintings."

"Wow, it must have been good. Wait until word gets around that Carolina Flanagan has discovered a new artist."

Carly frowned. She hadn't thought about that, she'd just *had* to have that canvas. Though she doubted it would have much effect on his sales – she was a software developer, not a celebrity. No one cared what she bought. She changed the subject. "How's the new job?"

Bridget sighed happily. "It's fantastic. Everyone is so

supportive and I've already got two projects on the go."

Her sister was a safety projects coordinator and had just started in her dream job. It was fantastic to hear her talking about work with enthusiasm, rather than the frustration she'd had at her previous job. Carly glanced in the rear view mirror at Jack. "How about at Dionysus?"

Jack remained at the oil refinery where Bridget used to work. There had been a huge incident only last month and the investigation was taking a lot of Jack's time.

"The accident really shook up a few people, and safety is now getting a much bigger voice. It's not a constant battle anymore."

They chatted until they arrived at the property where Zita and their mother lived. The main house was a big two-story place surrounded by lush gardens. Carly had helped her mother design it to make sure it was big enough for the refugee foster children she cared for. There were also smaller cottages where some of the older foster children lived, now that they were adults.

Carly sighed as Zita's two dogs raced out to greet them. She slowed the car to a crawl, afraid she might hit them, even though they kept their distance.

Getting out of the car, she then walked up the steps to the house. Loud voices could be heard inside, and as she pushed open the door, she saw Elena and Teresa in the living room arguing, and Alejandra was soothing her crying baby.

It was never quiet at Casa Flanagan. Carly loved it.

"Mama, we're here," Bridget called.

Carly went straight over to Alejandra, who appeared a little stressed. "Can I hold him?" The baby was only a couple of months old, and the fifteen year old was still getting to grips with having a child to take care of.

"Of course." Alejandra passed baby Julio over. Carly cooed over the little boy as she carried him into the kitchen where there were raised voices.

"Why did you invite him?" her mother asked Zita.

"Invite who?" Carly said, carefully maneuvering the baby so she could kiss her mother's cheek.

Zita sighed. "I invited Evan for lunch."

Carly stopped her gentle swaying with Julio. "The artist?"

Her sister rolled her eyes. "No, the fighter pilot."

Her muscles tensed. "Why *did* you invite him?" She didn't need to see him again. She didn't *want* to see him again. He was unsettling.

Zita pursed her lips and then her eyes twinkled, which meant she was up to no good. "Mama, I think Evan likes Carly. They met last night. He's a nice guy and this is the perfect opportunity for him to get to know her."

Mierda. Her sister was setting her up.

Carmen turned to her youngest daughter with speculation in her eyes. "Is that so?"

Zita nodded.

Carly wanted to scream.

"In that case, he *must* come." Carmen grinned.

"Poor guy doesn't know what he's getting himself in for," Jack murmured to Bridget.

The doorbell halted further conversation.

"That must be him," Zita said, wiping her hands on a dish towel and hurrying to the front door.

"I think Julio needs changing," Carly said quickly and headed for the stairs. The longer she could avoid Evan the better.

She wasn't sure what it was about him that unsettled her. He was an attractive man, sure, but she'd dealt with good-looking men before. Many of them either wanted to tell her how to run her company, or wanted a job, or her money. She got the feeling Evan wasn't interested in any of that. Which made her nervous. She couldn't trust her taste in men.

After changing the baby – not because he needed it, but because she hated to lie to her mother – she sang to him until he fell asleep in her arms. She watched him sleep for some time before gently laying him in his crib. As much as she wanted to, she couldn't hide out there all day, so she went downstairs.

Her eyes were instantly drawn to Evan. His black hair was tied back in a tiny ponytail and he was wearing jeans and a black and white checked shirt. He was talking with Jack, and seemed completely comfortable surrounded by the nine females in the room – her mother and two sisters, as well as the six foster girls staying at the moment.

As Carly walked in, Evan looked up and met her eyes. He smiled, a small, private smile, and nodded to her before returning his attention to Jack. She breathed deeply to slow her heart rate.

"How is Julio?" Alejandra asked as Carly walked in.

"He's asleep upstairs."

She closed her eyes and whispered a prayer of thanks. "He has not been sleeping well." Alejandra had fled El Salvador after she'd fallen pregnant. She'd been threatened by a local gang and, fearing for her and her baby's life, she'd left. She'd been granted refugee status and was being homeschooled until her English improved so she could go to school.

Carly ran a hand down the young girl's arm. "After lunch you should get some sleep yourself."

She nodded. "*Mamita* said the same."

Carly smiled at the name the girls had given Carmen – little mother. It was apt, because at just under five feet, she was even shorter than Carly.

"It is time for lunch," Carmen announced, gesturing them into the dining room with its long table. Carly moved to her usual seat at the head of the table opposite her mother.

"Carly, let Jack sit there today," her mother called. "You can sit next to our guest."

Carly smothered her groan. Carmen did like to play matchmaker. "How did the rest of the exhibition go?" she asked as she sat down.

"Good," Evan said. "I sold a couple more pieces."

"Congratulations." Carly didn't know what else to say. Usually she was fine with small talk, but right now all she could focus on was the heat coming from Evan's body. She frowned. It was so unlike her to get this flustered around a man.

"It's great, isn't it?" Zita said. "I knew the exhibition was a brilliant idea."

"Did anyone else sell pieces?" Carly asked.

"I think Isobella and Desmond both sold one painting," said Zita. "Stewart was happy. There was quite a bit of media there, so that should hopefully bring people in over the next two weeks."

Carly was glad the exhibition wouldn't be a complete waste

of money. When she'd seen the first few works, she hadn't been so sure.

"What kind of painting do you do?" Bridget asked Evan.

"I work in various media: watercolor, acrylic, pencils, but my favorite is oil painting."

"Is painting your full time job?" Bridget asked.

"I do some freelance graphic design work as well."

"That's a different skill set." He'd mentioned it last night, but Carly wanted to know more.

He glanced at her. "Yeah. There's a lot of work out there for graphic artists and it keeps the money coming in." He was very matter-of-fact about it.

Most of the artists she met were snobs who wouldn't dare risk their reputations by doing anything commercial. It was one reason why the developer of an indie game she was sponsoring was still searching for an artist to do the artwork. Evan's style would suit the story perfectly. "Have you ever worked on software, games and such?"

His arm brushed hers as he turned her. "No, but I've been intrigued by it. There are some beautiful games out there."

Carly ignored the rush of warmth through her body. "I have an indie developer who's looking for an artist. If you're interested, I can put you in touch."

"That would be great." He smiled then, and it was like a fire on a cold night.

She nodded. "I'll give you the details after lunch."

"Enough of this work talk," Carmen said. "Tell us about your family, Evan. You're not a Texan?"

Evan's smiled disappeared. "I'm from New York City originally. My folks and brother still live there."

"Do you see them much?"

"Not really." He shifted in his chair, looking decidedly uncomfortable.

"Why not?" Carmen asked.

Before Evan could answer, Carly said, "Mama, that's really none of our business."

Evan shot her a grateful look, which made Carly all the more curious.

"How long have you been in Houston?" Carly asked.

"About ten months," he said. "I really like the yard sizes out here; you get a country feel with city conveniences."

Did he like to be a little more isolated from everyone?

"I like my space," Carmen agreed. "Plenty of room for my garden."

Carly smiled. Her mother's "garden" was more like a small scale farm with almost every food imaginable grown in it.

"I must admit, gardening's not my strong suit. The garden is mostly grass in various stages of shock."

Carmen tutted. "A garden adds to the serenity. You *must* have one. I can help you if you like."

"Mama, not everyone loves gardening like you do," Zita said.

Evan grinned at her. "Some advice would be great. I'm renting, but the agent said I can plant the two empty garden beds at the front. I don't know where to start."

Carly suspected her mother wanted to know more about Evan, and this was her way of finding out.

"Jack and I have news," Bridget spoke up.

"You're getting married!" Carmen exclaimed.

Bridget rolled her eyes. "No, Mama. We've bought a house."

"Well, it's a step in the right direction," her mother muttered.

Carly smiled. "That's great, Birdy. Where is it?"

"Pearland."

She'd speak with Bridget later to see if they needed any financial help.

"What's it like?" Zita asked.

Bridget described the house, and by the time she was done, they had all finished eating. Carly helped her mother clear the plates and the younger girls stacked the dishwasher.

"Come and see my garden," Carmen invited Evan. "You can tell me what you like." She turned to Carly. "Carolina, you must come too. You have not seen the latest changes."

There was no point arguing. She walked past Zita on her way out and her little sister gave her an apologetic smile. Zita's turn would come soon enough.

***

Evan was amused by Carmen's unsubtle way of keeping

Carly and him together, but he was pleased. He'd had a slight attack of the guilts after Zita invited him to lunch, hoping he hadn't been too forward in getting what he wanted. He didn't know what Zita had told her mother, but it seemed like Carmen was scoping him out to make sure he was good enough for Carly.

He was looking forward to seeing the garden. The fence line between their properties was thick with bushes and trees, which didn't allow him to see further into the yard. Following Carmen outside, he then stopped in shock. Garden wasn't the right word for what he was seeing. It was an oasis, a food paradise, a productive farm. Everywhere he looked there were colors and textures, but more than that, it was lovingly tended. There were no weeds, no sick or straggly plants, there was just health and vibrancy. He wanted to paint it. Acrylics would be best to catch the intense colors.

"Are you all right?" Carly asked, stepping up next to him.

He nodded. "This is amazing." He took Carmen's arm and said, "You must be a dryad or a garden sprite."

The older woman chuckled, but waved him away.

"I mean it," said Evan. "I'd very much like to paint it, if you'd let me."

Carmen gaped. "This? My little *finca*?"

He wasn't sure what a *finca* was, but he nodded. "It's beautiful. It's nurturing."

Carly's mother lowered her eyes and patted his hand. "*Sí.* You can paint it, if you would like."

"Thank you." He was itching to get his sketchbook now and do some preliminary sketches.

"Carly, show him around." Keeping her eyes lowered Carmen went back inside.

Oh, hell. "Have I done something to offend her?"

Carly was silent a moment. "You've touched her," she told him, gesturing for him to follow her. "Not many people understand what her garden is to her, but you did. You've got a knack for seeing more."

"It helps to be observant when you're an artist." He wasn't sure what to make of the speculative look on her face. Changing the subject, he asked, "So what does she grow?"

"It would be easier if I told you what she doesn't grow." Carly laughed and he liked the carefree sound of it. This was the first time he'd seen her relaxed.

"Some of the fruit is from El Salvador and other places in Central America. She likes to help the girls feel at home. There's a big greenhouse over there for the tropical food."

Zita had told him a little about the foster girls and their circumstances and he'd wondered how comfortable they would be with strangers. It was obvious from the lunch that they felt right at home.

"Mama also grows vegetables. She says the stuff you buy in supermarkets has no flavor."

Evan didn't pay much attention to what he ate, as long as it wasn't too unhealthy, but he had to admit the meal he'd just eaten had been the best one he'd had in a long time. "Does she have an excess of food?" The garden beds went on and on.

"Sometimes. If she does, she gives it away. She's quite active in the migrant community and some of them struggle to make ends meet."

"How does she afford it all? Does she get government assistance? It can't be cheap to care for all those girls and keep the property running."

Carly scowled, her lips pursed together. "Casa Flanagan is run by my charity. We don't take handouts, but we do support these children who have fled for their lives."

"That's fantastic," he said. "The children need a strong support system once they've been accepted into the US."

She sighed. "Not all of them have been accepted."

"What do you mean?"

"We're running a trial for the government. Our latest three girls are waiting for their applications to be processed." She plucked a leaf from a nearby bush and held it up to her nose. "There's been a lot of discussion that children shouldn't be kept locked in detention centers for months while waiting to be assessed. Casa Flanagan has been chosen as one of the organizations to run a trial to explore if keeping the children in the community can work." She shredded the leaf and threw it into the garden bed. "There are many people against it, arguing the kids could be dangerous and escape into the community."

She waved her hands around, her tone angry. "They have no idea what the kids have been through, and we've got seven more weeks to prove it can be done."

She was fiery, passionate, so worked up.

She was magnificent.

Just listening to her talk about it made him want to support her. No one liked to be imprisoned.

"Have you seen enough? I think Mama mentioned dessert earlier."

"Sure." He followed her back to the house. There was far more to this woman than he'd ever imagined.

In the kitchen, Zita was making a fruit salad.

"Did Mama tell you Evan wants to paint the garden?" Carly asked Zita.

"No. She came inside and went straight upstairs, said she needed a minute's peace. "

"Should I go and talk with her?" Evan asked.

Carly shook her head, giving him a small smile. "No. She'll be down soon."

"And she'll be demanding you get started on the painting," Zita added.

He smiled. That he could handle.

"Come through to the dining room and we'll have dessert." Zita picked up the bowl and motioned for him to follow her. "Dessert's ready," she called.

Footsteps thundered down the stairs and the girls trooped in. Alejandra was carrying a baby.

"He's awake," Carly said, and ran her hand over the baby's head, cooing at him. Her whole demeanor softened and she lost the stiff façade. Evan found it fascinating.

She was someone else he'd love to paint. Not as her corporate image, but here, maybe in the garden, as she was at home. The softer, more vulnerable Carly. But it would take some time to convince her.

It was lucky he knew how to be patient.

<h1 style="text-align:center">Chapter 3</h1>

Carly was desperately hoping Evan would leave soon, but he didn't seem to be in any hurry. He sat chatting with her mother, explaining what process he would go through to paint the garden, and Carmen was hanging on his every word.

She was pleased to see her mother so excited, but Evan put Carly on edge. She couldn't quite work out who he was, what he wanted. Everyone wanted something.

She didn't like the way he examined her, like he was trying to figure her out. It made her uneasy. Part of the problem was that he'd invaded her home, the space where she could be herself.

"Carly, do you think we could go soon?" Bridget asked. "Jack's got to go visit one of the other refineries tomorrow and it's an early start."

"Sure." It was the excuse she was looking for. They all stood and started saying their goodbyes.

"It was nice seeing you again, Carly," Evan said.

She didn't trust herself to speak. She wasn't sure she agreed with him. Instead, she nodded and headed to her car.

***

When Carly got back to her penthouse apartment, it felt emptier than normal. Usually after a visit to her mother's she was pleased for a bit of peace and quiet. Today it felt lonely. Her only company was the fish in the large aquarium in the wall, and they weren't much for conversation.

She dumped her purse on the table and wandered over to the floor-to-ceiling windows that gave her a view over the city. It was immense. Way below, cars moved here and there, and people were specks on the sidewalk. She sighed and went into her walk-in-wardrobe to take off her high heels and change. After a shower, she put on her one indulgence – comfortable, yet highly dorky leopard-print footie pajamas. If any of her business associates ever saw her in it they wouldn't believe their eyes.

Grabbing her laptop, she curled up on the sofa. She didn't really want to check her emails now, but if she didn't it'd be more work for her tomorrow. She dragged them into categories: those asking for charity, those asking for investment, those asking for an appearance or endorsement, and then finally those that had something to do with her company. She flagged the appeals she was interested in, and her personal assistant Hayden would find out more for her. Then she read the business related emails.

She was about halfway through when she sighed and shut the screen. She'd had enough. There wasn't a single personal email amongst the two hundred in her inbox, no friendly banter between colleagues, nothing but polite business speak.

Her cell phone rang and hope sprang that it might be one of her sisters. The caller ID was set to private and Carly debated whether to answer. But she had to, it might be important. With a sigh, she answered. "Carolina Flanagan."

"Carly, it's Evan."

Her heart skipped a beat.

"I hope you don't mind me calling. Zita gave me your number after I realized I didn't get the game developer's contact details from you."

She brushed aside the thud of disappointment. Of course. Why else would he be calling? Quickly she flicked through her email contacts. "His name is Basil." She read out his phone number and email address. "Tell him I think your work would suit the game."

"Thanks. I appreciate it. Working on a game would be a new experience." He sounded genuinely interested.

"*De nada*," she said. She hung up before he could say anything else.

At least now she knew what he wanted from her. He'd got the business contact and she wouldn't hear from him again. It didn't bother her. She was always trying to help people on their journey.

It was just as well she wasn't interested in him. She was way too busy for a relationship anyway.

She continued working, ignoring the ache in her heart.

***

The following day, Carly arrived at her software company, Comunidad, at seven in the morning. She settled at her desk with her coffee. This was the best time of the day. Most of her staff didn't start until nine, so she didn't have people wanting anything from her and she could spend an hour doing what she wanted to do – like working on the new app she hadn't told anyone about.

Smiling to herself, she set her timer and got to work. She loved programming, loved working with the languages of computers to make them do what she wanted. At the moment she was working on an app to help people learn English. She had watched her mother's foster children struggle for years, and her aim with this app was to make it fun – to enable families to learn together, or for individuals to do it themselves. It would have implications for her social media platform, Comunidad, as well. She'd developed the platform in college as a way for migrants to connect with one another, to help form a community in the place they had moved to. People could connect with others from the same country, or with those who spoke the same language. They could help each other, explaining traditions that may not be familiar, new foods, and share support systems that were available. It had been Carly's way of helping people make the transition that she herself had found so difficult.

The timer's sharp ring cut through the silence, and Carly blinked. The hour had flown by. Soon people would begin arriving, and she needed to be ready for the day.

Saving her work, she opened the planner her PA had sent her on Friday. She had her usual Monday meetings, a lunch appointment with the owners of a small software company who wanted her to buy them out, and she had an hour blocked out to visit the indie developer hub.

She smiled. Downstairs, she had a whole floor designated as office space for indie developers and entrepreneurs. She leased the space to them for an insignificant amount, and they had access to meeting rooms, office space, and once a day, a Comunidad developer to help them with any technical issues they couldn't solve. It was such a vibrant hub of activity and she enjoyed being part of it.

"Morning, Carolina!" Hayden, her very efficient personal assistant, waved as he dumped his bag on his desk, hit the power button on his computer and then came and stood in her doorway. "How was the exhibition? Was it awful?" He sipped his coffee, his crisp white shirt contrasting with his dark skin.

Carly smiled at him. "There was one good artist."

"Let me guess. You had . . ." He paused as he looked up, thinking, "three artists who asked you to be their patron."

"Close. Two."

He pouted.

"I told Isobella and Desmond they could send through their business proposal. I've sent you their details."

Hayden's grin was wicked. "How low did their jaws drop?"

"Low enough," Carly admitted, trying not to smile. Hayden loved to be sassy, but he was also a damned hard worker and she appreciated him. "How was your weekend?"

"A group of us went out for drinks. You should have come with us."

The tug on her heart was easy to ignore. She couldn't possibly socialize with the people she worked with. She was the boss, they didn't really want her there. She'd just cramp their style. Plus, she'd had a dinner to go to. "How was it?"

"Great. I met a gorgeous guy and we're going to dinner tonight. Cross your fingers for me."

"Good luck." As he turned to go, she said, "I've moved the requests I've received to the normal folders and flagged the ones

I'm interested in."

He scowled at her. "Seriously, Carolina, I don't know why you hired me. You're efficient enough as it is."

She shrugged. "I was checking out something else last night and thought I might as well," she lied.

"You need to get yourself a social life." His tone was exasperated and there was pity on his face as he walked away.

Her body tightened. There was nothing wrong with her social life. She was out almost every day at dinners or lunches, and she always made time to go to her mother's every other week.

A little voice in her head reminded her those events were business, not social, but she shut it down. She was the CEO of her own company. She was busy.

She didn't have time for a social life.

***

"I'm heading down to the hub," Carly told Hayden as she walked past his desk later that day.

"Roger that. I'll hold all calls."

"Thanks." She needed to get away from all the nonsense she'd been dealing with today. Her executives had been squabbling about the direction the company should take. She'd had to firmly tell Lisa, her chief financial officer, that they were not going to increase the rental rates on the hub, and they weren't going to start charging for add-ons to Comunidad. Lisa wanted to increase the company's revenue, her eye firmly on profit, but that had never been Carly's goal. She didn't deny that it was a very nice benefit, but she was more interested in helping the community by providing opportunities she hadn't had. Plus, the company was making plenty of money from their software applications and from advertising revenue. She'd get Hayden to arrange a meeting with Lisa one on one. If the woman didn't agree with the company's ethos, then it would be better if they parted ways.

The elevator dinged and the doors slid open. Carly took a deep breath and tried to leave her stress behind. Here she was focused on helping others, not on building a business. As she stepped onto the floor, she waved to a couple of the developers who leased permanent space. It was all open plan, with desks covering most of the floor space, and the occasional divider to give people a bit of privacy.

She spotted Basil, the developer she'd told Evan about, and wandered over.

"Hey, Carolina. What's new?" Basil was of Italian descent with thick dark hair and dark eyes.

"I gave your name to an artist I met over the weekend," said Carly. "I thought he might suit your game."

"Evan, right? He called me last night and is coming in this afternoon to show me his portfolio. Thanks for thinking of me."

"No problem." She'd have to make sure she wasn't around when he arrived. "How's the game going?" She'd invested in its development and couldn't wait until it came out.

"I've got a couple of glitches I'm working through, but it's still on track."

She wanted to ask him if she could look at his code, see what he was doing, but knew it wouldn't be welcome. No one wanted an investor to get too involved. Instead she walked over to the desk where the developers booked appointments with the Comunidad representative. It was a first come, first served system, and depending on the help required, Carly might get to one person or several. Reading the details of the first person on the list, she noted his desk number and went over to help.

***

Evan stepped out of the elevator and scanned the floor, looking for the desk numbers so he could find Basil. Instead, he saw Carly sitting next to a guy, pointing at the screen and speaking rapidly. Her face was animated, her eyes eager, and the guy next to her nodded and began to type. After a minute, Carly said something and he nodded again, his focus not leaving the screen. Then she got to her feet and walked to a desk in the middle of the room.

She looked completely out of place there. She wore a pale blue skirt suit with a white shirt, and another pair of those killer heels in a matching shade of blue. Her straight brown hair didn't have a strand out of place, and she exuded confidence.

Everyone else around her was wearing jeans and T-shirts, with the occasional person in a collared shirt. Carly was the rose amongst the weeds. She examined a piece of paper on the desk and then glanced around the room. Her eyes met his and she stiffened.

He'd definitely made an impression on her. It just wasn't a good one.

That was a real shame.

Keeping his eyes on hers, he smiled and walked over. "I didn't expect to see you here." What was the CEO of a billion dollar company doing in their rental space?

"It's my day to help," she said. "You're here to see Basil, aren't you? He's over there." She pointed. "Excuse me." And then she walked away.

Well, she was to the point. Evan watched her for a minute, amused. What did she mean it was her day to help? He'd have to find out later. Right now he needed to be in business mode. He smoothed out his expression and walked across to Basil to introduce himself.

"Thanks for coming by, man," Basil said as he took the portfolio from Evan.

"After we spoke, I did a couple of preliminary sketches of what I thought you were after."

He held his breath as Basil opened the portfolio. He'd left them on the top so Basil would see them straight away. He stared at the sketches, glancing between the three of them, his eyes wide and his mouth slightly agape.

Evan waited. He knew from experience there was no point asking for an opinion until Basil had the chance to absorb his work. It didn't stop a few nerves jumping in his stomach, wondering if his efforts would be good enough. When he'd spoken with Basil the night before, he'd been so excited about the project. The game had sounded like a lot of fun and Evan was eager to try something new.

Finally, Basil shook his head. "These are perfect. Exactly what I had in mind."

The nerves danced a jig of celebration and settled. "I'm glad."

"We need to talk costs." He named a figure. "Does that

suit?"

Calculating the time it would take, Evan hesitated. It was a little less than he would have liked, but the game concept was interesting, and if it was successful it could lead to other opportunities. He had to find all the income streams he could as an artist. "What's the timeframe?"

"I've got a twelve-month plan. Each week I'll let you know what I'm working on and you can do the artwork. I'm working from here at the moment because Carolina is sponsoring the project."

That was interesting. "Is that why she's down here today?"

"No. It's her turn to be support."

"What do you mean?"

"This is the indie hub. Comunidad leases the space to indie developers and sends one of their experts downstairs every day for an hour to help. We generally help each other anyway, but if it's a tough one, sometimes they're the best people to solve it. Carolina is here at least once a week."

Carly was big into supporting the community. Evan liked that. She'd not lost sight of the average guy, despite her incredible success.

At the moment Carly was helping a young woman. She pulled the keyboard toward her and typed rapidly, her eyes fixed on the screen. Then she clicked the mouse and sat back. The woman grinned and hugged her. Carly beamed, looking younger and more carefree for a moment. It kicked him right in the gut.

"She must be good," Evan said.

"Who, Carolina? She's the best. There's something in her brain that picks up mistakes none of us can see, and the way she codes is like she was brought up speaking it." The admiration was clear in Basil's voice.

It was obvious Carly loved it. How much time did she get to do it these days?

"Often there's a glitch no one can solve. It stays on the sign-up list and ninety percent of the time it's Carolina who fixes it."

Evan knew there had to be a reason why her company had become so successful, and he guessed her technical skills were part of it. Her intelligence was quite a turn on.

Basil cleared his throat and Evan realized he was staring. He turned back to the man. He could watch Carly all day, but that wasn't being productive. "Do you want to develop a schedule?"

Working on a game was going to be fun.

***

An alarm beeped loudly, echoing through the room and Evan looked up as Carly sighed and pressed a button on her phone.

"I've got to get back," she said to the guy she was helping. "If you send me that code, I'll go over it tonight."

"Thanks." He pressed a few keys on the computer.

Evan stood. "I'll be right back," he told Basil. He wanted to speak with Carly before she left.

He caught her at the elevator. "Thanks for giving me the tip. Basil's hired me to do the artwork."

She stepped back, away from him, but gave him a small smile. "That's great. It's a wonderful project."

"You're sponsoring it, aren't you?"

She nodded. "It's an interesting concept."

The elevator arrived. He was going to lose his opportunity. "Do you want to go out to dinner with me?" he blurted.

Her eyes widened and her lips parted.

"Tomorrow night, seven o'clock?" he suggested. He held his breath.

She looked a little unsure. "I've got plans." She hesitated. "This week is fully booked." She stepped into the elevator.

"How about I call and arrange a time next week?" He hoped he didn't sound desperate, but he didn't want her to get away. No other woman had intrigued him like she did, or understood his painting the way she had.

"Sure," she said. Her eyes widened and the elevator doors slid to a close.

He grinned. She'd seemed a little bit surprised by her answer. He might not have an exact date, but it was a step in the right direction.

"Holy shit," someone said near him. "He got a yes."

As Evan walked back to Basil's desk, a few people stared at him. He frowned. "What's going on?" he asked Basil, who was also staring at him.

"You asked Carolina out!"

He nodded. "So?"

"She's never said yes to anyone who's asked, and most of us have tried."

Evan gazed around the room at the shocked faces and then chuckled. "Well, aren't I the lucky one?"

Chapter 4

The elevator doors closed and Carly shut her eyes. What the hell had she done? What in the world possessed her to say yes to Evan? She didn't do dates. The men who asked her out weren't really interested in her. She *knew* that. She hugged herself, her body stiff. But there was something in Evan's eyes that dared her to accept, and the "sure" had slipped out before she could stop herself. It was Hayden's fault. She was still hurting from his earlier comment about needing a social life. That had to be it. That was the only reason she'd said yes.

She'd have to tell Hayden to delay Evan when he called. Her schedule was pretty full anyway, so Evan would eventually give up.

The elevator doors opened and Carly stepped out, stopping briefly by Hayden's desk.

"How did it go?" he asked.

"Solved a few issues," she said, and hesitated. How could she phrase this? "You might get a call from an Evan Hayes. He wants to arrange dinner. Delay him, will you?"

Hayden made a note. "Which company is he from?"

"No company," she said and continued into her office before he could ask anything else.

Hayden followed her in. "What do you mean no company?"

She sighed. She should have known he wasn't going to give up. She sat behind her desk to give herself the position of

34

power. "No company. He's an artist who's working with Basil."

"So why does he want a dinner meeting?"

Carly didn't look at him. "It's not a meeting."

The absolute silence made her glance up.

Hayden stared at her, his mouth open, before he shook his head. "You agreed to go on a date with someone?"

She shrugged. "He caught me as I was leaving. I've changed my mind." She turned to her computer, hoping he would leave.

Hayden sat down. "Sugar, you've got to tell me more. Is he cute? What does he paint?"

She hated scrutiny, Hayden knew that. It was one of the reasons why she never dated. "Google him," she suggested. "Now I really have to get back to work." Her tone was sharper than normal, as was the stab of guilt. Hayden didn't deserve to be spoken to like that, even if he was being nosy.

"Sure thing." He got to his feet, his eyes a little hurt.

She sighed, on the verge of apologizing, but he was already out the door. It was for the best. She was his boss. They could be friendly, but they could never be friends. It would only complicate matters. It was far better if she kept the roles clear and defined. Far less messy that way.

But the guilt hung over her for the rest of the day.

***

Evan spent the afternoon nutting out the details with Basil and doing some preliminary sketches. He was fascinated by the game and had a much better sense of what was needed. He was packing up when a tall, slim, African American man walked over to the desk.

"Hey, Hayden," Basil said. "What's up?"

"Nothing much. I thought I'd drop in on my way past and find out how everything is going."

Basil frowned. "Carolina not happy with something?"

"Nothing like that. I haven't stopped by the hub in a while and wanted to check things out."

Evan waited patiently for an introduction. He wasn't buying Hayden's excuse. There was something overly casual about it.

"Sorry, we haven't met. I'm Hayden." He held out his hand and Evan shook it.

"Evan."

"Hayden is Carolina's personal assistant," Basil told him.

That was interesting.

"What is it you're developing, Evan?" Hayden asked.

"I'm doing the artwork for Basil's project."

"Fantastic. I know Carolina is really excited about it."

"She recommended Evan to me," Basil said.

"Really? How did you two meet?"

Evan didn't like the prying. He didn't know this guy, didn't know what his relationship with Carly was like, and he wasn't going to give him more information than he had to. "We met at an exhibition on the weekend."

"Ah. She mentioned there was a good artist there. It must have been you." He checked his watch. "I'd better get going. I'll see you around."

Evan watched him go. What the hell was that about?

Basil cursed quietly under his breath. "Do you think she's going to pull the plug on her sponsorship?"

"Why? Because her PA came down?"

Basil nodded. "Hayden never comes down here unless he's doing something for Carolina."

"I got the feeling he was checking me out," Evan said, hoping to allay his fears.

Basil snapped his fingers. "Of course. You asked her out. I bet he wanted to see who you were." He sighed. "That's a relief."

Was it? Who did this PA think he was – Carly's minder? Evan shook his head, not sure what he was getting himself in for. Did he want to put up with this kind of shit?

In his mind he saw Carly standing on the podium of the gallery, controlling her nerves, and then today, smiling so happily when she'd helped someone with their code. She was an enigma.

Yeah.

He definitely wanted to know more.

***

Carly shut down her computer at six o'clock. She only had an hour before she was meeting the organizers of a charity fun run to discuss details. They had chosen the location – The Wooden Spoon – and she had no doubt she'd be expected to pick up the bill. She sighed and took her change of clothes into her private bathroom. She wanted to have a shower, but she didn't have time to straighten her hair again. She'd have to make do with refreshing her makeup.

She braced her hands on the sink and closed her eyes. What she really wanted to do was go home and go to bed.

The lunch meeting with the owners eager to sell their software had gone nowhere. They had set a ridiculous sum on the sale price and weren't going to budge. They'd been reading too many stories of developers making it rich, but the fact was, their software wasn't different enough to warrant spending so much money. When she'd told them she wasn't interested, they'd become nasty, effectively ensuring she'd never do business with them again. On returning to her office, she'd had Hayden put them both on her blacklist.

She sighed. Some days she couldn't figure out how she'd come to this. It seemed like one day she was happily programming her software, and the next she was running a billion dollar company.

Her. The shy little no one from El Salvador.

After changing her outfit, she reapplied her makeup and then checked the time. She'd catch a cab to the restaurant. As she was about to call the number, her cell rang. She answered without checking who it was.

"Carly, I hope I'm not disturbing you."

She closed her eyes at the sound of Evan's voice. She'd forgotten he had her cell number. She'd have to have a word to Zita about who she gave her number to. "I'm just on my way to a work dinner," she said and then cringed. Why did she have to add "work"? She should have given him the impression she was a serial dater. That would scare him off.

"I won't keep you then. I wanted to organize our own dinner date. How about Saturday night?"

"Let me check." She reached for her tablet and opened her calendar. She was free. Her first free Saturday in months. What were the odds? She sighed. What should she do? Lie to him?

"With the weather cooling down, it might be nice to go on a

picnic," he said.

"A picnic?" She couldn't remember the last time she went on a picnic. She wasn't sure she had any appropriate clothing.

"Yeah. How about I pick you up at five thirty?"

The idea was intriguing. She yearned to say yes. But could she really risk it?

"I'll organize everything," he persisted.

That was the tipping point. The hope she was holding down bubbled up. The idea of not having to do anything was appealing as hell. "All right."

"Great. I'll see you then." He hung up.

Carly lowered her phone. Was she finally going mad? There was no way she should have agreed to the date. At a bare minimum, she should have put him off for a couple of weeks to check if he was really interested. But no, she'd agreed to go on a *picnic* of all things. She would definitely have to dig through her wardrobe to see if she had anything casual enough to wear. She wasn't sure she even had any flat shoes, except her tennis shoes. She'd got rid of anything without a heel when her stylist had told her she looked diminutive without them.

Her chest was already tightening at the thought. She'd just have to cancel. She'd call during the week and make some excuse.

But right now she had to get to dinner.

***

Evan hung up the phone and chuckled. Carly hadn't been expecting his picnic idea. He was pleased he'd thought of it. When he'd debated where to take her on their date, he'd immediately ruled out all the high class places. She'd be used to going to those, and anyway his budget didn't stretch quite that far. He'd also considered taking her to one of his favorite little restaurants, but he wanted to be alone with her. He had the feeling she wouldn't open up if she was surrounded by people. Which made a picnic the perfect idea.

The only problem was, he had no idea what food to take. Carly could be vegetarian, or allergic to something. He debated for a brief second about calling Zita. He could do with all the help he could get.

"Z, I need some help," he said when she answered.

"What's up?"

"I'm taking Carly on a picnic on Saturday and I forgot to ask her if there was anything she didn't eat."

"Wait. What? Carly agreed to go on a date with you?" She sounded incredulous.

His back stiffened. "Yeah. You got a problem with that?"

"No, not at all." She laughed. "That's fantastic. I can't remember the last time Carly had a date – at least one she told us about."

Evan relaxed. She didn't have a problem with him. "So, is she allergic to anything, or vegetarian?"

"Nope. She loves fresh, crusty white bread, but she doesn't allow herself to eat it very often. Oh, and you should definitely throw in some pâté and those little red pepper things stuffed with cheese. She loves those."

He grabbed a scrap of paper and made notes. "Does she have a favorite drink?"

Zita was quiet for a moment. "Go non-alcoholic. She often drinks at her lunch and dinner meetings and she likes to have a break from it. When we were kids, she used to love apple cider."

He could manage that. "Thanks, Z. I owe you one."

"Where are you taking her?"

"Hermann Park."

"That's nice. Find somewhere away from the crowds."

"Will do."

"Oh, Mama wants to know when you'll be around to paint the garden."

He wanted to stay on Carmen's good side, but with the work for the game it was going to be difficult. "How about Sunday?"

"Come around after church, say about ten?"

"I'll be there." He hung up and reviewed the list in his hand, an idea beginning to form. He'd do a tapas-style picnic. He wouldn't have to cook and they could eat whenever they got hungry.

He smiled. He hadn't been this excited about a date in a long time.

Chapter 5

Carly was a fool. She should have canceled the date *days* ago and then she wouldn't be having this conundrum. She had nothing appropriate to wear.

She checked the time again. Five o'clock. Not enough time to run out and buy something. She should have done that during the week, but she'd been meaning to cancel altogether. She'd run out of time. Forgotten. Whatever.

Huffing out a breath, she scanned her clothes. This was ridiculous. Surely she had a pair of sandals and a casual dress, or a pair of jeans buried somewhere in her closet. She kneeled down and sorted through her shoes, until finally she found a pair of flat sandals with cute diamantes on the straps. She'd bought them pre-stylist and had loved them, but had relegated them to the back of the wardrobe afterward. And from memory she had a couple of outfits she'd loved too much to throw out as well.

She stood and went to the back of her closet where she'd hidden her outfits. There was a cute floral dress – white, with huge red hibiscus flowers on it, which would work perfectly.

A small voice in her mind told her she couldn't possibly go out in public in anything less than her normal Carolina outfits, but the problem was, Carolina didn't do picnics. She did dinners and lunches in five-star establishments. She could hardly go on a picnic in her four-inch heels. It wasn't practical. Besides, she wasn't likely to run into anyone she knew.

Shutting out the voice, she slipped on the dress and shoes and turned her attention to her makeup. Just as she was finishing, the buzzer sounded. Her hand froze as she applied her lipstick and she slowly breathed out. Checking her appearance one last time, she hurried over to answer.

"There's an Evan Hayes to see you," Harold, her doorman, said.

"Tell him I'll be right down."

Nerves humming all across her skin, she grabbed her purse, locked her door and headed downstairs.

When the elevator doors opened, Evan turned from where he was chatting with Harold and looked her up and down. She braced herself, but he gave her a small appreciative smile. Her body heated. Ignoring it, she walked over. Evan was dressed in jeans, sneakers, and a blue T-shirt with some kind of image on it. It was sexy casual. "Ready to go?"

"Absolutely. I'm parked out front."

His car was an older model white station wagon that had seen better days. He held the passenger side door open for her as she got in. It smelled like paint and she smiled. She appreciated that he hadn't fussed over cleaning the car or hidden the smell with one of those way too strong air fresheners. Perhaps he didn't even realize it smelled.

As he got into the car, he said, "I thought we'd go to Hermann Park. Is that all right with you?"

"Sure."

He pulled into the traffic. "How was your dinner the other night?"

"Which one?"

He chuckled. "Monday night. How many dinners have you had?"

"Four."

He glanced at her, seeming surprised. "You sure are popular."

"My money is at least." She snapped her mouth shut. She shouldn't make comments like that to him. She didn't know if she could trust him yet.

"I'm sure that's not true. What were the dinners for?"

She sighed and then decided to tell the truth. Better he understood he had little chance of getting money from her now, than before she had a chance to get attached. "Monday's meeting was with a charity. I'm sponsoring a fun run and they wanted more money to buy bibs or shirts or something. I told them the amount I'd sponsored them was more than enough to cover all that and they weren't getting any more." They hadn't been happy. "Tuesday was a meeting with a very big company who want to buy Comunidad. I told them it wasn't for sale. Wednesday was another arts group – sculptors this time – who'd heard about the exhibition and wanted me to sponsor them as well. And last night was a session with a group of developers who have designed an interesting platform that could be used at Comunidad. I'm still considering it."

"Hell. So what did you do on your night off – sleep?"

She smiled at his disbelief. "I don't sleep much."

"I can see why. Thanks for spending time with me tonight. If I were you, I would have told me to try again next month."

She glanced at him. He was serious. "It was tempting." She chuckled. "But the schedule next month isn't much different from this month." It was nice he appreciated her time.

"Has anyone told you that you work too hard?"

"Only my family and Hayden."

"Hayden's your PA, right? I met him the other day."

She was surprised. "When?"

"Monday, when I was at the indie hub. He came down, I'm not sure what for. It almost looked as if he was checking me out."

Carly stifled a groan. She shouldn't have mentioned Evan to Hayden at all. She never expected he'd go and check him out though. "That's probably my fault. I mentioned you might call to set up a date. I forgot you had my cell number."

"Is he your gatekeeper?"

"He keeps the more annoying people away."

"Was he meant to keep me away?" Evan asked as he pulled into the parking lot at Hermann Park.

"Of course not," she lied, unstrapping her belt and getting

out of the car.

Evan took a picnic basket and rug from the back seat and joined Carly on the grass. "Would you like to go anywhere in particular?"

"No. I've not been here before." Was it sad that they had a beautiful park in the middle of the city and she'd never been there?

"All right. I know a good place."

They walked in silence as she followed him around the lake to a quiet spot. It was a beautiful evening – still, and with enough warmth in the air that she didn't need a cardigan. There were a lot of people taking advantage of the weather: joggers on their evening run, a few people walking their dogs, and a couple of families gathered around the barbecue facilities. Evan continued on until they came to a big shady tree away from everyone else. It had a lovely view of the lake, but was at a distance from the path so they wouldn't be disturbed. He spread the checked picnic blanket underneath and gestured for her to sit.

Carly did so as he began to remove things from the picnic basket.

"Would you like a drink?" He took a bottle out of a cooler bag and showed her the label.

Was he trying to impress her? She drank enough wine as it was. Dutifully she checked the label and laughed. Sparkling apple cider. "I'd love some." She hadn't had it since she was a child.

He poured and handed her the plastic champagne flute. Carly took a sip, allowing the bubbles to tease her tongue.

"Is it a good year?" he asked, his tone pompous.

"It's delicious."

He flashed her a grin that made her heart race. "Are you hungry?"

She nodded. She'd forgotten to eat lunch as she'd been working on her app. It was just as well she'd set an alarm for when she had to get ready, otherwise she would have been late.

Evan pulled containers out of his basket, taking off the lids as he did. "I've got stuffed peppers, chili olives, pâté and bread to start."

She stared at him as he laid out some of her favorite foods. Suspicion massed heavily in her stomach. How did he know? Was this part of his game? "Who told you?" Her voice was cold, the disappointment thickening. He *was* trying to play her.

"Told me what?" He put down another container and glanced at her.

She couldn't hold in her anger. "Who's your spy? Who told you what I liked?"

***

Evan held up both hands. "Don't be mad. I wasn't sure if you were vegetarian, so I called Zita. She gave me some suggestions."

Carly let out a long, slow breath.

Why was she so upset? "I'm sorry." He didn't want to get off on the wrong foot when the evening was just beginning, though he wasn't sure why he was apologizing.

"Forget about it."

He couldn't. Why would she be mad that he went to the effort to buy what she liked? Unless she thought he was manipulating her. If everyone she dealt with constantly wanted things from her, it was no wonder she'd look for ulterior motives. He was going to have to be really careful if he wanted to keep seeing her. Show her he wasn't interested in her money.

He handed her a plate. "Help yourself."

"Thank you." She gave him a small smile.

"Tell me," he said after he'd piled food onto his plate. "What does Carly Flanagan do on her days off?"

She swallowed her mouthful. "What days off?"

He frowned. "The weekend. What did you do today?"

"I dealt with a few queries, and spent the rest of the day working on an app."

"Surely there are other people who can do that?"

"It's what I like to do," she said, straightening her shoulders.

She was as prickly as a pear. "What do you like about it?" He remembered her sheer delight when she'd helped someone in the indie hub during the week.

She blinked. "It's like speaking another language. You code it, and then it does exactly what you want it to."

So control was important to her. "Is it difficult?"

Carly laughed. "I imagine it's a whole lot easier than painting a landscape. Programming can be taught."

"So can painting."

She shook her head. "Only to a certain extent. I think the really great artists see the world in a different way from the rest of us."

"I disagree. I worked my ass off to get where I am. There's no raw talent there, it's hard work." He hated the way people made art seem like some airy-fairy concept that only a few could do. He'd wanted to become an artist, had told his doubting parents he could do it, and had proved them wrong. It was in large part stubbornness more than talent.

"Your work is wonderful," she said.

Pleasure rushed through him, which surprised him. He'd worked hard not to care about what people thought of his work, he was just trying to make a living. He needed to lighten the mood. "Better than Isobella's and Desmond's?"

She hesitated. "Yes, but don't tell them I said so."

He mimed locking his lips.

"So what do you do in your spare time?" she asked.

That was a good question. He shouldn't make fun of her for working all the time because he wasn't much better himself. He'd been living in Houston for ten months, and aside from the artists at the center and Zita, he didn't have any friends. He spent his days painting or drawing, experimenting with new media. "When I'm not making art, I read, and I follow the Yankees."

"So you're a workaholic?" She raised an eyebrow.

He smirked. "Takes one to know one."

She nodded. "So what do you like about game art?"

"I'm always looking to diversify. Being a portrait or landscape artist certainly doesn't pay the bills unless you make it big. I like to try a new medium, get some new skills, and explore if it's something I want to continue with. Basil has such a clear idea of what he wants for the game and he can actually articulate it. It makes my job so much easier."

"If you could choose only one format, what would it be?"

"I love landscapes. Give me some oil paints and a canvas,

and I'm a happy man."

"If the first night of the exhibition is any indication, you may get to do just that. Selling three works in one night is a fantastic achievement."

It was, but he knew not to get his hopes up. "We'll see."

"Your parents must be so proud."

His laugh was bitter. "Not so much." He needed to redirect the conversation. "Do you have any hobbies, or guilty pleasures?"

Her eyelids lowered and he could swear she was blushing. "Carly?"

She cleared her throat. "Not really. No time. I do like antiques, but Bridget normally shops for me."

"How can she shop for you? Isn't it a personal thing?"

"Whenever she goes to Brenham she video calls me, shows me what they've got."

"You don't go yourself?"

"I never have the time."

Well, that was sad. Evan wanted to change that. There had to be some way he could show her how to relax, and maybe take some of his own advice at the same time.

"Do you want another drink?" he asked, gesturing to her empty glass.

"Please." She handed it to him. "How long have you known Zita?"

"Ten months. She came over and introduced herself the day after I moved in. I've got to say I was surprised. I wasn't expecting to get to know my neighbors."

"Zita likes to meet everyone," Carly said. "Did you move from New York?"

"No, I was living in Michigan. I was tired of the cold."

"And you mentioned you've got a brother?"

"Yeah, he's younger. He's an electrician, and still lives around the corner from my folks."

"Are you close?"

"We chat about once a month. There were no regular lunches at my parents' place, like you do with your sisters. That must be nice."

She nodded and took a sip of her drink.

He didn't want to talk about his family. He was far more interested in her. "So what did you do before you became CEO of your own company? What did a young Carly do for fun?"

She sat up, a little more alert now. "Not much."

"No? You didn't have boys hanging around?"

She laughed in disbelief. "Hardly."

"Really? Weren't you fighting them off?" She was beautiful with her darker skin, her deep brown eyes, and her curvy body.

"They didn't notice I was alive," she said. "I wasn't one of the popular girls."

"So which crowd did you fit with – the geeks, the marching band, the jocks?"

She shrugged. "None of them."

Evan gazed at her. He wouldn't have picked her as a loner. "A small group of friends?"

Carly looked away. "Something like that. What about you?"

"The artists, of course. I loved creating things." He rubbed the back of his neck. "May have even got into trouble for painting a graffiti mural on the back of the locker rooms, but they kept it there." That had been incredibly fun and exciting, two of his friends keeping watch while he painted a scene with the school's mascot and the different teams on the field training. It had taken all day during one summer vacation.

"Always the creative. Did you go to college?"

"Yeah. Rhode Island School of Design."

She raised her eyebrows. "That's one of the best."

"Got in on a scholarship." It had been one of the proudest moments of his life. He'd expected his parents to be thrilled for him.

He'd been wrong.

***

"What about you?" Evan asked. "Did you go to college?"

Carly was enjoying herself, but now she paused. How much she should tell him? "Eventually. I had a mentor who taught me how to code, and supported my first little software program. When I came up with the idea for Comunidad, I needed to learn more."

"So you were sixteen when you sold your first program?"

"Yes." It was the biggest thrill of her life. She'd been able to buy herself a new computer with the initial proceeds, and later when she'd found herself a distributor, she'd bought her mother a new car.

"What made you want to learn how to program?" His expression was interested, as if he genuinely wanted to know.

She hesitated. She actually wanted to tell him, and she felt like she could trust him. Was she being gullible?

The worst that could happen was he'd tell her story to the media, and she wasn't ashamed of her past. "I was a freshman in high school and was in the library after school." It was where she'd always hung out, away from people who wanted to make fun of her, with her books that made her feel safe. "One of the seniors was being tutored by an older guy and I listened in. It sounded fascinating. I never realized you could learn how to code programs. Afterward, I got out as many books on the subject as I could find, and every week I made sure I was in the library for the tutor session so I could listen."

"You didn't ask him to tutor you?"

"Mama wouldn't have been able to afford it. As it was, I had to use the school's computers to experiment with because we didn't have a computer at home." If the teachers had known what she was doing, they wouldn't have been pleased.

"So were you completely self-taught?"

"No." She smiled. "After about a month, the tutor noticed I was always there and he saw what I was doing on the computer." She'd been stuck on a piece of code and had chosen the computer close to the tutor in hope she could get a glimpse of the screen. "He was impressed and offered to help." It had been a little terrifying that the older man had even spoken to her, let alone wanted to help. She'd barely been able to squeak out a response. "From then, we used to meet at the library once a week. I'd ask him any questions I had and he'd answer them." Dennis had been retired and she suspected now that he'd got as much enjoyment out of their interaction as she had. He hadn't had any family close by.

"He gave me my first laptop. It was an old, slow thing that he didn't use any more, but it was so much better than using the library computers. It meant I could continue programming when I got home."

"What did your mother think?"

Carly smiled at the memory. "When I brought the laptop home, she was horrified. She wanted to know what this man wanted from her little girl. She demanded to meet him and he convinced her he wasn't taking advantage of me." She placed her empty glass on the blanket, leaning it up against the basket so it didn't tip over, and ate another stuffed pepper.

"When did you start work on your own software?"

"I made a couple of games for my sisters first. My tutor gave me instructions to build something simple. From then I knew I wanted to build something for myself." With her own computer she was able to spend all her school breaks coding. She'd been so incredibly shy that she didn't have any friends to hang out with.

"Are you still in touch with your tutor?"

She nodded. "He moved to Austin to be closer to his grandchildren, but I see him a couple of times a year."

"He must be incredibly proud of you."

Dennis wasn't the type to give effusive praise. And he'd tried to refuse when she'd given him shares in Comunidad, but she'd insisted. Without him, it never would have happened.

The light was fading. There were less people running on the paths and the families over by the barbecue facilities were packing up. Carly didn't want to go, but she wasn't keen to stay out here at night either. "It's getting dark."

"Do you want to get some dessert?" Evan asked. "There's a chocolate place not far from here. We could grab ice cream or a cake."

It sounded wonderful. She didn't often have dessert. "Sure." She helped him pack up the hamper and fold the picnic blanket. When he held out his hand to her, she took it without thinking, enjoying the warmth and comfort. They walked side by side, slowly back to the car. Carly hadn't ever been this relaxed on a first date. Evan had surprised her with the suggestion of a picnic and everything else had been so casual. It was "getting to know you" conversation, but it wasn't forced. For once, she didn't feel as if he wanted something else from her. He seemed genuinely interested in her as a person, not as a billionaire. Could he *really* be interested in her? Carly hoped so.

On the drive to the chocolate place, Evan broke the silence. "Zita introduced me to this place. She got me hooked on the triple crème truffles when she brought some over as a welcome gift."

When they arrived, it was full of people, and the rich aroma of melted chocolate captured Carly's attention. It smelled divine.

"Shall we grab something to go?" Evan suggested. "It's a bit crowded."

"Sure." She walked over to the cabinet, which displayed rows of chocolates, brownies, cakes and pies. She had no idea what to try. While she perused the menu, Evan ordered a dozen triple crème truffles and an ice cream cone. Deciding ice cream would be the easiest if they were getting take out, Carly pointed to the flavor she wanted and got her wallet out.

"I'm paying," Evan said.

"I can pay, you bought dinner."

He shook his head. "No, I've got this." He gently pushed away her hand.

It wasn't right to let him pay. She had more money than him. "I'm happy to."

"So am I," he said firmly.

The determination on his face made Carly put her wallet away. It gave her flutters in her stomach that he paid, like this was a real date. She took her cone from the shop assistant and followed Evan outside. "Thank you."

"You're welcome."

They wandered down the street until they found a park bench and took a seat. It was dark now, but still early. Carly wasn't ready to invite him back to her place, but she didn't want the date to end yet.

"So we've talked about family, childhoods and education. Now it's time to ask the tough questions," Evan said, his tone serious, but with a glint in his eye.

Carly's lips quirked. "What would they be?"

"Favorite color?"

"Emerald green."

"Favorite TV show."

"I don't watch television."

Evan sat back. "What, not at all?"

"I don't have time."

He nodded. "Fair enough. Favorite movie."

She pursed her lips together. That was a tough question. She didn't have much time to go to the movies either. "I don't know. What's yours?"

"*Die Hard*," he said instantly.

"What's it about?"

His mouth dropped open. "You've never heard of *Die Hard?*"

She shook her head, that old sensation of being on the outer swirling in her stomach. She wasn't familiar with a lot of pop culture references, had always preferred to be lost in her programming world.

"Bruce Willis, yippee-ki-yay?"

"Doesn't ring a bell," she said lightly, trying to think of another question to ask.

"That's a tragedy. I'm going to have to rectify that. *Everyone* needs to see *Die Hard*."

"What's so good about it?"

He opened his mouth and then shut it again, shaking his head. "No, I can't explain it. You have to see it for yourself. We could go to my place now and watch it?"

Carly got the feeling he was deadly serious, and this wasn't just a way to get her back to his place. She couldn't help smiling. But calculating the time it would take to get out there and back, she shook her head. It'd be a two-hour round trip and she couldn't ask that of him. "I'll take a raincheck."

"What about tomorrow? No, wait, I'm going to your mother's to paint."

"Really?" Her mother would be thrilled.

"Yeah. I'm looking forward to it." He sounded genuinely excited.

Carly finished her ice cream as he asked, "Any pets?"

"I have a tropical fish tank." It had come with the apartment, and maintenance on the tank was included in her lease. All she had to do was feed them occasionally. "You?"

"An Australian bulldog."

She'd never had a dog before and was never sure how to

behave around them. Zita's two dogs were so energetic and made her a little uneasy.

They walked back to the car. "Did you want to go to the movies tonight? There's still time," Evan said.

She would, but there was so much she needed to get done tomorrow. She really should get back to work, she'd had enough time off as it was. "I'm a little tired."

"Of course."

They were silent on the drive back to her apartment. After pulling up, Evan jumped out and ran around to the passenger side door to open it. Ridiculously pleased at the old-fashioned gallantry, she got out.

"Thank you for a lovely evening."

"Thank you for giving me some of your time."

She stood outside her apartment building. Was that it? Was he going to kiss her? Did she want him to? "Well, I'd better go in." She moved a step away and he took hold of her hand.

"Just one more thing," he said and he bent his head toward her.

Her breath caught moments before his lips touched hers. It was a gentle kiss, soft and sweet, but Carly's heart raced in response.

"Good night, Carly," Evan said as he stepped back.

Her legs a little unsteady, she nodded to him. "Good night." She fled inside.

Chapter 6

Evan felt pretty darn good when he woke up on Sunday morning. His date with Carly had been nice, casual. He'd had the opportunity to learn more about her, and what he'd learned left him wanting more. She was . . . reserved wasn't quite the right word. Cautious might be better, and he'd only just scratched the surface. When he'd arrived home, he'd done a quick sketch of her sitting on the picnic blanket, in her flowery summer dress, looking relaxed. That's the person he wanted to see more of. He didn't think the businesswoman Carolina was really who she was at all.

Then there was the kiss. He'd decided to keep it short, almost friendly, but the spark when his lips met hers had surprised and aroused him. There was so much hiding beneath her surface.

He made coffee and went out on the back deck to enjoy the morning sun. His bulldog, McClane, came with him and Evan tossed him a treat. McClane laid down next to his chair and munched on the bone-shaped chew. It was gone in seconds.

Evan liked his place. It might be a rental, like all of the other places he'd lived in since leaving New York, but this was the first place he'd felt settled. Everywhere else was more like a stop before his final destination. Still, he wasn't ready to make a commitment. The idea of having a mortgage was a little bit frightening, and he wasn't one hundred percent sure this was where he belonged. He may be feeling settled because the house had everything he wanted: a decent swimming pool so he could do laps, space from his neighbors so he could play music at whatever volume he liked, and it had a yard for McClane to explore on the odd occasion when he was feeling adventurous.

But that didn't mean Evan belonged. He'd never really belonged. New York had been full of hustle and bustle, but everyone was rushed, unhappy, going through the motions. His parents had been a prime example. They worked long hours, complained about their jobs, and spent every cent as soon as it came in. They were tied to their paychecks and too caught up in their own lives to remember to pick him up after class. Evan had vowed never to be like that.

After college he'd tried a small town in Rhode Island, but it had been too small, everyone wanting to know his business, and that didn't work for him. In each city after, he'd floated around, not becoming part of the community. None of the artist centers he'd joined had members who were full-time artists, they were all treating it like a hobby. He hadn't been able to convince anyone that his way of working actually brought in money. Not a fortune, that's for sure, but enough for him to live and keep doing what he loved.

When he'd left Detroit, he'd chosen to try a bigger town on the outskirts of a city. He'd discovered this place, and he'd even made a good friend in Zita. It was strange having someone to chat to and discuss ideas when in the past, he'd always had to rely on himself.

No one else was interested.

His mind veered away from that thought. Today he was heading over to Carmen's to do the first sketches of her garden. He hadn't quite decided what medium he was going to use, though he was leaning toward acrylics. Those details would come to him when he had a better idea of what he wanted to do, which angle to capture.

He was curious about Carmen. She had been genuinely moved by his offer to paint her garden. He'd bet Carly's willingness to help others came from her.

He smiled at the thought of Carly. Should he call her? Would it seem too eager to call straight after their date? Would she be too busy to chat? Probably. He'd been stunned when she'd listed off her appointments the week before, amazed she'd even agreed to go on a date on her one night free.

He didn't want to seem too pushy, and casual dating suited him just fine. He was uncomfortable with women who wanted to spend every second of the day with him, especially when he was painting. So he wasn't going to be one of those people for Carly. He'd leave things a couple of days and then call.

Pleased with the decision, he got to his feet and headed over to Carmen's.

***

At ten o'clock exactly, he knocked on the front door of Casa Flanagan. Unlike the other day, it was silent. Zita's two dogs wagged their tails next to him, looking up as if to say, are we going inside?

Perhaps Carmen wasn't back from church yet.

Evan debated what to do. He hated waiting, and there was no point going home and turning right back around to come back. He might as well get to work. The dogs would let him know when Carmen arrived. He took his things out of the car and walked around the side of the house.

The garden was as lush as he remembered, with colors and textures intertwining. He wandered the paths, working out which perspective he wanted to paint, and taking a few photos to get an idea of framing. A door banged shut and he looked up to see a girl in her early twenties walking away from one of the little cottages at the back of the property. Not wanting to startle her, he called, "*Hola*," and waved when she glanced over.

The girl hesitated and then walked toward him, keeping a garden bed between them. "Who are you?"

"Evan Hayes," he said. "Carmen said I could come and paint her garden, but she must still be at church."

The girl relaxed. "Zita mentioned you. I'm Daniella." She stepped back. "I need to get to work. The others shouldn't be long. I'll see you around."

He continued his meandering until he'd explored the whole

garden and had chosen two or three spots. As he walked back to the house, the dogs barked and a car pulled up the drive. Out front, a van drove into the garage and all the women poured out. Zita saw him first.

"*Hola*, Evan. I hope you haven't been waiting long?"

"No. I took a walk through the garden, found some spots I'd like to set up."

"That's great. Come inside and have a drink."

He greeted Carmen with a kiss on both cheeks and followed them inside to the kitchen where Zita made him a glass of horchata. He was itching to start drawing, but he had learned his manners from an early age. He had to do the small talk first.

Luckily, Zita recognized the signs. "Why don't you take the drink and get started? Give us a holler if you need a hand."

"Thanks." He carried his drink and equipment outside to the first place he'd identified. Placing his glass next to him on the garden wall, he began to draw.

***

Evan had drawn three sketches from different angles, but he wasn't happy with any of them. There was something not quite right, something missing. He picked up the glass of horchata, but he'd left it too long. The ants had found it and were swarming all over it. Sighing, he tipped the contents into the garden bed, hoping it wasn't going to kill anything.

Someone cleared their throat behind him. He looked up and his face heated. Carmen was standing there watching him.

Caught.

"Sorry, the ants got to it."

She waved her hand. "That does not matter. I did not want to disturb you. You seemed quite involved."

How long had she been standing there?

"I'm sorry. I tend to zone out when I draw."

"My Carolina is the same when she is on her computer. Like you, she does not hear when I am standing right next to her."

Had she spoken to him and he'd ignored her? "Did you need something?"

"I wanted to ask whether you would like to join us for lunch."

He glanced at his watch. It was midday. As if on cue, his stomach rumbled. "If you have enough, I'd love to."

"There is always enough for one more."

It was such a different sentiment from his own family. He'd never invited friends to stay for dinner, because his father would have kicked up a fuss about the extra mouth to feed. Yet his family earned more than Carmen. He closed his sketchbook and returned his pencils to his case before following her back to the house.

"Is the drawing going well?" she asked him.

He didn't want to answer. People sometimes panicked when he said it wasn't, and he didn't want to upset her. "It's going well for a first pass."

"Would you mind if I did some gardening after lunch? Will I be in your way?"

"Of course not. Please do what you need to and tell me if I'm in your way. This is your garden."

She nodded, pleased with his answer.

Inside, Zita carried a large bowl of salad to the table where the girls were seated.

"Have a seat." Carmen said, directing him to the head of the table. He hesitated, but at Zita's nod, he sat down.

Soon the room was filled with chatter. Next to him, Zita said quietly, "So how did the picnic go?"

Hell. He hadn't considered this aspect of asking for Zita's help. "It was nice."

"Nice?" Zita repeated, screwing up her face.

"Nice," he said firmly.

"Are you going to see her again?"

He chuckled at her persistence. "I am not going to discuss my relationship with your sister with you."

Zita pouted. "Just tell me this. Did she wear her high heels?"

He frowned at the question. Why would Carly wear high heels on a picnic? "No."

Zita beamed as if he'd told her the secret to the universe. "That's great!"

Not sure where this was going, he kept his mouth shut.

***

After lunch, Carmen put on a wide-brimmed hat and accompanied him out to the garden. When the path split, she took the right path while he continued to the next place he'd identified as a potential landscape. After maybe an hour, he put down his pencils. It wasn't working. He couldn't quite capture the story he wanted to tell – the hours of work that went into tending the garden to make it what it was.

He walked back along the path until he found Carmen crouched down, picking some peas. That was what he needed. Walking over to her, he asked, "Would you mind if I draw you in your garden?"

"Me?" She seemed surprised.

"Yes. Just keep doing what you need to do. I'll follow you around."

"You do not want an old woman in your painting," she protested.

"You're not old." He chuckled. "You are the mistress of the garden, the nurturer, the defender."

She waved him off. "If you want to."

Inspired now, he drew. It only took him a moment to notice she wasn't moving, she was posing. He swallowed his smile. "You don't need to be still. Keep picking the peas or whatever."

"How can you paint if I keep moving?" she asked, but reached for the next pea.

"I get a sense of your movement and then I can transfer it to the drawing."

She was silent for a moment as she picked her crop. "I hear you took my Carolina out to dinner," she said, catching him by surprise.

He stiffened. "Yes, I did."

"A picnic, Zita tells me."

"That's right." He continued to sketch, as he tried to ignore the tension in his shoulders.

"She is not worth taking out to a fancy restaurant?"

He couldn't quite pick her tone. "I figured she gets enough of fancy restaurants at work."

Carmen hummed, neither in agreement or disagreement.

"I thought she'd appreciate something different." Why was he defending himself? It was none of her business. He didn't have to live up to her expectations.

"I'm sure she did. My daughter works too hard. She has forgotten how to have fun." Carmen paused and looked over to him. "Do you know how to have fun?"

She was definitely testing him to see if he was good enough for her daughter. He was tempted to say something outrageous to prove he didn't care, but he controlled the urge. "My work is my fun."

"I do not believe it is the same for my Carolina. Not anymore."

He got the same impression, but Carly had appeared relaxed and happy at lunch the other day.

Carmen dropped the subject and he was able to focus on his drawing again, trying to capture the essence of the woman on the page. They worked side by side in silence, Carmen making her way around her garden harvesting produce and picking the occasional weed out of the soil. She kept a basket next to her, and a pair of secateurs hung from her belt so she could trim an unwieldy branch or stem. She hummed as she worked, a tune Evan wasn't familiar with, but it flowed into his head and stuck. He began to hum along with her.

The fading light was the first indication it was getting late. He checked the time. He'd been there all afternoon. He flicked through his sketchbook, reviewing the collection of drawings. There were probably more than he needed, but he'd enjoyed watching Carmen work. He couldn't remember ever being this relaxed with his own mother. Though he didn't remember a time when she'd been this serene.

"I should be going," he said, getting to his feet. "My dog will be getting hungry. Thank you for your time today."

"You have a dog? You could have brought him here."

"He'd probably trample all over your beautiful garden."

"They are just plants. They will recover."

Evan wasn't so sure. McClane always chose to lie directly on the most fragile plant – another reason why he barely had a garden.

"When shall I come and look at your garden?" Carmen said.

He'd forgotten about her offer. "You don't have to." He didn't want to feel like he owed her.

"I know. I would like to," she said. "How about tomorrow afternoon?"

He hesitated for a moment, but the look on Carmen's face suggested she wouldn't take no for an answer. "Sounds great." He'd be working on the game artwork, but could take a break in the afternoon.

Carmen reached over and stood on her tiptoes to kiss him on both cheeks. "You are a lovely man. I will see you then."

Heat rushed to his cheeks and he hurried away. He wasn't used to that kind of affection, especially from a parent. He blocked the feel-good vibes coursing through him. There was no point getting used to them, or needing them. The first time he did something to disappoint her, she'd change her mind about him. It's what always happened.

****

It was Tuesday, and Carly hadn't heard from Evan. Not that she was expecting him to call immediately, but some kind of follow-up would have been nice. He probably hadn't enjoyed himself. The disappointment was all too familiar to her, though usually it hit halfway through the date rather than a few days afterward.

He was the first guy since Andrew who was interested in *her*. Maybe that should be a red flag.

She'd been so young when Andrew had charmed his way into her heart and her pants, just out of college, and already a multi-millionaire. She'd been so excited that a guy seemed genuinely interested in her and she'd spent all of her free time with him. She'd taken his advice about needing a stylist and had bought them both new clothes. He'd coached her how to act like a businesswoman and she'd seen a remarkable change in how people treated her. She'd felt powerful for the first time in her life and had listened to all of his advice. She'd been so eager to please, eager to change herself into whatever he wanted, she'd even refurnished her apartment with things he'd liked and given him a key. When, after a few months of dating, he'd casually mentioned a project he was trying to get funded, she'd given him the fifty thousand dollars without hesitation.

That was the last she'd seen of him.

She'd been devastated. She never told her family what had happened, too embarrassed by the way she'd been conned to admit the truth. She'd simply said they'd broken up. When she finally recovered enough to examine their relationship, she'd realized that he'd never told her the details of the project, or much about himself. He'd been fully focused on her and that had been incredibly flattering.

But she'd learned from that mistake. He had taught her how to spot money-grabbers and made her less naïve.

Carly pushed thoughts of Andrew aside.

Evan was different. She'd been herself with him. Perhaps it was wearing different clothes, maybe it was the silly getting-to-know-you questions he'd asked, and he hadn't once asked about Comunidad. Maybe she should call him.

"Carolina, your two o'clock is here," Hayden's voice called through her intercom.

She took a deep breath. She had to stop thinking about Evan and focus on work. Her two o'clock was Lisa, and Carly wasn't sure how she was going to broach the subject she needed to raise. Letting out her breath, she pressed the button on her intercom. "Send her in."

She stood and went to the door to greet her. Lisa was in her early forties, with short, sleek black hair, and she wore dark suits that were always immaculate. Her style was effortless whereas Carly always felt fake. "Have a seat." She indicated the small meeting table.

"What can I do for you?" Lisa sat upright, her legs crossed. "Hayden wouldn't tell me what this meeting was about."

Carly hated confrontation. "Are you enjoying working for Comunidad?"

She blinked. "Of course."

"Is there anything that frustrates you that you'd like to change?"

Lisa frowned. "There's always something I would do differently from someone else."

She wasn't going to give anything away. Carly couldn't blame her. "Why don't you tell me what you would change?"

Eva shifted and crossed her legs the other way. "It's not my place to say."

"I accept suggestions from everyone in my company, so if you have ideas I'd like to hear them." Carly suspected she wouldn't agree with them, but that was the point of the meeting. She wanted people working for her who were happy, and who embraced the ideals the company stood for.

"All right." Lisa tucked a stray hair behind her ear. "We're not taking every opportunity we can to expand and improve the company. We're an important player in the industry, but there are bigger players than us and we need to keep up with them."

"Why?"

Lisa blinked. "To continue to be relevant."

"How do you suggest we do that?"

"Through expanding our advertising, charging for apps and add-ons, and not helping those who may become direct competitors in the future."

Carly frowned. "What do you mean?"

"The indie hub. We're basically supporting them to develop software that will be on the market competing against ours. The least we could do is ensure a percentage of their profits come to us."

Carly shook her head. Lisa didn't get it. It was damn hard to develop anything, but to get it to a stage where it was making money was a whole other step. "Our motto is Community, Sharing, Support. They're not words, they're actions. I never formed this company to make money. It came out of a desire to help people. We don't need to expand, we don't need to compete with the bigger players. We have our niche, and we can give our users a different type of service than anyone else."

"But that makes no business sense."

"We're not your typical business," Carly said. "I'm always happy for you to make suggestions, Lisa, but you need to keep in mind why we're here – to help people and build a community. That's our foremost goal – not to make money. If you don't agree with that, it's fine, but you might be happier elsewhere."

Lisa's eyes widened. "Are you asking me to leave?"

"Not at all. You're a fantastic asset to the company, but if you don't like what we stand for, you're going to be frustrated and unhappy. I don't want that for any of my staff."

She nodded. "I'll keep that in mind."

Carly stood. "Thank you for your time."

She waited until Lisa had closed the door behind her and then sat down again, letting out a deep breath. That was hard. She would hate to lose Lisa, because she was brilliant at what she did, but the truth was Carly wanted all her staff to agree with the company motto, otherwise they wouldn't embrace what she stood for.

"Carolina," Hayden's voice came through her intercom. "Are you in for Frederick? I've got him on the line."

With a sigh, she got to her feet and walked over to her desk. Frederick was her public relations manager and was bound to have a new idea for her to approve – something she'd have to be the face of, she was sure. "Put him through," she said and waited for her phone to ring.

***

By the time Carly was finished, she'd agreed to three different events, which would take up more of her time. Perhaps she needed to say no more often, but Frederick only ever pitched events that suited the company's motto. She could hardly refuse.

Her cell phone had rung twice while she'd been on the phone. The first message was business related and the second was from Evan.

A rush of warmth went through her as she heard his voice.

"Hi Carly. Are you up for a movie night soon? You still need to watch *Die Hard* and I'll watch whatever you want to see. Give me a call."

Carly smiled. A movie night sounded like fun. She went to call him back as a reminder flashed up on her computer. She had to be downstairs at the indie hub in five minutes.

She sighed. She'd have to call him when she was done.

Chapter 7

It had been three days since Evan had called and left Carly a message. Since then they'd been playing phone tag, leaving messages for each other, but being unable to connect.

She was constantly on his mind and he wanted to see her again, talk to her.

Today, he was going to the Comunidad building to show Basil the work he'd done. He called her cell phone and left another message, this time inviting her to lunch, then put his work together and headed into Houston. By the time he arrived, he still hadn't received a response.

Walking across the lobby of the building, he noticed Hayden carrying a takeout coffee and a satchel. He jogged to catch up with him.

"Hi, Hayden," he said.

Hayden turned from the elevator bank. "Evan, right?"

He nodded. "I've been trying to get hold of Carly, but I guess she's been busy. Can you tell me if she's free for lunch?"

"She's been crazy busy this week." He got out his cell and flicked through. "I've barely seen her. She hasn't had a minute to herself." He looked up. "She's got something blocked in at twelve, but she hasn't written what it is."

The elevator arrived and they both got in. Evan hit the button for the indie floor.

"You could always try and catch her then," said Hayden.

"She might be in her office, but I can't guarantee it. She might have something off site to do."

"Thanks." Evan got out at his floor, an idea forming.

***

At midday, Evan told Basil he was taking a lunch break. He dashed downstairs to a bakery he'd spotted on his way in and bought two subs with the lot. Then he headed to the top floor.

After checking the map, he made his way to Carly's office. Hayden's desk was right outside. He was typing at his computer, and he smiled when Evan stopped by.

"Is she in?" Evan asked.

"Just arrived back. Let me check if she's busy." He picked up his phone. "Evan Hayes is here to see you."

There was a pause and he put down the phone.

Hayden gestured him in. "Good luck."

Evan opened the door, a slight feeling of trepidation in his stomach. Perhaps she was busy and he was about to make a fool of himself.

Carly sat behind her desk, wearing a peach shirt, her hair clipped back with some kind of pearl encrusted clip. Her eyes were shadowed, but she smiled when she saw him. "Hi. I'm sorry we haven't connected. It's been so busy this week."

She looked tired, but her smile dissolved his concerns. Was it weird that just her smile could make him feel better?

"I took a gamble," he said, holding up the bakery bag. "Have you got time for a bite?"

She checked her computer. "Yes."

"Are you sure? Hayden said you had something blocked out."

She glanced down and then screwed up her face. "I sometimes put in appointments so I can have time to myself," she admitted.

"Good idea. But that means I'm stealing your free time again. I can leave the sub and let you take a nap or something." Was he going to constantly feel guilty about taking up her time?

She chuckled. "I like spending time with you. Just let me finish this email."

His heart beat a little faster at her words. He glanced around the office. All the furniture was polished dark wood, and there was a huge floor-to-ceiling window that looked out over the city. A painting hung on one wall and Evan wandered over to take a closer look. It was a farm scene, workers in the field and children playing nearby. The brushwork was intricate. He checked the signature at the bottom. It wasn't one he recognized.

"It reminds me of El Salvador," Carly said, walking over to him. "We had a farm like that."

"How old were you when you moved here?" he asked, moving to the table and placing the bag down.

"Eight."

They sat down and he handed her one of the rolls. "Why did you move?"

"It wasn't safe anymore. Mama and Papa wanted us to have a better life, but Mama didn't want to move to Ireland, which is where Papa was from. She said it was too far away from her family."

It was the first time she'd mentioned her father. "Your dad died, didn't he?" Zita had told him.

"Yes. Papa was killed before we left El Salvador."

He put down the food. "I'm so sorry."

"It is what it is. The civil war had ended, but there was still so much violence. He was killed after work one day."

"That must have been devastating for your whole family."

She nodded. "A week later we got our approval to migrate."

Evan sat back. It was tragic. He couldn't imagine losing a parent and then having to move to a whole different country. "Was the move difficult?"

Carly was silent as she chewed her food. "The girls coped all right. Bridget was five and starting school, and Zita was only three. They missed my grandparents and aunts and uncles, but they made friends quickly enough."

"What about you?"

"I was the shy girl with the funny accent. I was behind in my schooling and it took me a while to grasp some things."

He remembered what she'd said the other night about hanging out in the library as a teenager. Had she had no friends at all during school?

"Thank you for buying me lunch," Carly said, changing the subject. "The next time we go out it'll have to be my treat."

He liked she was thinking about the next time. "Fair enough. When are you free for that movie night?"

She scrunched up the empty wrapper and got to her feet. "I'm not sure. Let me check." She moved over to her computer and pressed a few buttons. "Not until next Saturday."

Damn. He hadn't expected it to be so long. "Seriously?"

She gave a small smile. "Yeah." She glanced back over her calendar. "Wait a minute. I've got lunch at Mama's this Sunday. I could come over afterward. Oh, but it's Bridget's turn to drive."

"I can drive you home."

She shook her head. "I can't let you do that. It's a long trip at that time of night."

He didn't care if he got to spend time with her, but she seemed adamant. Thinking of other options, he said, "Or you could stay the night, and I'll take you home in the morning."

At her raised eyebrows, he hurried on. "I'd take the couch and you can have my bed. Or I could drop you back at your mom's house." He didn't want to come across as creepy.

She was silent.

"McClane will be there as chaperone."

"Who's McClane?"

"My dog."

She hesitated. "Can we play it by ear?"

"Sure. It might still be early by the time we watch *Die Hard*. Unless there's a movie you want to see?"

"I'll think about it. What food do you want me to bring? We could order pizza."

"Sounds good. I'll make sure there's popcorn and drinks."

Carly shook her head. "No, it's my turn to pay. What do you normally have at a movie night?"

"The usual."

"Which is?"

He frowned. "Haven't you ever done a movie night?"

Her expression went blank. He'd hit a sore spot. Quickly he continued, "Microwave popcorn is a must, some sort of soda, and any candy you like."

She relaxed. "That sounds like fun."

"Great. Why don't you call me when you're finished at your mom's and I'll come and pick you up?"

"All right."

He grinned. He was looking forward to sharing his favorite movie with her.

Carly sighed. "This has been lovely, but I have to get back to work."

He stood up. He wasn't going to overstay his welcome. "No problem. I'd better get back as well. Basil will be wondering where I went." He bent toward her and gave her a quick kiss. Her eyes widened in surprise and he forced himself not to smile. "I'll see you Sunday."

Evan walked out, throwing a grin at Hayden as he passed his desk.

***

Carly really didn't know what she was getting herself into. Perhaps she should have just called Bridget and said she'd drive herself to mama's house. Then she wouldn't be in this conundrum. What if movie night was his euphemism for sex? She wasn't sure she was ready for that, no matter how attracted she was to him.

Yesterday she'd called Bridget to let her know she didn't need a ride home, and then of course she'd had to explain why. Now she was standing in front of her wardrobe debating whether she should pack an overnight bag. It made sense to be prepared for every eventuality. So should she pack her footie pajamas? It was definitely the most comfortable thing she owned, and it was what she slept in in winter, but it wasn't exactly stylish. What would Evan's reaction be?

But if she didn't take the pajamas, she'd have to take her boxer shorts and tank top, and that would be a little too revealing without a bra, and too cold. With a sigh, she packed both. She then checked her calendar for Monday and packed a skirt suit for work.

She let out a deep breath. She was ridiculously nervous and ridiculously excited. To think she was thirty years old and only just having her first movie night. She double checked to make sure she had everything and then headed downstairs to wait for Bridget and Jack.

When they arrived, Jack helped her put her things in the trunk and Carly climbed into the back seat.

"So, you and Evan, huh?" Bridget asked grinning.

Carly's face heated. "It's a movie night. He insists I watch some film."

"What's with the overnight bag then?"

She shrugged as if it was no big deal. "If it's late when we finish, I might stay over. It's a long drive back to my place."

"You could stay at Mama's," Bridget teased.

That was still an option if things got uncomfortable.

"What movie?" Jack asked as he got back into the car.

Relieved for the change of topic, she said, "*Die Hard*."

"Good film."

Who was she kidding? She really shouldn't be doing this. She had a hopeless track record with men. The guy she'd dated in college had moved on as soon as he'd got what he wanted, and Andrew had conned her. Since then she'd realized that most men were more interested in Comunidad than herself, which meant no one had made it past the first date.

But this was conceivably her third date with Evan. Did that count as being in a relationship? Of course not. It was just a couple of dates. Carly hadn't quite figured out what he wanted from her yet.

It was time for a change of subject. "When do you move into the new house?"

"In a couple of weeks," Bridget said. "I can't wait."

"When do we get to see it?"

"As soon as we get the keys. We're going to move straight in. The estate agent on our rental managed to find new tenants, so we don't have to finish out the lease."

"That's great." Pleased that she had distracted her sister, they continued to chat about the new house until they arrived.

***

It was four o'clock before Bridget and Jack made noises about leaving. Carly had decided not to mention to her mother that she was going over to Evan's place and had sworn her sisters to secrecy. She didn't want the inevitable questions when she wasn't sure where this was going herself. With that in mind, she couldn't have Evan pick her up, so she got Bridget to drop her off at his place instead. It felt like she was sneaking around. It was probably how teenagers felt when keeping things from their parents. But she was an adult. She could do what she liked.

As they drove up the long drive, a large ranch-style house came into view. It was far bigger than she'd expected.

"Do you want us to wait to make sure he's here?" Bridget asked.

She did, but that would be childish. They'd made a date and he would be there. "No. It's fine."

As she got her bag out of the trunk, a big white and brown dog came trotting around the side, its whole massive body wagging a greeting.

"You must be McClane." She awkwardly patted him on the head, pleased when he didn't jump up, and then said goodbye to Bridget and Jack. As they drove off, she walked up the front steps and knocked on the door.

There was no answer.

McClane trotted along the veranda and then looked over his shoulder to see if she was coming. With a sigh, she put down her bag and followed the dog, hoping he knew where he was going. As she went around the side of the house, she heard classical music. Tracing the sound, she found Evan in the backyard, standing at an easel, painting.

"Hello," she called, not wanting to startle him.

There was no response.

She walked closer. "Evan?" Still nothing. He was completely enthralled in his work.

Moving so she could see what he was painting, she discovered it was a familiar landscape. It was the view from her office. How could he recreate it when he'd been there only once? Shifting so she could see it better, Evan suddenly blinked and whirled to face her, his brush lifted.

Her heart raced as she stepped back and put her hand to her chest. "Evan, it's Carly."

"Sorry. You startled me."

"I called you twice."

"I didn't hear. Sometimes I get caught up." He gave an apologetic smile. "What time is it? Wasn't I supposed to pick you up?"

"Bridget dropped me off. It's about half past four. Am I too early?" Perhaps she should have called.

"No, no. I lost track of time." He put down his brush.

She hated to interrupt him. "If you need to finish something, go ahead. I can find myself a drink and a seat."

He glanced at the canvas and then her. "Would you mind?" he asked, his eyes hopeful. "It's coming through clearly."

She shook her head, surprised by the fact he wasn't pandering to her. It was a nice change. "Not at all. Just tell me where your kitchen is."

"Through the back door, on your right. I won't be long." Before she could respond, he'd returned to his painting.

She smiled. She'd never seen him this intense before, but she totally understood the focus. She hated being disturbed in the middle of programming.

Wandering back to the house, she admired the long lap pool, and the comfortable outdoor sofa on the veranda. She grabbed her bag from the front door and went into the kitchen. There were dishes in the sink, but aside from that, it was clean. She put the snacks on the table and after a quick search, she found a glass, and poured herself some soda.

She was tempted to have a look around his house, but she resisted, instead taking her drink outside. Evan was still painting. Taking a seat, she settled in to wait.

It wasn't long before McClane joined her, resting his chin against her leg and looking up at her with hope. She chuckled. "Are you after a bit of attention?" She scratched behind his ears and he panted happily.

The block was as big as her mother's, but there wasn't much on it. The yard stretched out toward the back with only a few trees and bushes to break up the grass. Evan had set himself up under one of the trees. He obviously wanted to work outdoors in the shade, because there was no other reason for him to be out there. He wasn't painting anything he was looking at.

Carly would have liked to watch him closer, but didn't want to disturb him. His hand was moving deftly over the canvas and he never hesitated. This was the master at work.

She took a deep breath, enjoying the peace and quiet, and let it out again. It was so lovely out here. She wanted to just sit there and enjoy the afternoon, but if Evan was working, she probably should too. Carly took out her phone and began reading through her emails.

***

McClane got bored before she did. He moved over to his food bowl and pushed it toward her. She checked the time. It was almost five-thirty and there was no sign Evan was close to stopping. Carly didn't mind. She had plenty to do.

Still, she got to her feet and picked up the bowl. She had no idea what the dog ate, but McClane went to the door and when she opened it, he moved straight to the pantry. Inside was a bag of dog kibble and a scoop. Carly filled it up and poured the food into McClane's bowl before placing it on the floor.

The dog gulped it down in seconds. He then sat down and stared hopefully at her. "That's all you're getting from me," she told him. She didn't want to risk overfeeding him.

Though now she was in the kitchen, she was a little hungry herself. She opened the bag of candy she'd brought with her and ate a handful.

How much longer would Evan be painting? Should she call herself a cab, or should she disturb him again? She didn't want to do either, but she could hardly do nothing.

Wandering back outside, she took a seat. She'd go through the rest of her emails and if he hadn't finished by then, she'd catch a cab home. She settled down and closed her eyes for a moment. As she relaxed, she fell asleep.

***

Evan placed the final flourish on the painting and stepped back. He nodded. It was exactly what he'd pictured. He signed his name in the bottom right corner and sighed. It hadn't taken him long to complete it. Carly hadn't even called yet.

He frowned. There was something wrong with that thought. Turning around, he saw her sleeping on his outdoor couch. The memory came flooding back of her scaring him and him saying he'd only be a few minutes more. He reached for his phone, already realizing it was late by the long shadows in the garden.

Six thirty.

Damn. She'd been here two hours and he'd ignored her. McClane would have normally disturbed him long before to make sure he got fed, but he was sleeping on the couch next to her.

Carefully he carried the still wet canvas over to the veranda. Carly didn't stir, so he carried the painting inside and propped it on a spare easel. When he'd finished packing and cleaning up, he went to wake her.

She was curled up on the couch, her expression calm, a slight smile on her face. It was sweet. "Carly," he said softly. She didn't stir.

"Carly," he repeated, running his hand gently over her arm. "It's time to wake up."

She murmured something he didn't catch.

"Come on, sweetheart. Wake for me."

Carly's eyelids fluttered open and she stared at him. "Oh, have you finished?"

He nodded. "I'm so sorry. I tend to get distracted when I paint. I've been a horrible host."

She uncurled and yawned. "Not at all. I must have fallen asleep."

"I'm surprised McClane didn't fetch me. He usually wants dinner by six."

"I fed him," Carly said, stretching. "I just gave him a scoop of the kibble in the pantry. I hope that's all right."

"That's great." He was fascinated by this relaxed, slightly sleepy creature in front of him. She didn't seem the least bit perturbed by the fact he'd neglected her for hours, and now she was waking up, she wasn't the least bit self-conscious. "Do you want to come inside and we'll order pizza?"

She brushed her hair out of her face and nodded, getting to her feet. "Did you finish the painting?"

"Yeah."

She followed him into the kitchen and he noticed she'd opened the packet of candy. She was probably starving.

"How did you do that?" she asked.

Confused, he turned to her. "Do what?"

"Remember exactly what the view from my office looks like."

She'd recognized it. He wasn't sure whether she'd even looked at the painting.

"I don't know. It's not exact. It's more a feeling of colors and shapes."

"Can I look at it?"

"All right." He took her into his studio, ignoring the damn nerves again. The studio was the biggest room in the house, the one that was meant to be a combined living and dining room. The skylight in the center let in plenty of light and he'd put several dropcloths over the wooden floors to protect them.

Carly walked straight over to the painting and stared at it. "It's like standing at my window," she said. "What will you call it?"

He hesitated. He knew exactly what to call it, but he wasn't sure if she'd like it. "Rapunzel."

She pursed her lips, a tiny frown between her brow. She gestured to the paintings stacked against a wall and the table covered in sketches. "May I look at some of your other work?"

She wasn't going to comment on the title. He didn't blame her. "Sure."

Over at the table, Carly perused his sketches. Her breath caught. "This is lovely. Has Mama seen it?" She was holding one of the sketches he'd done last weekend.

"Not yet."

"She's going to love them. It feels like I could call out and talk to her."

"Thank you." He constantly told himself he didn't need his work to be praised, but the truth was, it always gave him a buzz, always reiterated to him that he'd made the right choice by following his dream and not getting a nine-to-five job like his parents had wanted. "Do you want me to order the pizza while you go through them?" His stomach was beginning to rumble.

"I'll order it. It's my turn, remember? Do you want anything in particular?"

"Whatever you like. I'll take a quick shower." He was a messy painter and always ended up with a myriad of colors all over himself.

Evan took the quickest shower in history, not wanting to keep Carly waiting any longer than he already had. He threw on a pair of jeans and T-shirt and hurried back to the studio. She was sitting on the floor and McClane was sprawled across her lap with a look of pure adulation on his face. Carly was beaming. "You want to be a lap dog, don't you?"

"He would if he could," Evan said, as his heart beat a little faster at the lovely image.

Carly grinned at him. "I sat down to get a better look at the paintings and he climbed right on. He's a heavy thing, isn't he?"

"He is. Come here, McClane," Evan called.

McClane turned his head away from Evan as if he couldn't hear him, but otherwise didn't budge. Damn disobedient dog.

Carly laughed. "The pizza should be here in twenty. Are you still up for the movie night?"

"Of course. Do you want to help me set up?"

She nodded. "If I can get McClane to move."

Between the two of them, they shifted the stubborn bulldog and headed for the living room. He gestured to the couch and then realized it was covered in McClane's hair. "Wait a second." He brushed ineffectively at the cushions. It wasn't coming off and if Carly sat down, she'd get hair all over her clothes. He glanced around for other options. "You know I could bring my mattress in and we could camp out on the floor," he said. "That's what we used to do as kids."

She smiled. "Sounds like fun." They carried Evan's mattress into the room, pushing it against the sofa. They remade the bed and McClane claimed his spot in the middle of it.

"Have you thought any more about staying the night?" Evan ran a hand through his hair. "If you want to stay, it might be more comfortable to get into pajamas." He didn't want to make her feel uncomfortable. "No pressure, or anything."

She checked the time. "It'll probably be pretty late by the time you'll get home. Are you sure you're happy to take me to work in the morning?"

"Absolutely."

"All right. I'll get changed," she said.

She probably wanted a shower too. "I'll grab you a towel and you can use the bathroom."

He dashed out, grabbed the towel, taking it back to Carly, who now had her bag with her. "Bathroom's through there," he pointed.

He quickly swapped his jeans for tracksuit pants and the pizza arrived. Grabbing a couple of plates and the soda from the fridge, he carried it all back into the living room. McClane perked up at the smell of food.

"Not a chance," Evan told him sternly.

Hearing footsteps coming down the hall, he called, "Pizza just arrived."

Carly walked in to the living room and Evan's jaw dropped. He couldn't stop the smile from spreading across his face. She was wearing leopard-print footie pajamas, complete with inbuilt slippers. It was *not* what he'd ever imagined her wearing. When his gaze reached her eyes he realized she was a little unsure.

"That's fantastic," he said. He resisted the urge to snuggle her. "Take a seat." He put the DVD into the player and switched on the television. He handed her a plate. "Get it while it's hot."

They helped themselves to the pizza and he put the box on the table out of McClane's reach. "Are you ready for the experience of your lifetime?"

She nodded, smiling. He hit play and they settled back to watch the movie.

***

When they finished eating, Evan took their plates to the kitchen. Carly's eyes didn't leave the screen. He grinned.

By the end of the movie, she was a bundle of nerves, twitching and jumping at the slightest thing. He felt kind of guilty, but she was so fun to watch. He'd seen the movie so many times he could recite it almost verbatim, so he found himself watching her for her reaction to something that was coming up.

At the end she let out a long breath. "I'm exhausted."

"That's only the first one."

She shook her head. "I can't handle any more right now."

"Did you bring your own movie?"

"No. I couldn't think of one."

Evan offered her the bag of candy and she took a handful. "I'm not sure how I'll sleep tonight," she said.

It was still early as far as he was concerned, but he was a night owl. "Well then, if you don't want to watch a movie, and this is kind of like a slumber party, do you want to play truth or dare?"

Chapter 8

Carly stared at him wide-eyed, not sure whether he was joking. She'd heard about truth or dare games, and had always thought they sounded horrendous. Imagine being asked to tell one of your deepest secrets, or being dared to kiss a boy you didn't like. Though if she was honest, she wouldn't mind kissing Evan again. "Did you play truth or dare as a kid?"

"As often as possible. It was an excuse to kiss the girl I liked."

"I can't imagine you being shy."

He shrugged. "You're never really sure whether the girl likes you back."

Their eyes met and Carly felt a pulse between them. "I like you," she said, holding her breath, hoping she wasn't making a fool of herself.

He gave a half smile. "I like you too." He leaned forward, ever so slowly, and brushed his lips against hers, once, twice, before deepening the kiss. His lips were warm and tasted like chocolate. Carly shuffled closer, bringing her hand over his shoulder and around his neck so she could run her hands through his hair.

Swirly, zappy sensations spread through her, and when his hand brushed her breast, they went into overdrive. She moaned.

He kissed her cheek, working down her neck, and reached for her zipper.

Something snuffled between them.

Carly shrieked and leaped back. It took her a second to realize McClane had woken up and decided to check out what they were doing.

Evan swore. "You have the worst timing, mutt."

Carly pressed her hand against her rapidly beating heart and let out a shuddery breath. The timing was perfect.

Evan hefted the dog out of the way and grimaced. "The mood's gone, isn't it?"

She nodded, almost wishing it wasn't. But no, it was for the best. Perhaps she should tell him about her inexperience. Though it might scare him off. She wasn't averse to sex, she just didn't want to rush it. She squeezed her eyes shut, and then opened them and took a deep breath. "It's time for some truth." She curled her legs under her and faced him, crossing her arms. "It's been a while." Her face heated.

"What do you mean?" He looked concerned.

Was he going to make her say it? What if sex wasn't on his mind? She shook her head. Sex was always on guys' minds. She'd say it quickly, get it over with.

"The last time I had sex was over five years ago, and let's just say the order of fireworks must have gone missing." She felt like she was stepping out on a limb with no harness. "Can we take it slowly?"

"Of course." He ran his hand over her arm, in a soothing motion. "I've got to say I'm surprised. You're a beautiful woman. I would have thought you'd have no end of suitors."

She sighed. She said she'd tell the truth. "I was incredibly shy as a child. Moving to the United States was a huge culture shock, and I was always so terrified I would do something wrong, so I kept my mouth shut. That continued into college. There weren't many females in my courses and some of the guys didn't like that I could program better than they could." She ran a hand through her hair. "Then my software took off, and I was working all the time. By the time I noticed a guy was interested, it was clear they were only after my money."

"What makes you say that?"

"Experience. I trusted the wrong guy, gave him a lot of money and never saw him again. I should have realized, but I was too naïve. After that, I learned how to recognize the signs; all they wanted to talk about was themselves or my business. Sometimes they were after work, other times they wanted a loan. You're the first guy who has asked anything about me, and the only one who has ever paid for a meal." She sounded like the poor little rich girl and she didn't want that. "I figured they weren't worth my time."

Evan gaped at her. "Well, maybe I should thank those guys for being such douchebags. You fascinate me, Carly. You're intelligent, incredibly caring and generous, beautiful and brave. The way you spoke in front of all those people at the exhibition, despite being terrified, had me in awe."

She jolted. "How did you know that?"

"Know what?"

"That I hate public speaking."

"There was a tiny tremor in your hands as you held onto the podium. You didn't want to be there, but you did an excellent job of hiding it. I don't think anyone else realized."

Carly was stunned. No one had ever realized, she was sure of it. She'd practiced and practiced and practiced until she was certain no one would be able to tell, and yet Evan had picked it the first time he'd seen her.

"Your secret's safe with me," he said, brushing the back of his hand against her cheek.

She closed her eyes briefly. She believed him. She really felt she could trust him and hoped she wasn't making a mistake. "Thank you."

"What time do we need to get up in the morning?"

She blinked at the change of subject. It would take at least an hour to get to work, but probably much longer because they'd be getting all the rush hour traffic. Even if she skipped her hour of programming, they still needed to leave by six. "Five."

He raised his eyebrows and she chuckled. "Houston traffic is a nightmare at rush hour and I usually start work at seven. I'll make an exception tomorrow and start at eight, but I still want to allow a couple of hours for traffic."

"Next time we have a sleepover, let's have it at your place," he suggested. "I'm not a great morning person, so I'll apologize now if I'm not coherent tomorrow."

Carly felt bad. "I can catch a cab."

"No way. I invited you, I'll drive you home." He was adamant.

"All right." Carly grabbed her cell phone and set the alarm. She put it on the coffee table next to them.

"We should get to sleep." Evan switched off the television and the room went dark. McClane lay at the bottom of the bed, snoring quietly.

Carly slid down under the covers, her eyes slowly adjusting to the dark. She wasn't ready to go to sleep yet. She wanted to talk some more. She felt as if she'd told Evan all about herself, and yet she barely knew anything about him. Was that a warning sign? No, it was just that they hadn't got to talking about him yet. She'd make sure she asked about his past the next time they spoke.

Evan kissed her slowly. "Good night, Carly."

She smiled. "Good night, Evan." If he wasn't a morning person, it wasn't fair of her to rob him of his sleep. She turned onto her side and he wrapped an arm around her waist, pulling him close to him. Feeling incredibly safe and secure, she fell asleep.

***

A hideous, high-pitched beeping noise startled Evan awake. "What? Where?" It was still dark outside. Was it his fire alarm? Was his house burning down?

"Morning," Carly said.

Everything clicked into place. He wiped a hand over his eyes. "Already?"

She chuckled. "The offer still stands. I can catch a cab."

It was extremely tempting, but the dim light of Carly's cell phone illuminated her face. He'd take a couple of extra hours with her over going back to sleep. "Not a chance."

"Well, you don't have to get up right away. I'll be half an hour in the bathroom. I'll wake you when I'm out."

No, that'd be worse, and he suspected she wouldn't wake him again. He was tempted to ask to join her in the shower, but he remembered her request to take things slowly. It sounded like the guys she'd let get close had used her. Why had no one wanted to get to know her? It baffled him. "I'll get breakfast. What would you like?"

"I don't eat breakfast until I get to work. It takes a while for my stomach to wake up."

Evan frowned. Knowing how busy she was, did she actually remember to eat? "Coffee?" he suggested.

"That would be great."

Carly grabbed her bag and disappeared down the hall toward the bathroom. A few moments later, he heard the shower running. He got up and flicked on the light. McClane opened one eye, groaned at him, and then closed it and went back to sleep. Lucky bastard.

Evan trudged into the kitchen, turning on lights as he went. He couldn't remember the last time he'd woken this early. On auto-pilot, he switched on the coffee machine and opened the fridge. He'd meant to buy something nice for breakfast yesterday, but he'd got caught up in his painting. The best he could offer was toast or cereal. It was just as well Carly didn't want anything. He put on some bread to toast and made his coffee. He'd forgotten to ask Carly how she had hers so he'd make it when she got out of the shower. The water was no longer running, so she wouldn't be long.

Spreading his toast with peanut butter, he sat down with his coffee. McClane wandered in.

The smell of peanut butter always excited his dog. With a sigh, Evan got up, put another two slices of bread in the toaster and gave the bulldog one piece of toast. It was gone in seconds and McClane sat, waiting for the next piece. Evan grabbed his bowl and filled it with dog food. McClane ignored it and continued to stare at Evan.

"Last one," he said sternly as he gave the dog another slice. He wasn't going to let those puppy dog eyes sway him again.

By the time he'd finished his breakfast, Carly still wasn't out of the bathroom. Slightly worried, he wandered down the hall. It was silent inside. "Are you all right?" he called.

The door opened. "Just finished," she said.

Today's skirt suit was mint green, with a flared skirt. She was almost as tall as he was in those white heels. "You look great," he said, walking down the hall with her.

"Thanks."

"How do you take your coffee?"

"Black, please."

He filled a cup and gave it to her. Then McClane perked up and started to drool.

"Time you went outside," Evan said, and hustled him outside. There was no way he was going to give him the opportunity to drool over Carly's clean clothes.

"You didn't need to put him out because of me."

"Trust me. He's a hazard when he starts drooling, and you'd end up with love drool all over your shoes."

Carly chuckled. "All right."

"Toast?"

"No, coffee's fine."

He checked the time. Quarter to six. He needed to get a move on. "I'll take a quick shower and then we'll go."

She nodded, and he left her there drinking her coffee in his kitchen.

***

Getting into his car, Evan suddenly realized how grubby it was. Perhaps he had a clean towel he could put down. Before he could check, she was already seated. She was so different in her business clothes, almost untouchable.

As he backed out of the garage, Carly asked, "Do you mind if I check my mail?" She held up her phone.

"Go ahead." She was a busy woman, and if checking her email now while he drove helped her, he was happy for her to do it.

The drive was mostly silent, with Carly occasionally sighing or groaning as her fingers flew over her smart phone. Then it rang.

Who the hell was calling her at six thirty in the morning?

"Damn it," Carly muttered and pressed answer. "Morning, Matthew."

Evan heard an insistent voice coming from the phone, but couldn't make out any words.

"I appreciate your point of view, but I'm sorry I can't make it. I have a prior engagement." A pause. "Yes, I know attended last year, but this year I'm busy." She closed her eyes. "It's not my fault you told people I was going to be there. You only sent the invitation to me last week."

Evan glanced at her as she squeezed her hand into a fist.

"No, I won't cancel and no, I won't accept money to attend. Goodbye, Matthew." She hung up and when the phone rang immediately afterward, she pressed the cancel button.

"What was that about?"

She breathed in deeply and let it out slowly. "I attended a tech college's open day last year and gave a speech about how technology has helped me. The organizer, Matthew, was under the impression that because I'd attended once, I'd attend every year, but he only told me about it last week. It's next Saturday and I've got a software expo I'm committed to."

"If you didn't have plans, would you have gone?"

"Of course."

"Why?"

"It's my duty to give back to the community."

"Your first duty is to keep yourself healthy," said Evan. "You're allowed to give yourself a day off."

"I do. Every second week I go to Mama's. I don't give that up for anyone."

"And when do you give yourself a day for Carly – no events, no people, just you and a book, or a movie marathon?"

She frowned at him. "I don't need to do that."

"Everyone needs time out from the world, even if it's only a couple of hours."

"Hmm."

He dropped the subject. At least she was thinking about it.

Her phone rang again. "Hi, Hayden," she said when she answered. "Oh, you're not well? No, don't come in. I've got the schedule you prepared, I'll be fine." A pause. "No, don't bother calling a temp agency. I can answer my own telephone. You concentrate on getting better." She hung up.

"Hayden's sick?"

"Yeah. He sounded terrible. I must send him a get well basket." Her fingers darted over the phone.

Ahead, the traffic was congested so Evan focused on the road. By the time they'd arrived at Comunidad, Carly's phone had rung five times and each time her posture stiffened further. Did she go through this every day? It was no wonder she'd fallen asleep on his veranda. Shouldn't there be some kind of ban on calling people before nine o'clock if it was work-related?

"You can drop me off in the parking lot," she said, pointing to an underground garage. "It'll be easier."

He pulled in and Carly gave him a card to swipe.

"Do you want me to fill in for Hayden today?" he asked, the offer popping out before he thought about it. He didn't really know what personal assistants did.

She blinked at him. "No. It's fine. The work he's doing isn't urgent and I can answer the phone."

"If your work phone rings as much as your cell does, you'll never get anything done." It was a foolish idea as he had his own work to do, but for some reason he had an urge to help her.

"Those were all calls forwarded from work."

Evan frowned. "You forward your work calls to your cell on weekends?"

"I don't like giving my cell number out. Occasionally people need to get in touch with me out of hours about events I'm attending, so I need to be able to be contacted."

That was insane. "Get yourself a cell just for work then. Surely your purse is big enough for two phones."

She shook her head. "I don't take a purse to work. It gives men the wrong impression. All my clothes are made with pockets so I don't need one." She opened the car door. "Thanks for the lift."

"Wait." He wasn't ready for her to go. He cupped her face with his hand and drew her closer, brushing his lips against hers.

She sighed and he deepened the kiss, feeling her reaction all the way through him.

A car beeped behind them and Evan drew back, glancing in the rear view mirror as Carly sat back in shock. The car drove around them and she ducked her head.

"Are you hiding?" he asked, not sure whether he should be offended.

"I can't have my employees see me necking in the car." She smoothed out her skirt and her jacket.

He chuckled, kind of pleased she was flustered. "Are you free for lunch next Friday?"

She checked her phone. "No. I can do Thursday, though."

Evan was happy to change days. He'd tell Basil he'd be in on Thursday instead. "Great. I'll bring lunch."

She opened her mouth to protest and then closed it again. "That would be nice. See you then." She got out of the car and walked to the elevator.

She was so fascinating and so frustrating.

And he wanted to know everything about her.

***

As Evan arrived home later that morning, his cell rang. It was Carmen.

"I have the plants for you. Would you like me to come and plant them?"

Carmen had come over to his place last week and been appalled at the state of his garden. She'd insisted on taking some cuttings from her garden and said she'd fill the space in no time. Evan had had no clue what that entailed, but had agreed. She seemed more than happy to do it, and he could get some more drawings of her.

He really wanted to crawl back into bed, but instead he said, "That would be great. Come over whenever it suits." He hung up as McClane trotted out to greet him. Evan gave him a pat. "I hope you haven't been terrorizing the birds while I've been gone."

His dog panted happily. After he headed inside, Evan checked his cupboard to see what refreshments he could offer Carmen. The pickings were slim. It was time he went shopping.

He finished making a grocery list as a car pulled up outside. Carmen got out with one of the foster girls. He searched his memory . . . Teresa.

Carmen waved to him. "Teresa wanted to help me," she called as she went around the back of the people mover and opened the trunk. Evan jogged down the steps to help and his eyes almost bugged out of his head when he saw what was in there. These were not a couple of cuttings, these were full-grown plants.

"Carmen you haven't dug up your whole garden have you?"

She laughed. "Only a few things here and there."

This was not going to be the short planting session he'd envisioned. This would take all morning. And he could hardly let them do all of the work. "What can I do to help?"

"Leave it to us."

That wasn't going to work. He reached in and grabbed a couple of the plants. "Where do you want them?"

***

He was right. It was after midday before they finished. The garden beds looked amazing, as if the plants had been there for years. Evan was hot, sweaty, and covered in dirt, but Carmen looked as if she'd spent the morning sipping iced tea on the veranda. He didn't know how she did it. She'd worked far harder than he had, putting him to shame with her efforts. Teresa, on the other hand, was looking about as exhausted as he figured he did.

"Let me get some drinks," Evan said, inviting them into the kitchen. He flicked on the air conditioning and poured some cold water. "Thank you so much," he said, handing the women their glasses. He got out a box of cookies and offered it to them. Teresa took one, but Carmen declined.

"What do I have to do to make sure the plants survive?" he asked. He'd hate for all of them to die.

"Water them regularly until they are established," said Carmen. "I've given you plants that like the Houston weather, so they should be all right."

That was a relief.

When they'd finished their drinks, Carmen asked, "Where do you paint?"

"I have a studio. Do you want to see it?" They'd helped him today, so it was the least he could do.

"Yes, please."

He led them into his studio and let them wander around. Carmen walked straight over to the canvases, but Teresa drifted to the drawings he had scattered over the table. His pencils were spread out everywhere and one notebook was open to a blank page. He recognized the longing in Teresa's eyes. "Do you draw?" he asked, walking over to her.

She shook her head. "No. Not really." Her eyes never left the pencils.

Evan remembered that feeling, that intense *want*. After he'd discovered his love of art, he'd begged his parents for some colored pencils. They'd told him he was wasting his time and they couldn't afford it. He'd been so determined, he'd got himself a paper route so he could buy them himself. From then on, he never went anywhere without some kind of drawing implement and some paper.

"Take a seat," he offered, passing Teresa the notebook. "Give it a try."

"I couldn't."

"Sure you can. Carmen and I'll just be talking about the paintings." He smiled at her and walked over to Carmen who was watching them carefully.

"She is quiet, that one," Carmen murmured. "You are kind to encourage her."

It was hardly a kindness, but he didn't say that. Instead, he said, "Do you like any, Carmen?" He gestured to the paintings, and braced himself, waiting for the criticism. He'd thought he'd moved past his parents' rejection of his work. Carmen had been nothing but supportive so far, but it didn't seem to matter.

"They are beautiful. You have an eye for this."

He took a moment to absorb the praise, the tension leaving him.

"My Carolina bought one, did she not?"

"Yes." He walked over to his photo album. He always took photos of his work before he sold them. Flicking through, he found the one Carly had bought and showed it to Carmen.

She nodded. "Home and serenity. Two things my baby does not get enough of."

Evan was surprised by her astuteness.

Together they strolled around the room and returned to the table where Teresa was drawing. Evan looked at her picture – a sketch of him and Carmen – and surprise hit him in the chest. "That's amazing."

Carmen said something to the girl in Spanish and Teresa lowered her eyes modestly.

"You must have done some drawing back home," said Evan. She nodded.

He went to the cupboard and took out some new pencils and paper. "These are for you," he said, handing her the items.

"No. No, I couldn't." She shook her head.

"I insist. You need to keep drawing." He turned to Carmen. "She's good enough to go the arts center for lessons."

"I will make sure she does."

"No," Teresa insisted and spoke to Carmen in Spanish.

"She says it does not pay the bills and she can't afford it."

Anger welled up in him. That's what he'd always been told. "It pays mine." He put a hand over the girl's hand. "These are a gift. I would like you to have them. I remember wanting to draw so much when I was younger than you." Life wasn't all about earning money. There had to be pleasure in it as well.

She nodded. "*Gracias.*"

"We should go," Carmen announced. "I must be back for afternoon lessons. Zita will be finished."

"Thanks for your help," he said.

"Thank you for yours," Carmen replied, nodding toward Teresa, who had the pencils and pad clutched against her chest.

Pleasure welled up inside him as he waved them off. He'd paid the gift he'd been given forward. Encouraging Teresa the way his primary school teacher had encouraged him.

His day couldn't get better.

Chapter 9

By the end of the day, Carly had to concede that Evan had been right. Without Hayden there to answer her phone and field her calls, she'd got nothing done. If she hadn't already had meetings booked, she would have been chained to her desk all day. She called Hayden to find out how he was.

"Hello?" The quiet, pathetic greeting was enough to tell Carly he wasn't going to be at work tomorrow.

"How are you feeling, Hayden?"

"Like I could sleep for a hundred years. Thanks for my basket."

"You're welcome."

"I'm sorry, Carly, I don't think I'm going to be in this week. My friends who've had this have been laid low for a week."

"That's not a problem. I'll get a temp in to answer phones. You concentrate on getting better."

"Thanks. The temp agency number is in my contacts. Don't forget there's the gala ball on Friday night. You need to find another date."

Carly shook her head. He was as sick as a dog and still organizing her, though she had forgotten about the ball. Hayden was her plus one for it, and she'd have to find someone else. "Just get better," she said and hung up.

After finding the temp agency number, Carly called and explained what she wanted. Within minutes she had arranged someone to answer the phones for the rest of the week. She checked her schedule to see if there was anything else she needed them to do. Hayden was right. She did have the gala ball this Friday. It was raising money for medical research and she didn't want to go alone. Maybe Evan would be willing to keep her company?

She called him.

"Hey, Carly." His voice sent lovely shivers through her body.

"Hi. Are you busy on Friday night?"

"No."

"Do you want to go to a gala ball with me?" She held her breath.

"Sure. What's the deal?"

"It's a black-tie event raising money for medical research. If you don't have a tuxedo I can get one for you." She had no idea how much his paintings made him and didn't want him out of pocket for her event.

"I can manage," he said dryly. "Shall I meet you at your place?"

"Yes. About six?"

"Looking forward to it."

Carly hung up with a smile on her face.

***

The next day Carly was desperately missing Hayden. She hadn't thought answering a telephone would have been such a difficult task. The temp the agency had sent her didn't grasp the concept of putting a person on hold and checking whether she wanted to speak with them, or even checking her calendar to see if she was free. She'd spent just as much time going over the process with the bored twenty year old, as she would have doing the job herself.

She sent Hayden a box of chocolates to let him know how much she appreciated him.

Her cell phone rang late that afternoon and Carly debated answering it. She'd had as much as she could take from people wanting things from her. She checked the screen and sighed in relief.

"*Mi niñita, Cómo estás?*"

Carly smiled. "*Hola, Mamá.*"

"You sound tired. Are you getting enough sleep?"

"Yes, Mama. Hayden is away this week and the temp hasn't been very good."

"What is so difficult?"

"Nothing. She just needs to answer the phone."

"*Pfft.* I can do that. Would you like me to come in?"

It was a testament to how bad the temp had been that Carly was actually considering it. She couldn't afford another day of answering phones. Her mother would be more than capable, but she had her own work at Casa Flanagan. Plus, sometimes Carmen was a little abrupt with people. "You have the girls to teach."

"Zita can manage without me for a couple of days. I'll stay with you."

"I won't be around much, Mama. I have things scheduled every night."

"Then I shall feed your fish."

Carly glanced outside at the empty desk. The temp had said she had an appointment and had left an hour ago. She checked her calendar. The whole week was full of appointments. If Carly asked the agency for someone new there was no guarantee she'd be any better, and Carly couldn't be around to supervise a new temp. Hoping she wasn't making a mistake, she said, "It would be great if you could come in, Mama."

"*Bueno.* What time do I start?"

"Nine o'clock is fine." She wasn't entirely convinced she was making the right decision, but she was desperate.

"OK. Now, I must tell you about Evan."

Carly frowned. "What about him?"

"He is a gem. He gave Teresa some pencils and she has been drawing ever since. She is far happier than she was."

Her mother had been worried about her newest foster child. She hadn't opened up about why she'd left El Salvador and they didn't know what she'd endured.

"When did he do that?" He hadn't mentioned it to her.

"Monday. After we gardened."

She'd forgotten her mother had offered to help Evan in his garden. "That's nice."

"Yes. He is a nice boy."

Carly saw where this was heading. There'd be the not-so-subtle hint that she should date him. "I know. He's coming to a ball with me on Friday."

There was a stunned silence, and then, "Good. I'll see you tomorrow."

She grinned at the dial tone. She'd beaten her mother to the punch. She finished her work, feeling much better about the coming days.

***

Carmen arrived at Comunidad at precisely nine o'clock carrying a bag full of food, which she put in Carly's fridge. Carly didn't comment, instead she explained the phone system to her mother, pointed out the instructions Hayden had written, and showed her her calendar.

"*Madre mía*! That is a lot of appointments."

"It is," Carly agreed. "If someone calls and I'm in a meeting, take a message. If I'm not in a meeting, get their details, put them on hold, and then ask me if I can take their call."

Her mother nodded.

"Any questions?"

"No." Unperturbed, her mother got out a book and started reading.

Carly crossed her fingers, hoping it would work.

***

Carly had meetings all morning and hadn't heard a peep from Carmen. On her way into her office, she stopped at her mother's desk. "How's it going?"

"*Bien*. Here are your messages." She handed her a bunch of papers. "Your lunch is on your desk as your midday appointment canceled."

"Thanks, Mama."

"*De nada*. Are you coming to the Day of the Dead celebrations?"

Carly blinked at the change of subject. "Of course." It was this weekend.

"I didn't see it in your calendar."

"It's blocked out, I just haven't written what it's for."

Carmen checked and nodded. "Good. Oh, I almost forgot. Lisa wants an appointment with you, but you have no free spots until Friday."

"Check if she's free now. I have time."

"No. You will eat your lunch in peace."

"Mama—" Carly began.

"No. You need a break."

She let out a long quiet breath. Her mother was trying to take care of her. She headed into her office and picked up the phone. "Lisa, I've had a cancellation if you want to come to my office."

Her mother wasn't the boss here.

By the end of the day Carly was feeling a lot better about her mother working for her. There had been no other problems and all the phone calls had been handled professionally.

"Are you going home before your dinner?" Carmen asked, standing at the door to her office.

"No, Mama. I brought a change of clothes. I've told Harold you're coming, and he'll let you into my apartment. You might need to pick up some dinner on the way home. There's not a lot in the fridge."

Her mother nodded.

Carly felt bad about leaving her alone in her apartment, but it was better than her having to battle the traffic in and out of town for three days.

All in all, it was working out.

***

Evan couldn't wait to see Carly on Thursday. Yesterday he'd had the most amazing phone call, and he was desperate to share the news with her.

A New York gallery wanted to exhibit his art.

Someone had heard about the little exhibition in Houston, had seen his work and wanted to know if he had more. Evan calculated that he'd need to paint a few more works to have enough for the exhibition. This could really be his big break.

The only problem was, the work he was doing for Basil was going to eat into the time he had to complete the new paintings.

Though the project was already a bit ahead of schedule and Basil continued to be pleased with what he'd done so far.

Evan never imagined he'd have an issue with having too much work.

After collecting the food for lunch, he rode the elevator to the top floor. His footsteps faltered when he saw Carmen sitting at Hayden's desk.

She spotted him immediately. "Evan! How are you?"

"I'm well." When she stood up, he hugged her and kissed both of her cheeks. "What are you doing here?"

"Hayden is still ill. I am filling in. Are you here to see Carolina?"

"Yes. We have a lunch date."

She beamed at him. "Lovely. She is still in a meeting, but you can wait in her office if you would like."

"Thank you." Evan wasn't quite sure about Carly's mother sitting outside while they had lunch. He set the bag of food on the table and started to unpack.

Carmen stood at the doorway. "Teresa is much happier now she is drawing. Thank you for the lovely gift."

"That's great." He didn't know what the young girl had been through, but he was pleased he could bring some joy into her life. "Tell her if she wants any help, she can call me."

"That is very generous of you."

It wasn't really. He was happy to help her. It was hard when no one supported your work.

Carmen returned to her desk and he took a seat at Carly's meeting table to wait.

***

Half an hour later, Evan was still waiting. He became conscious of the little bubble of insecurity that he normally kept tightly under wraps, but he squashed it. He wasn't a boy anymore, no one was telling him his paintings were childish scribbles. Carly had merely been too busy to make lunch.

And not cared enough to call.

No. He knew the real reason she wasn't here. She'd forgotten about him, like his parents always had. He'd seen how good she was at avoiding things she wasn't interested in, so she could have easily ended whatever meeting she was in and made it to lunch.

The bubble broke free and rose to the surface. Who was he kidding? She wouldn't be interested in his news anyway. And he wasn't waiting around. He still had work to do for Basil.

His heart sore, he left the food on the table in case Carly was hungry when she returned, and went back downstairs.

***

Carly politely shook the hand of the CEO of Softco and forced a smile. "It was nice seeing you again," she lied. What she really wanted to do was tell him there was no way he was getting his grubby little fingers on her company and to get lost. Instead, she accompanied the Softco representatives downstairs, making polite chit chat the whole way. Her whole body was tense, but she stood straight and confident while the two men towered over her, purposefully standing close so she would feel tiny.

The moment they left, she let out a deep breath. How dare they try and intimidate her in her own building! Even if she wanted to sell, they'd be at the bottom of the list after that session. She wasn't going to give Softco any more of her time. It was clear they wanted to buy Comunidad, but they kept arranging meetings about different matters, before hounding her again, trying to pry more information about the company out of her. Well, she was done with them. They were going on her blacklist. Any business they could have done wasn't worth going through their pathetic power play. Her stomach was tied up in knots after each meeting and that irritated her.

Walking toward her mother, she was greeted with a dirty look. *Now* what?

"Where have you been?"

Carly sighed. "Mama, you have my calendar. You know I've been in a meeting with Softco."

"You are an hour late."

"Yes, Mama. It was a tricky discussion." Not wanting to explain herself, she walked into her office and stopped still when she noticed the food on the table along with a bottle of champagne.

Mierda.

She'd had a lunch date with Evan. No wonder her mother was giving her the evil eye. How could she have forgotten?

She'd blocked the time out in her calendar, but she'd marked it private rather than putting Evan's name on it. She'd assumed it was time she'd marked out for herself. And instead of finishing the meeting when it was supposed to finish, she'd let Softco dictate, hoping what they were proposing was worth it. She'd been foolish. She could have been having a nice lunch with Evan instead of all the politics.

She picked up the phone and called him. "I'm so sorry. I got caught up."

"It's fine." His tone was flat. "Throw out the food if you've already eaten. Listen, I'm busy. I'll talk to you later." He hung up.

Chapter 10

Carly stared at the phone. She'd never heard that disinterested tone from him before. He was upset.

It was no wonder. She'd stood him up. How could she make it up to him? She should go downstairs and apologize in person. But if he was busy, would he be annoyed at the interruption?

Her mother buzzed her. "Your one o'clock is here."

Damn it. Carly was sick and tired of back-to-back meetings and not having any time to herself. She debated for a second whether to postpone it for ten minutes while she went to talk with Evan. But she couldn't, it wouldn't be fair on the person she was meeting. Quickly she put the food Evan had left in her small refrigerator.

Then she went to the door to welcome her guest.

***

Just before three o'clock, Carly had a ten-minute break. "I'll be back shortly," she said to her mother as she walked out of her office and headed for the indie hub. As the elevator doors opened, she crossed her fingers, hoping Evan would still be there.

He was.

But now she was here, she didn't know what to say to him, or how to get him alone. She greeted her regulars and walked over to Basil's desk.

"Hi Carolina, how are you?" Basil asked.

"I'm well, thanks, Basil. Can I steal Evan for a minute?"

Evan had glanced up at Basil's question and was watching her, no smile or greeting.

Nerves jiggled in her stomach.

"Sure. As long as you're not trying to steal him for one of your projects."

Carly laughed and shook her head. "Evan, can I speak with you?"

He got to his feet. "Lead the way."

She moved over to a section of the floor where no one was working. "I'm so very sorry for missing lunch today. I'd blocked the time out as private, but hadn't put your name down. I figured it was one of my attempts to have some space and I ignored it."

"Forget about it."

She couldn't. "Can I make it up to you? Do you have plans for dinner?"

He sighed. "I'm not sure if I can. I've got some paintings I need to do for an exhibition."

Disappointed, she asked, "What exhibition?"

"A gallery in New York wants to feature me." He said it as if was no big deal.

"That's fantastic!" She hugged him. "You must be so happy." And then she remembered the champagne on the desk. "I can't tell you how sorry I am for missing lunch. You wanted to celebrate."

"Yeah, well, it's no big deal."

Of course it was, but for some reason he was pretending it wasn't. She'd never seen this fake indifference from him before, but she recognized it as his way of protecting himself.

She had a similar method herself.

She took hold of his hand and squeezed it. "It's a *very* big deal. I get it, really I do." She leaned forward and kissed him. "I'm so happy for you. If I can do anything to help, let me know."

He gave a half smile. "Thanks."

"If you need to paint tomorrow night, I understand," she said. If he had work to do, she didn't want him to feel obligated to attend the gala ball.

He let out a breath. "No, I'll be there." He took hold of both of her hands. "Thanks for understanding."

It was easy to. "Well, if you're coming, you could stay at my place afterward. It's going to be a late night."

He raised an eyebrow and her skin heated.

Maybe he wasn't interested anymore. Or maybe she was being too forward. She'd been thinking about their movie night all week, wondering what would have happened if McClane hadn't interrupted. "You don't have to."

"I'd like to."

She hesitated. She wanted to invite him to her mother's party over the weekend as well, but he might be too busy. "On Sunday Mama's having a party. It's the Day of the Dead, which is always a huge celebration in our family. Would you like to come? You may get some ideas for your paintings."

He hesitated, and then smiled for the first time. "Yeah, I would." He brought his arms around her. "I'm sorry. I was disappointed you missed lunch."

She brushed her lips against his. "So was I."

He rested his forehead against hers. "I'll take a raincheck tonight, but I'd love to stay Friday night and go to your Day of the Dead celebration."

"Great." She kissed him. "I'd better let you get back to work."

He nodded.

She turned, and about twenty pairs of eyes suddenly shifted back to their computer screens. "You might get a few questions," she murmured to Evan.

"I'd bet on it," he agreed with a grin.

When they reached his desk, she said, "I'll see you tomorrow."

Walking back to the elevator, she felt all eyes on her, but she ignored it. Inside, she smiled. Carly Flanagan had a boyfriend.

****

Evan stood at the easel, staring at the blank canvas in front of him. Nothing would come to him. Each time he decided what he wanted to paint, he'd second-guess himself. The painting had to be good – no, it had to be excellent, and he couldn't choose which of his ideas to go forward with. Whatever he chose was going to be exhibited in New York, at the gallery he'd walked past every day when he went to draw in the square, the gallery whose windows he'd stood in front of longingly, dreaming that one day his work would hang there.

And now it was coming true.

If only he could figure out what the hell to paint.

Disgusted, he threw down his paintbrush and strode outside. Staring at the canvas was getting him nowhere. He stripped off his T-shirt and dived into the pool. The cold water sent a shock through him, but he pushed through it, swimming to one end and then turning and swimming back.

While he swam, he let his mind drift. He needed to come up with a theme to tie all the pieces together. That would help him figure out what he should paint next.

But what kind of theme? He'd always painted whatever he wanted before. For the exhibition Carly had sponsored, he'd been told to provide four of his best works and they'd all sold in the end. He had the painting he'd done of the view from Carly's office, and he'd started several paintings of Carmen's garden, but they didn't really tie together. One was of a city, and one was of a garden. But Carmen's garden was also part of the city, just a different part.

He pushed against the wall of the pool as he turned again. Maybe that was the key. Maybe he could show different aspects of the city, make the theme "urban landscapes". He stopped swimming and examined the idea. Yes, it would work well. There were dozens of different angles he could take. He quickly got out of the pool, grabbing a towel and drying himself. He threw his shirt back on and went inside to paint.

***

At three o'clock, half a dozen alarms rang, shocking Evan out of his painting trance. He put a hand to his chest and chuckled, relieved they'd worked. He did not want to miss the ball. He surveyed his studio. He'd finished one painting today and worked on two others, which were coming together nicely. He cleaned his brushes and took one last look at the painting he

101

was halfway through. He was happy with the mix of colors and the flow of movement. It was a scene of New York that took him back to his childhood.

His phone rang and he walked out of the studio as he answered it.

"Evan, how's things?"

He smiled. He hadn't heard from his younger brother Karl in a while. "Great. What about you?"

"I'm getting married."

Evan sat down. "Congrats, man." He searched his memory for the name of the girl Karl had been dating. "You finally popped the question to Sarah?"

"Yeah. I still can't believe she said yes." The love and amazement in Karl's tone was clear.

Evan grinned. "So when's the wedding?"

"We haven't set a date yet, but we're having an engagement party in a couple of weeks. It'd be great if you could come."

Evan's happiness for his brother faded. An engagement party would mean seeing his parents. He doubted that would end well.

"I'd love to, but it's probably not a good idea."

"Evan, you can't keep avoiding them. It's been ten years. Things have changed."

Had they really? "I don't want to risk ruining your day."

"The only way you could upset the day is by not coming."

Damn it. His little brother was usually a quiet, mild-mannered sort, but every now and then something would get him riled and he was persistent. The thing was, Evan did want to go to the engagement party to celebrate with them, but that would mean facing his parents. He'd made a success of himself, so there'd be no "I told you so" they could throw in his face, but there were still all the snide remarks he'd have to put up with.

"When is it?" he asked.

Karl told him the date. It was the weekend before his exhibition opening. He'd have to be in New York about then anyway.

Could he handle all of the remarks about how pointless his art was, right before the biggest exhibition of his life? He closed his eyes and Carly's face appeared. If she could do all those public appearances when she clearly hated them, he could handle one engagement party.

"All right. I'll be there."

"Thanks, man. I'm so glad. I'll see you then."

Evan hung up and let out a deep breath. He'd be fine. But now was not the time to worry about it. He had a ball to get to.

***

Evan was ridiculously nervous as he rode the elevator to Carly's apartment. He'd never been to a gala ball before, and had no idea what to expect. He just hoped the tuxedo he'd bought was good enough. He hadn't been able to afford the top of the range, but he'd spent a little more than he'd wanted to, knowing he'd be expected to wear one to the New York exhibition opening as well.

He knocked on the door. This was his first time to Carly's apartment and he was curious to see where she lived.

The door opened and Carly stood framed in the space. His whole body jolted to alert as his eyes roved over her. She was wearing a mid-length black dress that hugged her curves and strappy heels that accentuated her legs. "You look stunning."

"So do you." She gestured him in. "Leave your overnight bag by the sofa for now. We should be going."

He did as she asked, taking in the floor-to-ceiling windows, the antique coffee table and day bed, and the huge tropical fish tank on one wall. It was all class.

Carly walked toward the door.

"Wait a second," he said, turning her toward him. He had to greet her properly and some things couldn't be rushed. He lowered his head and kissed her. She had the most luscious lips, so incredibly kissable, and he wanted to keep going. Instead, he pulled back. "How important is this event tonight?"

Her laugh was a little shaky. "I'm starting to think not very important."

He grinned at her and moved closer, but she stopped him with a hand on his chest. "I *do* need to go."

"All right," he agreed, pleased he'd even made her consider staying.

Carly grabbed her handbag and keys and he followed her out.

They took her silver BMW to the hotel where the ball was being held. It was a damn sight cleaner and newer than his car. What had she thought when she'd seen his station wagon? Was she enjoying slumming it with him?

Evan shook his head. He was being ridiculous. Lack of money had never been an issue for him before.

There was already a crowd of people mingling when they arrived. The ballroom had tall marble columns with arching ceilings and had been decorated for Halloween, with fake cobwebs draped artistically across the walls and jack-o'-lanterns adding extra lighting.

As Carly handed over her tickets, Evan gazed into the throng. The women all wore stylish dresses and sparkling jewels, while the men wore tuxedos. He was reminded of a documentary about Birds of Paradise that did extraordinary dances to attract a mate. There wasn't any dancing yet, but there was definitely a lot of preening and fluffed-up plumage. If he painted it, he would have to call it The Dance.

As they walked down the steps into the ballroom, Carly was greeted by an older gentleman with graying hair and a stiff posture.

"Carolina, it's lovely to see you."

"Hello, Bernard. Let me introduce you to Evan Hayes."

The man's shook Evan's hand.

"Bernard is the organizer of this event," Carly explained.

"You've got a great turnout," Evan said.

"Naturally." He turned away to focus on Carly.

Evan swallowed a grin. Obviously he wasn't worth the man's time. Too amused to be offended, he stood next to Carly and listened to the conversation.

"We have some fabulous items for auction tonight," he said. "But we need to raise so much in order to make this a reality. Can I count on you for an additional donation?"

Evan couldn't believe it. Carly had literally just walked into the ballroom and he was hitting her up for more money. Evan wasn't sure how much tickets were for the event, but he'd guess they weren't cheap. He wanted to say something, but it wasn't his place.

Carly smiled politely. "Let's see how the evening goes first. You may be surprised."

Bernard opened his mouth to say something else, but Carly was quicker. "Excuse us, Bernard, I need to introduce Evan to a few people." She took Evan's hand and walked away.

Evan grinned. "Nicely handled."

"I've had a lot of practice." She glanced around. "Now I need to find someone to introduce you to, so it's not obvious I was lying."

Before she could, they were approached by a woman wearing a peacock-blue dress and the most ostentatious diamond earrings Evan had ever seen.

"Carolina!" the woman cried, kissing both of her cheeks. "How are you?"

"I'm fine, thank you, Margarite. How are the fun run plans going?"

"Marvelous," she said, spying Evan. "And who is this?"

"Evan Hayes, Margarite Smith. Margarite is organizing a fun run to raise money for breast cancer awareness."

Was she the one who'd requested extra funds for shirts?

"What is it you do, Evan?" Margarite asked.

"I'm an artist."

"How lovely," she said. "Carolina sponsored an art exhibition the other day. So nice of her to give those hobbyists a chance to show their work."

"I sure appreciated it," Evan replied, keeping his expression deadpan.

She sucked in her cheeks and widened her eyes. "Oh. Well, I must go. Have a nice evening." Margarite fled.

Evan chuckled quietly and as Carly turned to him, she grinned. "Margarite has never moved so fast."

"Is everyone here so pretentious?"

"Well, no." She looked around as if trying to find someone to prove her point. As she did a handsome man came up behind her and slid an arm around her waist, pulling her close.

"You've got to save me," he said.

Evan scowled. Who the hell was he?

Carly took a step away, laughing. "Who's after you tonight,

David?"

"Every single woman under fifty it seems." The blond-haired, blue-eyed guy glanced over and noticed Evan. He took a step back.

"David, this is my date, Evan Hayes."

"Darn it, sorry. Carolina usually comes to these things with Hayden." He held out his hand and Evan shook it. "Nice to meet you."

Evan was reserving his judgment, but he said, "Likewise."

"David is the CFO at Dionysus Oil and Gas, and the heir to the company. He's the most eligible bachelor here."

It was the first time Evan had seen Carly genuinely pleased to see someone. He couldn't prevent the twinge of jealousy.

"Carolina constantly resists my charms, though."

"Oh, stop. You're not interested in me."

David grinned at Evan. "Carolina keeps me sane at these things. I help her fight off the money grabbers and she saves me from the husband hunters."

Evan relaxed. The guy seemed genuinely nice, and not interested in Carly in that way. "You'll have to teach me some of your tricks," he said. "She's been propositioned twice already and we've just arrived."

"All right." David nodded seriously. "You can't let them get to the pitch. Ask them about themselves, and before they get to the pitch, move on. Usually they love to talk about themselves so they forget for a minute why they came to talk to you."

"Thanks." He could do that.

"It's not so bad. They need money and I have it," Carly said.

"You work hard for it. These people don't."

Dinner was announced and they moved toward the tables. David sighed. "Into the lion's den." He saluted them and went to find his table.

"He was nice."

Carly nodded. "I met David at the first big event I attended after I made some money. We were the youngest ones there and we drifted together. He was much more experienced at the whole thing, having grown up rich, and he helped steer me through all the requests and conversations."

"You two never dated?"

She shook her head. "He was more like a brother or a guardian angel to me. It's funny, we never meet up outside of these events."

The green-eyed monster was tamed.

***

Carly's steps faltered as she saw who they were seated with. It had to have been specifically arranged.

"What's wrong?" Evan murmured.

She sighed. "Nothing." She greeted the three men, who were all executives at Softco. She introduced Evan, said hello to their wives and took her seat. It was going to be a long night.

The master of ceremonies spoke about the medical research they were raising funds for and then the first course was served.

"When does the auction start?" Evan asked her.

"Not until after everyone has eaten, probably around nine o'clock."

"Carolina, have you had a chance to consider our proposal?" The CEO Neil was sitting on her right.

"Not yet, Neil. You know how it is, I have to prioritize."

"What is it you do, Neil?" Evan leaned forward.

"I'm the CEO at Softco."

"What does Softco do?"

Neil frowned. "We're a software company. We design databases, platforms, operating systems, and a whole lot more."

"So does that make you a competitor of Carly's?"

Carly wasn't sure whether she wanted this conversation to continue, but before she could speak, Neil said, "No. Comunidad focuses on the front-end experience, while we supply the back-end software. We are looking at expanding, however, and we're trying to convince Carly to sell."

"Why Comunidad?" Evan asked.

It was a very good question and one she hadn't got a straight answer to.

"It has a diverse range of products, from the social media platform, to apps and well-tested software."

"But you just said you were a back-end guy." Evan grinned. "What do you need with Carly's products?"

"It's good to diversify."

"Not always," Evan disagreed. "You put too many balls in the air, and you're likely to drop one eventually."

Carly smiled. Neil looked a little annoyed at all the questions.

"What does your staff know about the stuff Carly's company does?"

The man shifted in his seat. "If we bought Comunidad, we would keep most of the staff and use their expertise."

"Would you keep Carly?"

Neil glanced at her. "It's not usually a good idea to keep the original owner. There are often conflicts when changes need to be made."

It was another reason to say no to them. Carly's company was her baby. Softco would change its direction and she wouldn't be able to stop them.

"So you'd put Carly out of a job?" said Evan.

"She would be more than financially compensated." Neil smiled at Carly. "You'll see there's a very generous figure in our proposal."

"We both know it's not about the money," Evan said. "Carly's wealthy enough without selling. What changes would you make?" Evan was definitely determined to get some answers from him, and it was kind of nice to have someone go into battle for her.

"I won't know until we get a good look at the company."

"I guess the big question is, do you want to sell?" Evan looked at Carly with a raised eyebrow.

"No," she said firmly.

"Then you're out of luck," he said to Neil. "So, what do you do in your spare time?"

Carly swallowed a grin as Neil opened and shut his mouth a couple of times. He'd been effectively railroaded and hadn't seen it coming. She could kiss Evan right now.

The second course was served and Neil turned his attention to his wife on the other side.

"Thank you," Carly whispered to Evan.

His wicked grin sent a shot of lust through her. "That was fun. I must thank David later for giving me the tip."

"He'll enjoy the story."

Neil didn't bring up the subject of buying Comunidad again.

Instead, Carly chatted to Evan and bid on a few auction items. When the auction was over, the band began to play.

"Would you like to dance?" Evan asked.

Carly shook her head. "I can't dance." It was the one thing she'd always wanted to learn, but she had two left feet and absolutely no rhythm.

"Really?"

She nodded. "I inherited my father's sense of rhythm." She remembered him trying to keep in time to the music at some of the Salvadoran festivals, but he never succeeded.

"This one's a slow one," said Evan. "You don't even have to move your feet, just sway with me." He drew her onto the dance floor.

Carly's chest tightened. If she made a fool of herself, everyone would see.

"It's all right, Carly, I've got you." His voice was soothing as he took one of her hands and used the other to draw her close to him. "Just sway."

Trusting him, she did as he said, trying to feel the melody.

"Relax," he said, whispering into her ear, and caressing her back.

Carly forgot to be nervous as the sensations spread through her. It felt so good being held in his arms. She'd never been held like this. It was comfort and support, and it was sensual. She was so aware of her body's reaction to him, and felt as if she could let down her guard, as if there was someone on her side. She closed her eyes and swayed to the music.

"This isn't so bad, is it?"

"It's nice," she admitted. It was more than nice. Every caress of his hand sent heat pooling in her core. She wanted to drag him off to a dark corner and explore her attraction to him, and she was stunned by the intenseness of her want. She'd never felt like this about anyone. She'd never considered herself a sexual person.

The song ended and was replaced by an upbeat one. Carly stepped back and swallowed, trying to get her reactions under control.

Evan's eyes were darker than normal. "Is it too early to go?" he murmured.

The suggestion was clear and her response was immediate. "Not at all."

It was time to find that dark corner after all.

Chapter 11

Carly's belly squirmed as they rode up to her apartment. They'd chatted about the evening on the drive home, but she'd been acutely aware of the sexual tension zapping between them. It had been years since she'd had sex, and Andrew had never cared much about her pleasure. She wanted it to be different with Evan, she didn't want to be so passive.

She unlocked the door and flicked on the light. "Would you like a drink?"

Evan smiled at her. "A glass of water would be great." He wandered over to the window to look at the view.

Some of her nerves calmed. He understood she was nervous. He wasn't going to rush her. She stepped out of her heels.

"This is a great view."

"I guess so." It had never interested her. She'd bought the penthouse apartment because it was within walking distance of work.

After filling two glasses with water, she crossed over to him and handed him a glass.

"Have you lived here long?" he asked.

"About six years." She walked over to the couch and sat down.

"The fish tank's cool."

"It came with the apartment." Though she did like watching the fish swim back and forward. They had such a simple life.

Evan came over and sat next to her, and her nerves began to hum. She was no good at this kind of thing. She didn't know whether she should make the first move, whether they should neck on the couch, or she should invite him into her bedroom. Her body tingled as she remembered their dance and the way his hand had lazily brushed her skin.

Evan took her glass out of her hand and placed it on the coffee table with his. He turned to her. "Carly, we don't have to do anything tonight, if you're not ready. We could just get into our pajamas and go to sleep."

He was leaving it up to her. She had to make the move, but it also meant she was in control. Pretending to be braver than she felt, she said, "Let's see where this goes." She leaned over and kissed him, and then sunk deeper into the kiss, tasting him.

Warmth pooled in her belly as his hand swept down her back and then across her breast. Long-forgotten sensations poured into her body as he kissed her neck, his thumb caressing her cheek. And then his hand moved lower.

Her body was alive. This was what she wanted.

"Tell me if I'm going too fast," he whispered, reaching for the zipper of her dress.

Cool air touched her skin briefly before the warmth of his hands covered her lower back. Luscious jolts went through her at each stroke. She wanted to touch him as well. Wanted to see whether she could make him feel like this. She untied his bow-tie and started on his buttons. She wanted to run her hands over his skin, feel his heat.

He took a deep breath in as her fingers caressed his chest. "I'm trying to go slow," he said, his voice strained.

Carly glanced at him. Was she having an effect on him? She brushed a thumb over his nipple and he closed his eyes.

She was. She actually was. Power surged through her, giving her the confidence to push his shirt off his shoulders. He quickly rid himself of it and she was surprised by his muscle-tone. Lowering her head, she kissed his chest, and then licked his nipples.

He hissed.

He was enjoying it. The knowledge made her brave, made her want to explore what she was capable of. She stood, stepped out of her dress, and the cool air on her breasts made her pause for a second.

"You're so beautiful," he said, his tone reverent.

In that moment, Carly felt beautiful, and she wanted more. She held out her hand.

He took it without a word and followed her into her bedroom.

Inside the doorway, Evan wrapped his arms around her and kissed her again. Her breasts pressed up against his chest and her groin pulsed. She wanted him. His thumbs caressed her breasts and she forgot to think. He brought her mouth back to his, kissing her with a passion that took her breath away.

It was so much more than she'd ever experienced.

He pried off his shoes while she undid his pants, pushing them down, and then they were both standing in their underwear.

Evan's lips made their way down her neck. "Are you sure, Carly?"

She nodded. "Yes." She wanted him as much as he wanted her. She led him to the bed. He laid her gently down on the bed and she scooted up to lean against the pillows. He followed, crawling toward her like a lion on the hunt. Her heart raced and she smiled at him.

"You're a temptress," he said. He kissed her and then continued down her body, doing things with his tongue that were driving her insane.

"Evan," she breathed as he crouched between her legs, his mouth on her, separated from her skin by her underwear. She arched against him. "Take them off."

"With pleasure." The grin he gave her was pure seduction and she only had a second to appreciate it before her underwear had disappeared and his mouth was on her.

She lost her breath as his tongue teased her and his finger entered her. The sensations rose in her so quickly she couldn't stop them and she shuddered as she climaxed.

As her body calmed, her embarrassment rose. They hadn't had sex yet.

"You're a Goddess." Evan moved up the bed, kissing her body.

The embarrassment faded as her body continued to sing under his lips.

"Ready for round two?" he asked, nibbling at her neck.

"Yes." But it was her turn to take charge. She wanted to make him feel as amazing as she felt. She just hoped she could.

Pushing him onto his back, she straddled him, feeling his hardness pushing against his underwear. She would get to that.

Like him, she began her slow journey down his neck, over his chest and to his crotch.

"Carly, you're killing me," he groaned.

She grinned, smug excitement flooding through her. She peeled off his underwear and took him in her mouth. His hips bucked. "Holy shit."

A heady rush of power swept through her as she tasted him and his breath hissed out. "I'm not going last if you keep that up." He passed her a condom, and after a moment's awkwardness, she sheathed him. Her eyes on his, she slowly slid onto him. He moaned as he entered her. She took a moment to get used to him and then she began to slowly move. She kissed his chest as the sensations began to build again. She was in charge and he wanted her. The tension built and she embraced it, loving the way her body was responding to him. When they came together, she'd never felt so powerful.

***

Carly's breathing slowly returned to normal as she lay on top of Evan. Her whole body was pleasantly relaxed and she couldn't stop smiling. This was what good sex was supposed to be like.

He nuzzled at her neck and she slid off him so he could clean up. Then he joined her under the covers and pulled her close.

"How are you feeling?"

"Amazing," she said. "You?"

He grinned. "Pretty damned good."

Her insides squeezed. She hadn't been bad, which is what she feared. She closed her eyes. Her body was so heavy, so pleasantly sated and it was hard for her to concentrate. There was supposed to be small talk afterward, she was almost sure of it.

"Sweet dreams." He kissed her head and the heaviness took her under.

***

The first thing Carly noticed when she woke the next day was that she wasn't alone in her bed. She watched Evan sleep, his dark hair was mussed and his expression was as relaxed as she'd ever seen it. He was so different from any other man she'd met. He wasn't the least bit interested in her money, or in awe of her success, he just wanted to spend time with her. It was such a lovely feeling.

They hadn't talked about what they were going to do today, but he had all those paintings to do. Knowing he wasn't a morning person, Carly quietly slipped out of bed and padded to the bathroom. She'd take a shower, and then head out to get some breakfast for them both.

The warm water was soothing on her skin and she stood under the spray, letting the water cascade down her. Her body felt satisfied. She grinned at the memory.

She was in a relationship.

The whole idea was so foreign to her. She wrapped her arms around herself. She'd almost given up on ever finding a guy who wanted to be with her.

After she'd dried herself and dressed, she debated straightening her hair. Peeking in at Evan, she saw he was still fast asleep and she didn't want the noise of the hair dryer to wake him. Instead, she toweled it dry and put on a large floppy hat. She scribbled a note and left it on the bedside table in case he woke, grabbed her purse, and headed out.

When she returned half an hour later with muffins and bagels, he was still asleep. Should she wake him? It was already eight o'clock, but some people considered it early for a Saturday.

She didn't want him oversleeping and being annoyed that he'd missed out on painting time, so she sat on the edge of the bed and said quietly, "Evan, breakfast is ready."

There was no response.

Louder this time, she said, "Evan, it's time to wake up." She ran a hand down his arm.

"Don't want to," came the sleepy reply.

Carly grinned. He sounded like a petulant child. "I've got bagels and muffins."

"Hmph."

Carefully she leaned over and brushed a kiss across his cheek and then over his lips. "Are you sure you don't want to wake up?"

His eyes flashed open as she sat back. He blinked a couple of times. "Carly?"

She nodded. "I've bought breakfast. I didn't know how late you wanted to sleep."

He examined her for a moment. "Your hair is different."

Self-conscious, she placed a hand on the hat covering her curly hair. "I didn't want to wake you drying it."

He pushed himself up to a seated position. "It's curly."

"That's what it tends to do when it gets wet."

"Show me."

Hesitating, she lifted the hat from her head. Evan motioned her closer.

She shuffled nearer to him and he ran his hand through her hair. "It's gorgeous. Why do you always straighten it?"

"I was told it looks more professional. It's so hard to manage when it's curly, it goes its own way."

"Whoever told you that was an idiot," Evan said. "You look powerful, untamed, exotic."

Her skin heated. "It was my stylist. She taught me how a business executive needs to dress."

He shook his head. "She didn't know what she was talking about. I love your hair like that. When I paint you, I want to paint that hair."

Carly blinked. "You want to paint me?"

"Absolutely. I want to paint you in all sorts of ways." He grinned. "And not in the slightly creepy way that sounded."

She laughed. "We'll see." She wasn't sure what she thought about him painting her. He saw too much. She didn't want others to see her the way he saw her. It would make her too vulnerable. "Do you want breakfast now?"

"As long as it comes with coffee."

"Of course."

She left him to dress and went back to the kitchen to make the coffee. A few minutes later, he came out, wearing shorts and T-shirt.

"You know it's only early, right?" he said as he took the coffee she handed him and kissed her.

"Eight o'clock is late for me."

"It's the weekend."

"My body clock's set for five no matter the day. I slept in today by comparison."

Evan shook his head in disbelief. "Nine's my usual wake up time."

She didn't know how he got anything done by waking up so late. "So what are you doing today?"

"I want to continue work on a couple of paintings for the exhibition. What about you?"

"I've got a few things I need to work on."

He put down his bagel. "Working seven days a week isn't good for you, Carly."

She shrugged. "This is stuff I want to do."

"Really? Like what?"

She hadn't told anyone else about the app she was developing. It was her little secret. "I'm creating an app."

"To do what?"

She hesitated. "Teach people English."

"Wow. That sounds challenging. How's it going?"

"Slowly. I don't get much time to work on it."

"I'm a big believer in making time for the things you love to do."

She nodded. "It's why I get up so early. I get to do an hour every day before work."

He shook his head. "You're amazing."

She shrugged. She did what she had to do, that was all.

"Do you want to come to my place?" he said. "We could hang out today, each doing our own thing, and you could stay the night. Then we can go to your mom's tomorrow for the party."

The idea was appealing. She didn't need more than her

laptop to do her work. Plus the thought that Evan wanted to spend more time with her was thrilling.

"Sure."

***

Evan wasn't entirely certain why he'd invited Carly to join him at his house. Normally when he painted he preferred solitude. That way he could get caught up in the work. He didn't have to stop at a given time, or worry about the other person feeling neglected. But the invite had slipped out, and he *did* want to spend more time with her.

They drove separately to his place so that Carly could drive home. When he arrived, McClane trotted out to greet him. Zita must have already dropped him off. He hurried inside to check the state of his house. He'd been in painting mode up until he left and it could be a complete pigsty, for all he remembered.

He shoved dishes into the dishwasher, quickly changed his bedsheets and tidied the living room. As he was checking what else needed to be done, Carly arrived.

McClane trotted to the front door to greet her, wagging his tail furiously, which was about as animated as he got these days.

"He's definitely taken a shine to you," Evan said.

Carly smiled. "I've never been very good around dogs." She crouched down to rub McClane's head. "But you're just the sweetest thing, aren't you?"

McClane panted happily in agreement, then licked her.

She got back to her feet. "Where are you going to work?"

"In the studio. I'm halfway through a couple of pieces."

"A couple of pieces?"

"Yeah. I tend to have a few works going at once, depending on my mood." He walked down the hallway and she followed him into his studio.. "You can pick your spot. There's a table in here, or the kitchen, or outside if you want. If you prefer the sofa, you know where it is."

She nodded and set up her laptop on the table.

After making sure Carly had everything she needed, Evan examined his painting. It was the place he used to hang out, drawing sketches for people to earn some money throughout high school. He could have painted it blindfolded.

Mixing the color he needed, he got to work.

***

Evan finished the painting and stepped back. It was good. It was just what he remembered. He'd even drawn himself in it, as a teenager, doing his sketches. He turned to say something to Carly, but she was gone. Concerned, he dumped his brushes in a cleaning solution and wandered through the house to find her.

She was sitting on the outdoor couch, her laptop on her lap, and McClane lying at her feet. She looked perfectly at home, as if she belonged. He blocked the yearning from his heart before it could take hold and checked the time. It was midafternoon and he hadn't even offered her lunch.

"Are you hungry?"

She didn't respond, her fingers flying over the keyboard.

He grinned, not so worried now that he hadn't noticed her leave the studio. She was as involved in her work as he had been with his.

"Carolina," he said, mimicking the way her mother said her name.

Carly jolted and looked up. "Sorry, did you say something?"

"I was wondering whether you're hungry. We missed lunch."

"Did we?" She checked the time on her laptop. "So we did. I'm a little hungry now you mention it."

"I'll see what I can find."

He put together a couple of sandwiches, grabbed his sketchbook and headed back outside. "Here you go," he said, putting the sandwich on the table next to Carly.

"Thanks," she murmured, her eyes never leaving the screen.

Evan chuckled. He was sure he was like that when he was painting. Eating his sandwich, he watched her. Her focus was absolute and the tap on the keyboard was almost constant. Whatever she was doing, she was fully involved. He loved the concentration on her face and the way she absentmindedly brushed her curls away when they blocked her view.

He picked up his sketchbook and began to draw.

***

Evan's stomach was grumbling when he finished. He

grabbed his half-eaten sandwich and took a bite. Carly was still totally absorbed. He debated disturbing her again, but he hated to be interrupted while he was painting. She'd get hungry soon enough and stop. Finishing his sandwich, he went back inside to start his next painting.

The blank canvas mocked him as he tried to decide what to paint next. What he really wanted to do was paint a series of images of Carly. It would take some time to convince her to let him use the images in an exhibition, but that wasn't the main purpose of painting her.

He shook his head. No, right now he needed to concentrate on the present exhibition, the urban landscape.

Closing his eyes, visions of Carly filled his mind. The urban stuff would have to wait. The pull to paint her was too strong.

Chapter 12

Evan looked up at the movement in the doorway. He must have been attuned to Carly to notice her walk in.

"Thanks for the sandwich," she said.

He checked the time. It was close to dinner. "Did you just surface?"

She nodded. "Sorry. I must have completed blanked out."

"Don't sweat it. Happens to me all the time. Was it productive?"

"Yeah. I've finished the first stage." She wandered over to him. "How about you?"

He gestured to the painting drying on one easel. "I've finished one and started on another."

"Can I have a look?"

"Sure." The nerves twitched in his stomach.

Carly walked over to the easel. He held his breath. She was silent for a long moment, scrutinizing the painting.

"Is that you?" she asked, pointing to the teenager drawing.

"Yeah." He was surprised she could tell.

"It's so detailed. You've captured the whole ambiance of the square; the hustle and bustle and the community of it. It feels like everyone there is friendly and knows one another."

The nerves settled. "Thanks. It was a fun place to hang out."

"What are you working on there?" she asked.

He hesitated. How was she going to react?

"Take a look," he invited. He'd finished painting Carly, but had yet to add the background.

She gasped. "That's me."

He nodded, waiting.

She squinted at it. "I look powerful, in charge." She paused. "Untouchable."

Evan wrapped an arm around her waist and pulled her close to him. "Carolina is a formidable person."

She shook her head. "If I met that person, she'd scare the hell out of me."

He frowned. "Carly, you *are* that person. At least when you're doing business."

"I never realized." She seemed a little sad. "I've been pretending I know what I'm doing for so long."

"I'm pretty sure you've got that down pat." He kissed her forehead. "Why do you hide behind that face?"

She squeezed her eyes shut. "When I first started making money, I had all these people giving me advice. They told me I had to look professional, show no fear, be assertive. I hired a stylist to show me how to present myself, and had a mentor to tell me how to deal with requests. It was a big learning curve and I had to work on it constantly. I guess it became who I am."

He shook his head. "No. The real Carly is the woman who goes and helps out in the indie hub, the one who is so involved in her programming that she doesn't register lunch being put in front of her, the one who goes to her mother's every couple of weeks and spends time with her family." He grabbed his sketchbook from the table and showed her the picture he'd drawn.

She stared at him. "When did you do this?"

"While I was having lunch. You were distracted."

She examined the drawing. "It's like a completely different person." Her fingers entwined themselves in her hair. "I look so different with curly hair."

"I like it."

With a sigh, she put the sketchbook down. "This isn't the type of person who runs a billion dollar company."

Anger stirred in Evan. "You can look however you want. Steve Jobs wore turtlenecks, for heaven's sake."

"But he was a man."

"So?"

"A woman is seen as more vulnerable by the men around her. Why do you think Softco arranged for me to be at their table the other night? They thought they could get to me."

Evan had no experience in that kind of thing. He had no idea if she was right, but it galled him to think that maybe she was. "Surely the way you wear your hair doesn't matter."

She shrugged. "Maybe, maybe not. Should we think about dinner?"

He let her change the topic. It was getting dark, and on cue, his stomach rumbled. "Yeah. I'll grill a couple of steaks and make a salad."

"Sounds good."

He led her into the kitchen and grabbed the makings for a salad out of the fridge.

"You've got far more in your fridge than I do," Carly said.

"It's too much of a hassle to go out every time I need to eat."

Evan fed McClane, who had turned up as soon as he'd heard them in the kitchen. Carly chopped vegetables for the salad and he marinated the steaks. He tried to remember the last time he'd had a woman in his kitchen, the last time someone had helped him prepare dinner. It had to have been in Michigan, but he struggled to remember details. Normally the women he dated didn't stick around for too long. They got tired of being ignored while he painted, thought he should drop everything to be with them when they wanted it, because being an artist wasn't really work.

He and Carly had slipped into a rhythm without any fuss. They saw each other when they could, and she was even busier than he was. It didn't faze her when he worked for hours, because she did exactly the same thing. There weren't any expectations from her. Evan appreciated that. He'd spent way too much of his life not living up to his parents' expectations.

"Do you want a drink?" He held up a bottle of sparkling apple cider. He'd made sure he had a bottle in his fridge since the picnic.

She grinned. "Yes, please."

Her smile sent warmth through him and he put the bottle down and pulled her into his arms. She fit snugly against him and he kissed her. A shiver of lust went through him as her arms encircled him and she kissed him back just as fiercely. This woman was incredible. How could no one see it?

He reluctantly broke the kiss, and Carly looked up at him with desire in her eyes. He wanted to drag her off to bed, but then they'd never get dinner. He cleared his throat. "I'll get you that drink."

When everything was ready, they decided to sit outside to eat.

"What should I expect tomorrow?" Evan asked. He'd been to Halloween parties before, but never to a Day of the Dead event.

"We'll go over early and honor the dead. Mama will have already built the altars for each person."

"What do you do with the altar?"

"We decorate it and then tell stories of the person we are honoring."

It was different from anything he was used to. "Who will you be honoring?"

Her smile was a little sad. "My father, two of Mama's brothers and Mama's father and grandparents. The girls will all have people to honor as well. You'll get to meet some of the foster girls Mama has cared for over the past nine years."

"And after that?"

"Then we party. Food, drink, music and celebration. Mama invites whole communities around and we celebrate together. You might want to bring your sketchbook."

"That wouldn't be inappropriate?"

"Not at all. We're celebrating life and you'd be capturing it. Though you may want to dance instead."

"I didn't think you danced."

She shook her head and her curls danced around. "I don't, but it's mandatory to have at least a jig."

He wanted to see that. He wanted to see Carly really relax and let go.

"It goes until late, but I usually leave early because I need to work the next day."

"Why don't you crash here again? That way you'll have a chance to rest before driving." And he could spend another night with her.

"All right. That would be great."

He liked that she wasn't presuming to stay. He didn't have to deal with her disappointment if he had wanted to paint instead.

"Do you have some more work you want to do tonight?" he asked.

"No, I'm done. My brain can only take so much at once."

There was a twinge of disappointment. He'd wanted to finish the painting of her tonight.

"If you've got more painting to do, I can watch the next *Die Hard* movie with McClane." She stretched. "Though that might even be too much for me right now."

"You wouldn't mind?"

"Of course not. You've got the exhibition coming up. I don't want to stop you getting your work done. It's important."

She understood. It was probably the first time that anyone really understood what he did. "Thanks."

After they'd cleaned up, he set her up with the movie and some popcorn and went back to his studio.

She was his kind of woman.

***

It was past midnight when Evan signed the bottom of the painting. Had Carly come to say goodnight and he'd ignored her? He couldn't remember any interruption. He cleaned his brushes quickly and then walked into the living room. Carly was lying on the couch asleep, and McClane had climbed up next to her. The DVD menu screen kept repeating over and over.

Carefully, he sat on the edge of the couch. "Carly, you need to go to bed."

She slowly opened her eyes and stretched. "Did I fall asleep?"

He nodded.

"What time is it?"

"After midnight."

She sat up. "I didn't see the end of the movie."

He raised his eyebrows in mock outrage. "You fell asleep on John McClane?"

"Yes."

"That's it! We can no longer be friends."

Carly sat up, put her hand on his arm. "I'm sorry. I didn't mean to." She was genuinely concerned.

"I was kidding." He kissed her lightly. "Come on, let's go to bed."

He helped her up, flicked off the television, and followed her to his bedroom.

What kind of life had Carly led that she couldn't recognize his joke?

Probably a lonely one. He should be more careful with her.

***

Evan's stomach was imitating a washing machine as he and Carly walked with McClane over to her mother's house on Sunday. It would not stop churning. This was a family event and not just some random lunch. He was going as Carly's partner, not Zita's friend, and that made it seem serious. He didn't do well with family stuff.

They strolled up the drive and Zita's two dogs raced out to greet them. McClane wagged his tail and soon all three of them were running around the front yard together.

"I give McClane about five minutes before he's run himself ragged," Evan said.

Sure enough, by the time they walked up the steps of the house, McClane was lying panting under a tree.

"Is he going to be all right?" Carly asked.

"Yeah. I'll get a bowl of water from Z and he'll be fine."

Carly opened the door and called, "Mama, we're here."

Her mother appeared wearing a traditional bright red skirt and a white shirt, her hair loose. "*Hola, mi niñita!* Evan, how are you?"

"Great, Carmen. Thanks for having me."

"You are practically family," she said, kissing both his cheeks.

He froze. Did she really think that? He and Carly had only

been on a couple of dates. The mantle of belonging tried to settle on his shoulders, but he shrugged it off. He knew better than that. Carmen was just being polite.

"How is the painting?" Carmen asked.

He blinked. He wasn't sure if she was referring to his painting of her garden, or painting in general, so he simply said, "Fine."

He was relieved to find Zita in the kitchen. After greeting her with a kiss on the cheek, he got the bowl of water for McClane and called him around to the backyard. By the time his dog was settled with Zita's two, Bridget and Jack had arrived, and there were also a dozen or so young women chatting excitedly, mostly in Spanish. He made his way over to Jack, who also appeared completely adrift.

"You understand any of this?" Evan asked.

"I catch the occasional word is all," Jack replied. "They talk so fast."

Carmen clapped her hands together and called, "It is time." She took a large basket from the bench and walked outside. The others filed after her, also picking up bags or baskets to take with them.

Evan fell in next to Carly. "Where are we going?"

"To the altars."

She took his hand and they wound their way through the garden to the back of the property and a large clearing surrounded by big, shady trees. There were over twenty white crosses set up around the clearing, each with a name on it. It was almost like a graveyard.

Carmen stopped in front of the cross in the center and everyone encircled it. Carly squeezed his hand and he looked at her, but she was staring at the cross. It had the name Brendan Flanagan on it. It must be for her father.

Carmen made the sign of the cross, and took a deep breath. "My husband, Brendan, the father of my three girls, taken from us too soon." She placed a small bottle of whiskey beneath the cross. "You always loved a drink, always ready with a story or to help others. You appeared in my life like a comet, bright and mystical, and swept me off my feet. You gave me three beautiful daughters, who you loved with all your heart." She knelt and placed a harmonica and a packet of cards on the altar. "To keep you entertained like you always entertained us." She turned to face the group. "The day I met Brendan was *Semana Santa*. We were going house to house with the priest and this tall, pale man caught my eye. He was ever so handsome." She put a hand to her chest and sighed. "He joined the procession and walked next to me, not saying anything. I felt him there every step of the way. By the time the ceremony was over, I had to speak with him."

Some of the girls smiled.

"He spoke only a few words of Spanish but it did not matter. Our hearts spoke to each other. From that day on we were inseparable."

Carmen stepped back. Carly let go of Evan's hand and moved forward.

"It is usually so difficult to decide which story to tell about Papa, but recently I saw a painting of the beach and I knew."

Was she talking about his painting? Bridget was smiling and nodding, Zita just looked sad.

"It was a hot summer and we lived inland, far from the ocean. One day, Papa said he'd had enough of the heat, so he packed us all into the pickup and drove almost two hours to the beach. None of us had seen the ocean before, and it was like he'd taken us to another world. We splashed in the water, built sandcastles and chased birds. I must have fallen asleep in the car on the way home because when I woke up I was in bed, and wondered whether it had all been a lovely dream." She stepped back, her eyes glistening.

Evan squeezed her hand. This was why she'd been so sad when she'd seen his painting. It had reminded her of a happier time when her father had been alive. Bridget stepped forward to tell her story, but he wasn't listening. He put his arm around Carly and pulled her close to him. A single tear ran down her face and she brushed it off.

It had been over twenty years since her father had died and still it brought her to tears. He didn't know what to say. He'd never lost anyone close to him.

Bridget finished her story and Zita stepped forward. "I remember him putting me to bed, kissing me goodnight." She stepped back.

If Carly had been about eight when her father died, it meant Zita was only three. Perhaps she had few memories of the man who fathered her.

Carmen was finishing her prayers for her husband when Bridget spoke.

"Mama, will you tell us how Papa died?"

Her mother put a hand to her chest. "Today is not the time for such stories."

"Please, Mama. I always thought he died at work, but Carly told me recently I was wrong."

By his side, Carly stiffened and then sighed.

"No. Today is for happy memories," said Carmen.

"Mama, the girls are old enough to know the truth," Carly said, moving over to put a hand on her shoulder.

Carmen looked at her daughter. "What do you know of it?"

"I was awake when the soldiers brought the news."

She shook her head, sorrow on her face. "No. Not now. We must honor the others first." She moved on to the next altar.

Evan wanted to ask what that was all about, but Carmen had already begun to speak, in Spanish this time.

"The rest will be in Spanish," Carly whispered. "The others we are honoring do not speak English."

Evan nodded. He was happy to stand and listen. There was a lot he could tell from the tone of someone's voice and the way they stood. He didn't need the exact words.

They moved from altar to altar; each time the person who spoke would leave gifts for the deceased and tell a story. When it came time for the foster girls to speak about their families, they often stood alone, or if they were upset, one of the other girls would comfort and support them.

It was a lovely tradition, so far removed from the cheap, commercial Halloween celebrated in the United States. It would be far nicer to celebrate all those people who had passed out of your life, to remember what they had meant to you.

When they were finished, Carmen said something in Spanish and the foster girls all moved back toward the house. Carmen went to join them, but Carly stopped her.

"Mama, it's time."

Carmen hesitated.

"Please Mama," Carly said. The older woman sighed. She walked over to a shady spot and sat under the tree. Her daughters followed, and when Carly glanced over her shoulder and indicated he should come, Evan joined them with Jack at his side.

"Your father was a good man," Carmen insisted. "He helped everyone he came in contact with, whether it was carrying a heavy bag for an old woman, or helping to harvest the fields. Everyone loved him." She took a breath. "The civil war was difficult. Salvadorans were fighting Salvadorans and each side believed they were right. Your father supported the rebels against the government whenever he could." Tears welled in her eyes. "The government was corrupt, and your father always supported the weak. When the war officially ended, I thanked God he hadn't been found, that he hadn't been killed. But then rumors began to circulate that supporters of the government were still searching for people who had helped the rebels, and the tension in our village was awful. We had all secretly supported the rebels. We decided to leave, to go to the United States." Her hands scrunched up in her skirt. "Your father was such a good man, he kept helping the people rebuild. He stopped at one of the rebel leaders' houses after work one day. There was an incident, no one could tell me exactly what happened, but shots were fired and your father was killed."

Evan sucked in a breath. How horrific for the whole family. It was no wonder Carmen hadn't told the truth to her young girls.

"Did they ever catch who did it?" Bridget asked.

"Again, there are rumors, but no one was punished."

Evan glanced around the circle. Carly was calm, but she'd already known the story.

Zita gaped at her mother. "Papa was murdered?" she asked as tears ran down her face.

Carmen nodded and stroked her daughter's back. Zita shook her off and stood.

"How could you lie to us like that? How could you leave without finding the culprit?" She whirled around and strode into the garden.

"Zita, wait," Carmen called after her.

"Let her go, Mama," Carly said. "It's a shock. I'll follow her."

Carmen turned to Carly. "This is why I never said anything." She sighed, getting to her feet. "I must see to the others." She walked out of the clearing.

Bridget groaned. "I shouldn't have brought it up today."

Jack hugged her. "You had a right to know."

Carly nodded. "It's best everyone knows. Why don't you go and talk with her and I'll find Zita?"

"All right." Both Bridget and Jack got to their feet and left.

Carly stood. "I'd better go talk with Zita. Will you be all right on your own?"

"Sure." Evan could take care of himself. "Good luck."

Chapter 13

Carly followed the path her younger sister had taken. There was one spot Zita always ran to when she was upset.

Sure enough, Zita was sitting, her knees pulled up to her chest, on the lower branches of the big oak tree on the boundary of the property.

"How are you feeling, ZZ?" Carly called.

"Go away."

Carly sighed. She recognized the tone. Zita was angry and upset. Bracing herself for the abuse that was bound to follow, she said, "I'm sorry you're upset."

"Of course I'm feckin' upset. It's bad enough I don't remember my father, now it turns out I don't even know how he died!" Her eyes widened and she slapped her hand over her mouth.

Carly took a step back. Zita didn't remember him? But she always had a story to tell on the Day of the Dead. "What do you mean you don't remember him?"

"I was *three*, Carolina. How much do you remember from that age?" The anger was clear, and she wrapped her arms around herself again.

Carly had never considered it from Zita's point of view before, she'd assumed because Zita had always said something, that she could remember him. Sadness swept through her. "I'm so sorry, *niñita*. I never realized."

Tears poured down Zita's face.

Carly took off her shoes. She was hopeless at physical activity and climbing a tree had to be one of the worst things she could do, but her sister needed her and wasn't coming down on her own. Carly grabbed the trunk and then stretched out for the first branch. It was nowhere near her reach. She jumped at it and missed, stumbling a few steps past.

"What are you doing?" Zita asked, wiping her tears.

"Trying to climb up to you." Carly grunted as she jumped toward the branch again. It was times like this her lack of height was a real problem.

Zita hiccupped, half-cough, half-laugh.

If it made her sister laugh, Carly was happy to continue making a fool of herself. She took a couple of steps back and tried a run up, smacking hard against the trunk.

"Ow."

"Feck, Carly. Don't hurt yourself, I'll come down."

Relieved, Carly held her scratched arm as her sister nimbly climb down. When she reached the bottom, Carly hugged her. Zita was much taller than she was, but she felt like a child in Carly's arms as she started crying again.

"Hush, *niñita*. It's all right. We can get out the old photos and go through them, tell you all the stories we remember of Papa."

"No. Mama can't know."

"Why not?"

"Because she's *always* talking about him. She expects me to know everything, and half the time what I say are things I've heard her repeat over the years. It would break her heart."

She didn't think Zita was right, but now wasn't the time to argue. "Then we'll have a girls' night, just you, me and Bridget. We'll look at photos and tell tales of Papa."

"All right." She sniffed.

Carly didn't know why Zita had kept it a secret all these years. Why she hadn't admitted she didn't remember their father? No one would have been upset. She'd been little more than a baby when it had happened. She hugged her sister. "How are you feeling?"

"I'll be OK." She wiped her face with her hands.

"Why don't you sneak upstairs and wash your face?"

Zita nodded and together they walked back to the house. At one of the forks in the path, Zita went left to avoid the party. The voices were loud and the music was happy.

Carly scanned the crowd of people who had arrived, and finally found Evan with Jack. She was pleased he had someone to talk to, because most of the people there were speaking Spanish.

Bridget moved toward her. "How is she?"

"She's OK. I'll talk to you about it later." Now wasn't the time.

Bridget nodded. "Thanks for bringing Evan. Jack doesn't feel quite like the odd one out."

Carly smiled. Jack was always sure of himself, so she didn't think he would have had a problem if Evan hadn't been there.

"So how are things with the two of you?" Bridget asked.

Carly didn't want to talk about her love life with her sister. "He's nice."

Bridget raised an eyebrow. "Is that all?"

She didn't want to tell her he was the first man to ever get her, to ever want to know who the real Carolina was. It would be admitting she already felt too much for him. "We're having fun."

"Well, if you ever need someone to talk to, I'm here. I appreciated your advice about Jack."

Carly nodded. She'd helped Bridget talk through some issues she'd had with Jack, but she didn't want to talk about her relationship with Evan. She just wanted to enjoy it. "I'll go pass around some food," she said and walked off.

She'd learned from an early age if she had a plate of food in her hand, she was able to go up to people she didn't know. Her mother had always insisted she mingle and be a good hostess, and passing around food appeased her. Carly had hated it at first, but had adapted. Making her way through the crowd, she caught up on the latest news, fielded requests for school and university fees, which she was happy to pay, and chatted with some of her foster sisters who had moved out and were making their way in the world.

Noticing Jack was chatting with Bridget, she glanced around

for Evan and found him sitting on one of the garden walls, sketching. As she walked over to him, she saw Teresa watching him.

"Pasteles?" she asked, offering him the plate.

He glanced up. "Thanks." He took one and she sat next to him.

"What do you think?" she asked.

"It's incredible. There's such a community here, so much support and love. No one's related are they?"

"There are a couple of families, but mostly we're all migrants or refugees. We've become each other's family, because it's so difficult starting over in a new place without a support network."

"That's what your social media site does, doesn't it? Brings together communities into a support network."

"Yes."

"Can many refugees afford a computer?"

"No. Comunidad recycles and reformats our old computers. We also take donations from the community, and then we wipe the hard drives, load the basic software, including a link to Comunidad, and teach families how to use them. It was one of the first things I set up."

"You mentioned a while ago that some of your foster sisters hadn't had their application approved yet, didn't you? Have they been accepted now?"

She shook her head. "No. Teresa, Elena and Beatriz are still waiting."

"Teresa?" He sounded surprised. "She came around with Carmen to do my garden."

Carly smiled. "She's part of the trial I spoke about. She's allowed to live with us instead of in a detention center. I'm giving a talk at the refugee symposium next month, which will hopefully convince the powers that be that it's the best option."

"There's nothing you can't do."

She shrugged and glanced down at his sketchbook. It was already a lovely snapshot of the people there. "Are you enjoying yourself?"

Evan nodded. "Thanks for suggesting I bring my pencils. I would have been itching for them otherwise."

Carly felt a bump against her leg and saw McClane at her feet. He lay down against the garden wall.

Evan laughed. "It's too much excitement for him."

She smiled, and then noticed Teresa was still watching them. She waved the girl over. "Teresa, you know Evan, don't you?"

She nodded.

"Hey, Teresa. Have you had your sketchbook out?"

She nodded again.

"I'd love to have a look if you want to share," Evan said.

Teresa took a small breath in. "Really?"

"Sure."

"Why don't you get it now?" Carly suggested.

She hurried off.

"She's got talent," Evan said. "With a little bit of guidance, she'll be excellent."

"I'll tell Mama. Drawing might be a way to bring her out of her shell."

"What will happen if her application is denied?"

"She'll be sent back to El Salvador."

Evan frowned and opened his mouth to say something when Teresa returned, clutching her sketch pad to her chest.

"May I?" Evan asked.

She handed it to him. Carly examined the pictures as he flicked. They were excellent. The drawings depicted scenes of family, of houses and streets in what looked like El Salvador.

"Is this your home?" Carly asked in Spanish. Teresa still hadn't completely opened up about her past.

She nodded, tears welling in her eyes.

Carly stood up, wrapping an arm around the girl. "It's hard, isn't it? To leave everyone behind?"

"I had to go," she whispered in Spanish. "I had to escape."

"Escape what?"

Teresa shook her head. "No. It is too awful. I cannot say."

Carly felt for her. Many of the girls who came to them had been sexually abused and felt like they would be hated or blamed if they admitted the truth. "You're safe now."

"There's no guarantee I'll be allowed to stay. And even if I can, my sister might be in danger. She's younger than me, but they might force her —" She pressed her lips together.

"Force her to what?" Carly asked gently.

"Force her into prostitution."

Carly's heart grew heavy. She placed a hand on Teresa's arm. "Is that what happened to you?"

She nodded.

Mierda. What could she say to that? She wasn't any good at counselling the girls, but she had to help. "I want you to tell Mama about what happened to you. Tell her everything you can, and there may be some way we can help your sister. How old is she?"

"Twelve."

Still a child, but that wouldn't necessarily protect her. "We'll do what we can."

"Thank you." Teresa sniffed, her eyes full of tears.

Evan looked up from the drawings and hesitated when he saw her tears. He glanced at Carly and she nodded for him to speak. "These are really good, Teresa," he said gently. "Do you want to sit here with me and do some more?"

She gave a cautious smile, brushing away the tears. "Yes, please."

Carly gestured for her to sit. "I'd better keep serving food."

She walked away, her heart full of concern for Teresa and her sister.

***

Evan offered his pencils to Teresa and began on a new sheet of paper. The Day of the Dead celebration was nothing like he'd expected. The earlier ceremony around the altars was a beautiful tribute, and then the revelation about Carly's father's death had been something else. He was worried about Zita. He hadn't seen her return and she'd been so upset. At least Carly wasn't worried. He'd wait a little longer and if Zita hadn't appeared, he'd go looking for her. She was a big softie and her heart was fragile. He hated to see her hurting.

Keeping one eye out for her, he continued drawing.

Evan loved crowds. He loved watching people interacting, observing their body language, making up their conversations. He'd put his own interpretation on the scene when he painted it, using lots of riotous color to match the clothing of those gathered, all wearing traditional clothing of their mother country.

His eyes followed Carly as she served the food. She didn't understand the meaning of the word relaxation, he was sure of it. Or perhaps she felt obligated to play hostess. He'd have to ask her about it later. She moved from group to group, stopping for a few minutes and then gracefully moving to the next group.

People watched her go. She had a presence about her, even when she wasn't in business mode. Today he'd convinced her not to straighten her hair, and she was wearing the traditional dress as well, so she blended right in. It was such a change. She seemed a little more relaxed than normal.

Seeing Zita walk out of the house, Evan stood up. "Excuse me a moment," he said to Teresa and walked over. "How's it going, Z?"

Her face showed no trace of her tears, but her eyes held so much sadness.

"I'm fine."

He hugged her. "You can always talk to me if you need to. Feel free to come and chill at my house any time."

She hugged him back. "Thanks, Evan. It was a bit of a shock, is all."

Evan didn't think that was all, but he didn't push it. Zita would come around if she needed to talk. Sometimes she visited him when she needed a bit of peace and quiet. "I'm here for you."

"I know."

He gave her another hug and then returned to his seat. What he'd said was true. He *was* there for her, just as she'd be there for him. Aside from his brother, he'd never had anyone he could rely on before. Not that Zita really needed him. She had such a wonderful community around her, a support network he envied.

Teresa gave him a shy smile as he sat. He didn't know what she'd said to Carly after she'd brought out the sketch pad, but she seemed a little happier. "The meeting at the art center is tomorrow," he said. "You should come."

She nodded, but he wasn't certain she'd understood. He'd have to tell Zita as well.

Not long after, Carmen, Zita and Carly carried out massive bowls of food and placed them on the table.

"Looks like it's lunch time," said Evan. It smelled incredible.

Teresa stood. "I will help."

Evan tucked his pencils back in their case and carried his sketchbook inside. Then he went to see how he could help too.

***

Carly woke on Monday morning with her head feeling like cotton wool. She hadn't drunk that much at the celebration, but perhaps it was because she'd been on her feet for most of the day. She shut off her alarm.

"Thank Christ. What time is it?" Evan groaned.

"It's five. Go back to sleep. I'll get ready and go." She hadn't been able to resist the invitation to stay at Evan's, but now she needed to leave as soon as possible to deal with the traffic.

"I'll make you breakfast," he said, but didn't move.

Carly smiled and kissed his cheek. "Don't bother. I'll pick up something at the office."

She got out of bed, and by the time she'd reached the door, he was fast asleep. She chuckled. No, he definitely wasn't a morning person.

The shower did little to clear her head, and her muscles felt a little achy as well. Absolutely too much time on her feet.

In the kitchen, McClane opened a sleepy eye, wagged his tail once and fell back asleep. Like owner, like pet.

The drive to work was long and Carly seemed to catch every red light. Her eyes were heavy and she focused every bit of energy on the road. By the time she arrived, she was exhausted. She'd never been so tired after a Day of the Dead celebration.

She changed into the spare set of clothes she kept in her office, and as she turned on her computer her cell phone rang. It was Hayden.

"Carolina, I'm buying bagels to celebrate my return to health, do you want some?"

The mention of food made her stomach roll. "No, thanks. I'll see you when you get here."

She hung up and stared at the screen for a moment, trying to remember what she was doing. That's right, email. Opening her email she reviewed her messages.

***

Sometime later Hayden walked into the office. "Morning, Carolina."

Carly blinked. She'd only read the first email in her inbox. She glanced at Hayden. He was as well-dressed and perky as usual. There wasn't any hint he'd had the flu.

"Morning. I'm glad you're better. I missed you."

He grinned. "What can I say? I'm one of a kind."

She nodded. "I gave up on temps after the first one was a failure and Mama offered to come in."

"Your mother?"

Damn it. She wasn't going to tell him that. She wasn't thinking properly. "Yes. I was desperate."

"I wish I'd met her."

Carly shook her head. "I'm not sure what she might have done to your computer, so don't be too enthusiastic until you've checked it out."

She shouldn't have said that either.

Hayden squinted at her. "Are you feeling all right? You look a little pale, and with your skin tone, that's some feat."

Carly ran a hand over her forehead. "I'm fine, just a little tired. I'd better get to work."

Hayden left and she leaned back in her chair. It was too much effort to sit up straight.

"Carolina?" Hayden's loud call had Carly sitting up straight in her chair again.

"What?" She looked around, but he wasn't in her office. It must have been the intercom. Before she could answer him, he was at the door.

"Geez, Carolina, you look like death warmed up. You must be coming down with what I had. You should go home."

Carly shook her head briefly and closed her eyes to stop the dizziness. "I have meetings."

"I'll cancel them."

"No, I'll be fine."

Hayden hesitated, and then he put his hands on his hips. "If

140

you don't go home, I'll call your mother."

Carly frowned. "You don't know my mother."

Hayden grinned. "She left me a lovely note, with her contact details, and told me to call if I had any questions about the work she'd done."

Carly groaned. She did *not* need that. "You can't call her." She'd never be able to get rid of her. Carmen had a way of smothering her children when they were sick. It definitely made them get better more quickly.

"I can and I will if you don't go home. Seriously, Carly, if you've got what I had, you need to go to bed. It knocked the hell out of me."

There was too much she needed to do. She couldn't be sick. "I'm fine. I'll take a couple of pills." She went to stand up, but her balance was off and she stumbled, grabbing hold of her desk.

"I'll take you home myself," Hayden said, hurrying to help her.

She didn't have the energy to protest. She pried off her high heels and sat back down again. "I need my laptop."

"You won't be able to use it," Hayden said.

"Pack it anyway." The nausea was getting worse. Hayden was right, she had to go home. One day in bed wouldn't hurt.

Hayden did as she asked and then helped her to the elevator. She leaned on him far more than she intended to. He drove home in her car and then accompanied her up to her apartment. She was too weak to protest.

"Which way to the bedroom?" he asked.

She pointed and he helped her into the room.

"I'm going to get you some water and some pills. Have you got a medicine cabinet somewhere?"

"In the kitchen above the oven."

"All right. You get changed and into bed."

With intense concentration, Carly managed to change into a tank top and boxer shorts and slip under the covers.

"Are you decent?" Hayden called.

"Yes."

He walked in and gave her the pills and a glass of water. She swallowed them carefully.

"Trust me, Carolina. Go straight to sleep. I'll sort out all your appointments. You call me if you need anything." He went to leave.

"Thank you, Hayden."

He turned and smiled. "We all need a little help sometimes."

Not her. She was the one who helped everyone else.

She fell asleep before he left the apartment.

Chapter 14

Evan was in a great mood as he wandered into the local arts center. As much as he made fun of Isobella and Desmond, he did enjoy coming down and talking with the different artists about art: new techniques they'd discovered, new media to explore and new canvases. He liked to keep on top of what was happening around the place.

The moment he arrived, Isobella pounced. "Evan, we haven't seen you since the exhibition. It went really well for you, didn't it?"

He swallowed his groan. "Yes, it did. You sold a painting too, I hear."

"Of course."

Desmond joined them. "Evan, good to see you. We wanted to talk to you about the proposal."

"What proposal?"

"The one for Carolina Flanagan. She asked us to submit a proposal about her becoming a patron of the center."

He'd forgotten about that. "Why do you need me?"

She waved a bit of newspaper in front of him. "You went to the gala ball with her. I thought you might be able to put in a good word for us." Isobella smiled at him.

He controlled his initial reaction, which was to tell them to go to hell, and reached for the newspaper. The social pages had a clear picture of him dancing with Carly, his hand brushing her back. The jolt of surprise was unpleasant. He'd not even noticed a photographer, too caught up in Carly, and now their intimate moment was in the paper for all to see. He handed the article back to Isobella. "I have nothing to do with the way Carolina runs her business. I suggest you submit the proposal directly to her."

"But we don't know how to write one. We're *artists*!" Isobella said.

"Then I suggest you google it," he said, walking past. How dare they use his relationship with Carly to get what they wanted?

"Evan, this is your art center too. Don't you want it to flourish?" Desmond asked.

"It's doing fine, as far as I can see."

"Don't you want to just be able to create?" Isobella asked. "Not to have to work, but spend your time being creative."

"I already do," he told her.

She gaped at him. "How? Is Carolina supporting you?"

He glared at her. "I've been making a living from my artwork since I was a teenager. I take all the jobs I can get." He walked off.

Desmond and Isobella didn't deserve any of Carly's help. They weren't willing to help themselves. They saw their work as masterpieces, took months to perfect one piece, and wouldn't consider having more than one work going at the same time. It was no wonder they couldn't support themselves. He thought about the three paintings he had in his studio, each at a different stage of completion. Each suited a different mood, and all were not far from finished.

He moved away and scanned the room. Two women walked through the door and he smiled, striding over to them.

"Zita, Teresa. I'm glad you came." He kissed both Zita's cheeks and smiled at Teresa.

"Thanks for suggesting it."

"I can introduce Teresa around and bring her home afterward, if you like. Save you coming out again."

Zita glanced at Teresa, who looked a little alarmed. "I'll stick around. Who knows, art may be something I'm good at."

The coordinator called the meeting to order and they took

their seats. The agenda was always the same – a member would demonstrate a new technique, people would try it themselves, and then they would continue with their own work, swapping news with whoever was there. Today's technique was painting using a squeeze bottle. It was an interesting concept, but not one that excited Evan. He'd brought his sketchpad with him, and he sketched as people around him chatted. Teresa sat beside him, and her drawing of the gathering was fantastic. It almost looked like a photo. Beside her, Zita was chatting to the person next to her.

"Zita, darling, how are you? I must thank you again for arranging the exhibition for us."

Evan's eyes narrowed as Isobella hugged Zita.

"I'm glad it was a success," Zita said.

"Absolutely. With your sister supporting it, how could it not be? That's why we asked her to be our patron."

Evan gritted his teeth. Where was Isobella heading with this?

"Really? That's great. Did she say yes?"

Isobella pouted. "Actually, she wants us to write a proposal. I'm not sure why she'd think artists would know how to write a business proposal."

"Oh." Zita looked a little unsure. "I'll talk to her if you like."

Isobella beamed.

"No." The word was short and sharp. Both women turned to him. "Carly asked for a proposal and so you'll give her a proposal. You shouldn't be asking Zita so you can get out of some work." He turned to Zita. "I know you're trying to help, but you're not helping Carly. You're adding more work to her already full workload."

Zita bit her lip and Isobella glared at him.

"How would you know?" Isobella demanded.

He ignored her question. Didn't Zita realize how much Carly worked, how hard she tried to give everyone something, and yet never took any time for herself? People like Isobella should be struck straight off the list because they were too lazy or self-important to do what was asked of them. It wasn't right.

"Not all of us are able to sleep with her to get what we want." Isobella realized she'd said the wrong thing immediately, as she slapped her hand over her mouth, her eyes wide.

The room had gone silent.

His anger was swift but he controlled it, getting to his feet. She didn't deserve any response. He gathered his things and walked out.

Behind him, Zita said, "How dare you? You're insulting both Evan and my sister. Don't come asking me for favors anymore."

He'd reached the car when Zita called out.

"Evan, wait."

He breathed slowly out before he turned. Zita hurried up to him, Teresa hanging back. He felt bad for the girl. The art center might have been good for her.

"What do you mean I'd be adding to Carly's workload?" she asked. "I was just going to ask her a question."

He shook his head. She had no idea how this worked. "Z, why do you think Carly asked for the proposal?"

Zita shook her head.

"Because she knows most people will find it's too hard and won't bother. If they *do* bother, she can get Hayden to review it for her. If you ask her, it's back on her plate and she has to deal with it directly. She already works way too much."

"I never realized. She never said anything."

"That's because she loves you too much to say no. You do know the only day she takes off each month is when she goes to your place for lunch?"

Zita's eyes widened. "No."

"You've got to stop asking her for so much. Sure, she's rich in money, but she's poor in time."

Zita was looking increasingly guilty. He hugged her. "I know you're doing it because you've got a good heart, Z, but someone needs to take care of your older sister."

She examined him. "It seems like you've nominated yourself for the role."

He wasn't so sure. He glanced at Teresa. "If you don't want to come back here, I can always give Teresa lessons, or help you find another center."

"A center would be great. She's not real comfortable around most men."

"I'll look around and give you a call." He checked his watch.

"I'd better get back to it." He had a whole lot of painting to do and he would have to find a new arts center for himself. He wasn't sure he wanted to deal with Isobella and Desmond again.

He got in his car and waved the girls goodbye.

***

It was dark when Carly woke. Disorientated, she closed her eyes and waited for her head to clear. It didn't. All the muscles in her body ached and her head pounded. She sat up carefully and turned on the light, hissing at the brightness. It was eight o'clock. She must have slept the whole day.

Very slowly she got up, went to the bathroom, and then shuffled into the kitchen to get some water. Her stomach grumbled, but the thought of eating made her feel nauseated.

She should call Hayden. Make sure there was nothing that had come up at work. She dialed his number while she checked her fridge for something she might be able to keep down.

"How are you feeling, Carolina?"

"Like death," she admitted, her voice croaky. "Anything happen at work today?"

"The whole company went under because you weren't there."

"What?!"

"Kidding, Carolina. It was fine. There were no issues rescheduling your appointments. I got Lisa to represent you in a couple of meetings and I took the minutes as normal."

"How did Lisa go?"

"She was great. She's changed recently, not so obsessed with money."

Carly sighed in relief. "I'll check my emails now I'm up and I'll be in tomorrow."

"No, you won't. You'll go straight back to bed, and if you do anything, then you can watch some television. I don't want to see you this week."

Annoyance stirred at Hayden giving her orders. "Sure," she lied.

She hung up and found some dry crackers in the cupboard. She ate one, drank a glass of water, and was exhausted. But she couldn't go back to bed, she needed to check her email. A shower would make her feel better.

Halfway to the bathroom, she changed direction and headed to her bed. Crawling under the covers, she fell asleep again.

***

Evan hadn't heard from Carly in two days. He wasn't exactly surprised, because he'd seen her calendar for the week. Still, he was a little hurt. He'd meant to call her, but didn't want to disturb her at work, and then he'd get lost in his painting and not come out until the early hours of the morning. He'd sent her a couple of text messages instead, which she hadn't responded to.

Today he was going into the city for a meeting with Basil. He arrived a little early, so he went to the top floor to check if Carly was in.

Hayden was back at his desk.

"Glad to see you're better," Evan greeted him.

Hayden raised his eyebrows. "How did you know I was sick?"

"Carly told me. Is she in?" He didn't want further questions.

"No. I passed on the flu. She's been off all week. I'm a little worried about her. She didn't call to check in yesterday." There was real concern in Hayden's eyes.

Evan frowned. It had to be something awful for Carly to be away from work at all, let alone for three days. "Is anyone looking after her?"

"Not that I know of. I'm under strict instructions not to call her mother."

That sounded like typical Carly. "I'll drop in after I've finished my meeting."

"Thank you. I didn't want to overstep my boundaries."

"I'll give you a call." He took one of Hayden's business cards and handed him one of his own before going to his meeting with Basil.

***

Two hours later, Evan walked into Carly's apartment building and smiled at the doorman. "I'm Evan Hayes. I'm here to see Carolina Flanagan."

"One moment, sir." The man rang a number and waited. "There's no answer," he said as he hung up.

Evan frowned and rang her cell. It went straight to voicemail. Concern shifted through him. What if she was unconscious, or lying injured and couldn't respond?

"Have you seen Carolina Flanagan today?" he asked.

"No, sir."

"I was supposed to meet her, " he lied. "She's been sick, and I'm a little worried she might need help. Is there any chance you can let me into her apartment?"

The doorman checked on the computer and shook his head. "You're not on my list, I'm afraid, Mr. Hayes."

"What list?"

"Residents can authorize access to certain people."

"Who's on her list?"

"I'm sorry, I can't tell you that."

Who would Carly trust? It had to be her sisters and her mother. He turned away and dialed Zita's number.

"Hey Z. Have you spoken with Carly in the last couple of days?"

"No. Not since the party."

"I dropped in to visit her at work and Hayden tells me she's been sick all week. I'm at her apartment now and she's not answering. The doorman tells me some people are authorized to get access, are you one of them?"

"Yes. Let me talk to Harold."

He handed the phone to the doorman. "Zita Flanagan wants to speak with you."

A minute later Harold handed the phone back.

"I've got you access," Zita said. "Call me back and tell me how she is."

"Thanks Z." Evan hung up and took the key Harold handed him. "Thank you."

By the time he got back up to Carly's apartment, his heart was pounding. He opened the door and walked in. "Carly?"

Nothing was disturbed in the living area, so he made his way straight to her bedroom. She was lying in the middle of the bed, the sheets tangled around her legs as she tossed from side to side. Evan rushed over.

"Carly, are you all right?"

She moaned.

"Wake up, Carly." Her forehead was boiling and her skin was damp.

"Papa?"

Was she hallucinating? "It's Evan, Carly."

"Evan?" Her eyes fluttered open and she squinted as if trying to figure out what he was doing there.

"How are you feeling?"

There was a pause, before she finally said, "Awful."

"Have you had anything to eat or drink?"

"Water." She pointed to the empty glass on the bedside table.

"Let me get you some more." He raced to the kitchen, filled up a clean glass with water, and then checked her fridge and cupboard for food. There was barely anything in there. He returned to her room and helped her to sit. She was so incredibly weak. How had she managed two and a half days like this? She should have called him.

"Drink up," he said.

She took a couple of sips and put the glass down, her hand shaking a little.

"Drink some more," he insisted, holding the glass near her mouth. She did as he said without complaint. "Have you eaten?"

"No."

There was nothing in the apartment, but he didn't want to leave her alone. The closest person who could help was Hayden. Evan grabbed his phone.

"I need a favor."

After he explained what he needed, Hayden said. "I'll be there in thirty."

"Who did you call?" Carly asked when he hung up.

"Hayden."

"You can't get him to run personal errands for me." She was horrified.

"He's getting some medication and food, is all."

She shook her head and then closed her eyes and put a hand to her forehead. If it was possible she looked even worse.

"Stop moving, sweetheart. You're only making it worse.

We'll get some food and fluids into you and you'll feel much better." He hoped. "Just let me call Z back. She's worried about you."

He walked out of the room and called Zita to fill her in on her sister's condition.

"I'm due at the courts this afternoon," said Zita, "but I'll come and look after her when I'm done."

"No, it's fine. I'll move in here for a couple of days." Evan didn't question the overwhelming urge he had to care for her. "Can you take care of McClane?"

"Oh. Sure."

He could tell she was surprised. "I'll grab my things later. I can work from here."

"Thanks for caring, Evan," Zita said quietly and hung up.

He did care. More than he thought he was able to. Carly had touched something in him that he'd thought was long dead. But he didn't have time to examine it now. Carly needed him.

She was still sitting up when he went back into her room, but her eyes were closed. She looked vulnerable and young. He watched her for a while until Hayden arrived holding two big shopping bags.

"I got fluids, chicken noodle soup, and all her favorite foods, for when she feels like eating again. For me it was about five days before I started on anything solid." He unpacked the bags onto the kitchen bench.

"Thanks. I appreciate it."

Hayden glanced toward Carly's bedroom and lowered his voice. "I'd do anything for her. She's the best boss I've ever had, and she doesn't take care of herself nearly enough. She's so selfless."

Evan nodded. "Can you clear the rest of the week for her?"

"Already done. I slept for the first four days, only waking when my roommate fed me. If Carly hasn't been eating, it might take her longer. Give me a call if she's not getting better by Saturday and I'll clear next week's appointments too."

"Thanks." He shook Hayden's hand and walked him to the door.

When he was gone, Evan heated the soup and took a bowl in to her. "Carly, it's time to eat."

She opened her eyes. "I'm not hungry."

"I know, but you need to try. It's chicken noodle, guaranteed to chase all those nasty bugs away."

She managed a smile.

He held the bowl for her while she took some spoonfuls.

"What are you doing here?" she asked after a while.

"Hayden told me you weren't well. When you didn't answer the door, Zita convinced your doorman to give me a key so I could check on you."

"Oh. Thank you."

She ate about half a bowl before she put the spoon down.

"Do you want to take a shower, or are you going to go back to sleep?"

She yawned. "Sleep." She shuffled back down into bed.

If what Hayden said was true, Carly should sleep for a few hours, which would give him time to go home. "I've got to go grab a couple of things, but I should be back by the time you wake."

"OK." It was a testament to how ill she was that she didn't question why he was coming back or what he was doing.

Evan waited until she'd drifted off to sleep, made sure she had a full glass of water next to her, and kissed her forehead. Then he went downstairs, told Harold that Carly was all right and that he'd be back, before driving home.

***

It was over a two-hour round trip by the time Evan arrived back at Carly's apartment. Harold gave him access to the parking garage, so he parked his car and loaded his gear into the elevator. Carly was still sleeping, so he took another couple of trips to get the rest of his stuff, and then set it up in the living room near the windows, being careful to spread out his dropcloth so he didn't splash paint on the floor. When he was finished, he heard Carly stirring. Quickly he went to her bedroom where she was sitting on the edge of her bed.

She gasped when she saw him. "I thought you were a dream."

He smiled. "No, I'm real. Are you hungry?"

"I need to go to the bathroom."

"Do you need a hand?" He wasn't sure how steady she was on her feet.

"I should be able to make it." She stood and swayed a bit as she took her first step.

"Let me help." He put his arm around her and helped her across the room to the adjoining bathroom. He waited outside until she emerged again, and then helped her back to bed. He handed her a glass of water and she took a sip.

"Why are you still here?"

"I'm taking care of you," he said.

"I'm fine. You've got work to do."

"I can do it here. I've been home to get my things. I'm going to take care of you until you're better."

"But you might catch what I've got."

He shrugged. "Doesn't matter. You need someone to help you."

"I'm fine," she said again.

"No, you're not." Frustration rose up in him. "You were barely lucid when I got here, Carly. You scared me, and you worried Hayden. I'm going to stay here until you're well again. Now, do you want some more soup?"

Carly stared at him for a moment and then said, "Yes, please."

But by the time he got back from the kitchen, she'd fallen asleep.

He propped a note against the glass of water, which said, *Call out when you wake up* and went to paint.

***

Evan set his alarm each hour and set the phone to vibrate. Each time it buzzed, he put down his paintbrush and went to check on Carly. Her skin was still very hot but she was sleeping solidly. It was six o'clock before she woke again and he heated her some soup.

"You're determined to make me eat," she said, taking a sip.

"And drink," he said, handing her a glass of an electrolyte mixture.

"Thank you." She smiled at him.

When she was done eating, Evan helped her into the shower,

153

and quickly changed the sheets on her bed while she was in there. When she got out, he dried her hair for her, and helped her back to bed again.

By that stage she was yawning and went straight to sleep.

He sat there watching her for a while. She had become such an important part of his life in such a short amount of time. Should he be worried? He hadn't had anyone important in his life before, hadn't allowed himself to need anyone. Not after his parents had constantly let him down. But Carly was different. She didn't expect anything from him, didn't need him, and for the first time in his life he wished she would. He wanted to be needed by her.

Wasn't that ironic?

He got to his feet. He had more painting to do.

Chapter 15

It was Saturday before Carly had the energy to get out of bed. She woke up early and Evan was asleep next to her. He'd been by her side constantly throughout the past three days and she'd worried he hadn't slept, but here was proof. Carefully, she got out of bed and stood for a moment to make sure she didn't get dizzy. She crept out of the room to the kitchen and opened the cupboard. She was definitely hungry today.

Inside, there was a veritable array of food, including her favorite raspberry and white chocolate muffins. She grabbed one and took a bite, before switching on the kettle. She'd have a cup of tea, because she wasn't sure her stomach would handle something as strong as coffee yet. While waiting for the kettle to boil she turned to look out of the window and stared.

Carly's living room had been transformed into a studio. There were three easels lined up, and multiple canvases spread out across the floor, and the dining room table was covered in a collection of different paints.

So this is what Evan had been doing.

She was glad. She'd been worried he wasn't going to have the time to paint while he was nursing her. She strolled over to peek at the paintings. The first was of the Day of the Dead celebrations; there was color and laughter and community. The next was of an office lobby with a doorman who looked suspiciously like Harold, and the third took her breath away. It was her mother in her garden, looking as content as Carly had ever seen her. It was beautiful. It was as if she could reach out and touch her.

"Carly, are you OK?" Evan was rubbing his eyes, dressed only in a pair of boxer shorts. Her heart gave a thud. He looked so tired, but so sexy.

He frowned at her standing by the paintings. Surely he didn't mind her looking at his work?

"Evan, these are magnificent."

He ran a hand through his hair. "Thanks. How are you feeling?"

"Much better." She walked across to him and gave him a hug. "Thank you for taking care of me."

"You're most welcome. You were a pretty easy patient, what with all the sleeping."

The kettle clicked off. "Do you want a drink?"

"I'll get it. You sit down." He accompanied her to the bar stool and she sat.

Carly had never been fussed over by a man before and it was kind of nice.

"Hayden called last night," Evan said as he made her a cup of tea. "He said everything is fine and wanted to check how you are. I told him I'd call him if you weren't going to be at work on Monday."

Work. Hell, she hadn't even thought about it. Had been too sick to even contemplate it. "I should check my emails," she said starting to rise.

"You should drink your tea," he said, putting a mug in front of her. "You can check them after you've eaten."

Irritation rose. Who was he to tell her what to do?

Carly sighed. He was the person who'd taken care of her when she'd been at her worse. She should listen to him, although now that work had entered her mind, she was anxious to check what had been happening while she was gone. She'd never been away from her company for so long. What meetings had she had missed? And she'd had dinners scheduled all week.

"Oh for goodness' sakes, Carly," Evan said, plonking her laptop in front of her. "Check in. I can practically hear you fretting."

Carly blinked and looked up at his frowning face. No. She could wait. She could have a nice breakfast with him without bringing work into it. She was sure of it.

She smiled at him and pushed the laptop away. "How many more paintings do you need for your exhibition?"

"I haven't decided. They gave me a range, depending on the size of the canvases. I need to go through what I've done and confirm which ones I want to use."

"So you get to choose what they display?"

"Yes."

It was a different world to what Carly was used to. "What about pricing? Who decides that?"

"I do, but the gallery will give me some advice on how they compare to similar artists."

"Are they expecting many people to attend?"

"It's one of the most popular galleries in New York. I used to go there on weekends and dream of having an exhibition there." He smiled, obviously remembering.

This was a *huge* deal. Carly hadn't quite realized. She'd been so busy with work, and Evan wasn't one to blow his own trumpet. She had to remember that, had to make sure she asked more questions about what he did.

"How is the game art going?"

"Really great. Basil's happy with my work so far. We had a meeting on Wednesday, which was when I discovered you were sick."

She only had vague memories of Hayden helping her home and then everything was fairly foggy until Evan arrived. She reached out and took his hand.

"I appreciate you taking care of me. You really put yourself out."

He growled. "You should have called me when you got sick. I would have come right away."

"I wasn't thinking clearly. All I knew was that I didn't want Mama coming because she tends to smother me in love, and besides, she and the girls all have to work." Carly shrugged. "I'm not used to having anyone else I can call."

"Well, you do now, so don't forget." He said it with an intensity that warmed her.

"I won't." Her stomach grumbled.

He chuckled. "What would you like for breakfast?"

"I had a muffin."

He grinned. "Hayden said they were your favorite." He got up.

"Hayden?"

"Yeah. He was so worried about you. After I found you, he brought over medication and food."

"I must thank him."

"You've got a loyal friend there."

Friend. No, she couldn't call him a friend. They were colleagues, she was his employer. "He's just taking care of his boss."

"That's crap, Carly. I saw how worried he was."

"Evan, he works for me. How can we be friends?"

He sat back. "Is that what you really think?"

She nodded. "No matter what happens, I hold his job in my hands, and that creates an imbalance of power."

Evan shook his head. "I'm not sure he'd agree with you. Have you ever been out for a drink?"

"There's the Christmas party each year."

"No, I mean a random, 'let's go for drinks'."

"I've always got meetings after work."

"Perhaps you should get a better work/life balance."

It wasn't possible – she was the CEO, she had so much responsibility. But she didn't want to argue with Evan.

She ate her breakfast and afterward had a long soak in the shower. The water felt incredible on her skin.

There was a knock on the bathroom door. "Are you all right in there?" Evan called.

"Yes." She shut off the taps and dried herself. She was feeling better, but still a little tired. Slipping into her footie pajamas, she then opened the door to Evan. She grabbed her hair dryer.

"Let me help," Evan said. He took the hair dryer from her and made her sit at the dressing table.

"I should straighten it," Carly said. She was always slightly fearful that if she didn't straighten it each day she'd forget how. She wasn't naturally good at styling, it took a lot of effort.

"No. You're not well. It just needs to be dry." He ran his fingers through her hair as he fluttered the hair dryer over it.

It felt good, so good, so Carly closed her eyes and let him do what he wanted. She wasn't going out, so it wouldn't matter for one day.

When he was finished, he kissed her on the forehead and they walked back out into the living room.

"Are you sure you're up to being out of bed?" he asked.

She nodded. "I've spent far too much time there."

She wanted sunlight and a different view. She settled on her chaise lounge. She couldn't avoid her responsibilities any longer. She opened her laptop and started to work through her emails.

Hayden had sent a complete summary of what had happened during the week. She smiled. He'd kept her informed. He outlined the appointments he'd rearranged, attached minutes of the meetings she missed, and summarized the issues that had come up while she'd been away. Carly was surprised. There was nothing to worry about. Hayden had even sent a couple of executives to the different lunches and dinners she'd had booked, and they had each emailed her a summary. It didn't appear as if she'd missed anything at all.

She frowned. Perhaps the world wouldn't end if she didn't do everything.

"Something wrong?" Evan asked.

"No. Everything seems to be fine."

"And that's a bad thing because . . .?"

"I expected there to be something. I never take time off."

Evan put down his paintbrush and walked over to her, sitting on the edge of the lounge. "That's great. It means you've set up your company so it doesn't fall apart when you're not there."

She'd always felt like she had to be there, she had to take care of everything. Perhaps she was wrong. Her list of responsibilities seemed less overwhelming, but she'd been in control for so long that the idea of letting go was scary as well. "It's nice."

She went back to her emails and the next one she read had her muscles cramping. It was from Softco. Why couldn't they understand she wasn't going to sell her company? She growled and set up an auto-forward to Hayden. She wasn't even going to bother meeting with them again.

"What's up?"

"I blacklisted Softco, but they keep emailing."

"Speaking of blacklists, do you want to add Isobella and Desmond to it as well?"

"Why?"

"They tried to get out of writing the proposal by asking Zita to talk with you, and when I told them it wasn't right, Isobella suggested not everyone was able to sleep with you to get what they wanted."

The hurt came first, a stabbing pain – the implication that Evan was sleeping with her just to get something. She knew it wasn't true – he hadn't asked for anything except her time, but the insecurity was never too far away. That made her angry. Carly's eyes narrowed. "Is that so?"

He nodded, watching her.

She dashed out an email, adding them both to her blacklist. "I won't be sponsoring them for anything again, but let me know if the art center needs anything."

"No." The word was hard, angry.

"Why not?"

"I'm not dating you for your money. I'm not going to ask you to help, just because you're rich. You have enough people begging you for money. If the art center needs funds, we'll raise it on our own."

"Evan, I'm happy to help."

"No," he said again. "There are other people who need your help more. Hell, spend the money on yourself for a change."

She sat up straighter. "Look around you. Don't you think this place cost a pretty penny?"

"Yeah, but it's not *you*, Carly. It's someone's perception of the way a billionaire should live. Your apartment, your clothes, your car – none of them represents the true person."

It was still disconcerting how easily he saw through the trappings. "So what do you think I should do?"

"What do *you* want? If you could live anywhere, where would it be?"

She thought about his painting that was now hanging in her

bedroom. She could imagine herself living there. Should she tell him that?

"What kind of car would you drive?" he continued.

"A Mini," she said instantly. "Small like me."

He grinned at her. "What color?"

That was hard. Her training told her white or silver, something classic, but her gut said, "Red."

"There you go. What about a house?"

It was kind of liberating playing the "what if" game. She placed the laptop on the coffee table. "I'll show you." She led him into the bedroom and pointed to his painting. "There. I'd live there."

Evan gaped at her. "Really?"

She nodded. "Peace, serenity, away from everything."

"You're a closet recluse, you know that?" he said.

"Does that place exist?"

"Only in my imagination."

She yawned so widely, it felt like her jaw might split in two.

Evan laughed. "You've had enough excitement for one morning. Why don't you go have a nap? You're still recovering."

He was right. She wasn't as worried about work now that she'd checked her email. "Wake me at midday?"

"Sure thing. I'll have lunch ready."

"Oh, no. You need to paint. We can order something in." She climbed into bed, the exhaustion starting to wash over her. The last thing she saw as she closed her eyes was Evan smiling down on her.

And it was then she realized she loved him.

***

By Sunday, it was clear to Evan that Carly was almost better. She'd decided not to go to her mother's for their usual lunch, because she didn't want to risk giving her family the flu, so they spent a lazy day, chatting and working.

Carly took a sip of her apple cider as she sat curled up on her lounge, watching him paint. "I don't know much about your family."

Evan's hand paused mid stroke. He didn't look at her as he said, "Not much to tell." He continued painting, hoping she'd drop the subject.

"There must be. You know pretty much everything about mine. You've got a younger brother, right? He's an electrician?"

"That's right. Karl. He set up his own business recently." He was proud of his little brother. He'd broken away from the hand-to-mouth existence his parents were still living and was successful in his own right.

"What about your parents? Are they still working?"

"Yeah. I can't see them ever retiring."

"Workaholics like us?" she asked.

The bitter laugh slipped out. "No."

Silence followed and he looked up. Carly was waiting for him to elaborate. Shit.

"They'll keep working until they die, because they can't afford to do anything else."

"I'm sorry."

"Don't be. It's their own fault. The second they earn anything, they spend it, sometimes before they've even got the money in their hands."

"That must have been hard growing up."

"Let's just say I was always 'sick' for school excursions." He didn't want to talk about it.

"I never told Mama about my school excursions, because she would have gone without something to send me."

He stopped painting. "That's the difference between Carmen and my parents. For them, their needs came first, but they never saw it that way. They always had to have the latest television, a brand new car, a designer garden, but then they had no money to pay the bills, or for clothes for us, or school excursions." He'd stopped believing their promises that he could go on the next excursion when he was in elementary school. "By middle school, I'd learned not to rely on them for anything after they'd forgotten for the third week in a row to pick me up from the art class I'd paid for."

It was ridiculous. His mother was a personal assistant and his father was a manager at a local department store. Between them, they earned a decent income, but they didn't know how to save for a rainy day, or any day really.

"They must be proud of you, though. You're incredibly

successful."

Evan put down the paintbrush and debated for a split second whether he should lie to her. But he couldn't. "I don't think they know."

She frowned. "What do you mean?"

"I haven't spoken to my parents since they kicked me out of home."

Carly gasped. "Why would they do that?"

"They always told me I was wasting my time painting. They thought I'd never earn a living and I had to get a real job like them. They never supported my drawing in the square, but I didn't let them stop me."

He hadn't told them how much he earned each week. If he had, they would have asked him for a loan or made him put it into an account they had access to. They'd done it to his brother – 'borrowed' money from his account that he never got back. Instead, he'd hidden it in his room until he was old enough to get an account without needing his parents' signatures.

"Then I got a full scholarship to Rhode Island School of Design. They said I was wasting my time and refused to pay for the bus ticket there. I had enough saved and I told them I was going." He'd thought they'd be proud of him. "They told me not to come home when I failed. They weren't going to support a freeloader. I haven't been back since."

It had been equal parts terrifying and freeing to leave. Evan had stepped out into the big unknown without a safety net, but he had followed his dream – and someone had believed his work was good enough to warrant a scholarship.

"They never tried to contact you?"

He shook his head. "I emailed them when I arrived, told them where I was staying, and never got a response. I kept in touch with my brother, and he's still in contact with them, but I don't know whether they talk about me."

"It makes your achievements all the more amazing," said Carly. "I always had my family's support, no matter what I did. I wouldn't have been brave enough to do this if they had been against it."

"I was probably more stupid than brave. If you check the statistics, there aren't many artists who make an income above the poverty line. Most have to work other jobs."

"Most obviously don't take the opportunities you do." She got to her feet. "Don't sell yourself short, Evan. People like Isobella and Desmond would never do game artwork, graphic design, or other more commercial work in order to make a career. You seize everything you can, and that's why you're successful. Yes, you're the most talented artist I've seen, but you also work damn hard for it." She stood in front of him, her hands on her hips, her eyes fired up with passion.

His heart swelled. No one had ever stood up for him. No one had ever understood that he worked hard to get where he was. He hugged her fiercely.

When he let her go, she took a step back and put a hand to her chest. "What was that for?"

His cheeks warmed. "You get it. Not many people do."

"Well, you get me too. Not many people do."

It was true. Somehow they'd found each other.

All of a sudden his stomach started to churn.

***

Carly was refreshed and ready to go when she strode into work the next morning. She was a little later than usual, because Evan had stayed the night again and he'd distracted her in the shower. Her cheeks warmed at the thought. She loved him so much, and it was equal parts thrilling as it was terrifying. What if he didn't feel the same way about her?

Hayden was already at his desk and he gaped at her, then checked his watch. "I didn't think you'd be in today."

"I'm not late, am I?"

"For any normal person, no, but for Carolina Flanagan, hell yes. Are you still ill?"

She was in too good a mood to be offended. "I feel great. Thank you so much for helping me home and picking up those things for me."

"Any time." He followed her into her office, his head tilted to the side. "You are looking good."

"Thank you. What do we have on today's schedule?"

By the time he'd finished telling her, her good mood had dissipated. She sighed. "It never ends, does it?"

Hayden hesitated. "Can I make a suggestion?" He twirled his pen around and around in his fingers.

"Sure." She indicated he should sit.

He pulled out a chair and sat on the very edge of it. "Last week proved you don't need to do everything, Carolina. We managed fine without you."

The relief was strong, but she couldn't prevent the tiny bit of hurt that she wasn't missed. She worked hard for her company.

"That's not to say you're not the cornerstone of the company," Hayden went on, "it's just that you don't need to attend everything. That's why you've got executives and managers and me."

Rationally, she knew he was right. Nothing had collapsed when she'd been sick. Could she really delegate a few things so she had more time to herself, more time to be with Evan?

Her chest tightened. She'd be giving up control, but she had to. She hadn't really been living before she met Evan.

She printed out her week's schedule, put it on the desk between them and braced herself. "All right. What do you suggest I delegate?"

Hayden blinked at her. "Seriously?"

"Yes. You know everything that goes on around here. You probably have a better idea of what people are capable of than me." The tension was tight in her chest and she regulated her breathing. It was all right. All she was doing was investigating the possibility of letting go of some things. It didn't mean she had to do it.

Hayden stared at her for a moment and then grinned. "This is going to be fun."

Chapter 16

Carly's head was spinning by the time they were finished. "You think I can delegate *that* much?"

The amount Hayden had highlighted on her schedule was terrifying. But the scariest thing was the excitement beginning to simmer in her stomach. The idea she could let go of so many of the things she hated to do was so tenuous, she was afraid to hope.

Hayden grinned. "Not only do I think you can delegate that much, but I also believe you can make it seem like you're giving them all a prize. A lot of your executives would love to go to all these lunches and dinners. They're envious. If you split it up evenly between them – charities to one, business to another, and the schmoozing and networking to someone else, they'll love it. You go to the meetings that mean the most to you, and then divide up the rest."

It was so damn appealing. It had never occurred to Carly that her staff might actually *want* to do it. For her, it had always been a chore. She was the head of the company, which meant she *had* to do it all. There was really only one thing she loved to do and that was the work with the refugees and with Casa Flanagan, but she could continue that. She squeezed her eyes shut and then opened them again. "Let's do it. Can you arrange a meeting?"

Hayden whooped and made a note.

"What about these regular meetings?" She had different weekly meetings almost every day. "Surely I have to go to those so I'm aware of what's happening in the company?"

He tapped his pen against the table. She'd never seen him this nervous.

"Too far?" she asked.

"No. I, ah, I was thinking perhaps I could go in your place?"

"You?" She was surprised. "Don't you have enough to do? Why would you want to?"

He chuckled. "Not everyone hates meetings as much as you, Carolina. I can go and give you the summary. But that's only if you trust me enough."

"Of course I trust you. You're my right-hand man."

He looked relieved. Did Hayden not realize how much she valued him? She'd tried to show him.

"But I don't want you to be overworked," said Carly. "Do you really have time?"

He hesitated and then got to his feet. "Hold on a second." He dashed out and retrieved a document from his desk, clutching it to his chest. "I've been working on this. It's only an idea, you might not like it. It's probably a bad idea."

She held out a hand, giving him an encouraging smile and he gave it to her.

It was a very detailed proposal. He'd obviously been working on it for a while. It listed all of his regular tasks, added the tasks he wanted to do, and highlighted those he could delegate to others. He made a case for hiring an administrative assistant to work with him. Carly checked the figures, and the workload. It was more responsibility than he'd had before, but he was up to the task, she was sure.

"Would you *really* be happy with this much work?"

Hayden stopped tapping the pen and nodded. "There's not been a lot of challenge lately, because my boss does most of my work."

She rolled her eyes at him. "All right." It was an easy decision. "Write a position description for the assistant and do a new one for yourself. You might want a new title too. Send them to HR when you're done. I'll tell them to expect it."

"Really?" He seemed surprised.

"Of course."

He beamed at her. "Thank you, Carolina. You won't regret it."

The use of her full name saddened her. Evan's comment from the other day echoed in her head. "Call me Carly."

He grinned. "Thanks, Carly." He got up to go.

"Wait a second." She scribbled a figure on a piece of paper and handed it to him. "Would you be happy with this new salary?"

He glanced at the paper and his jaw dropped. "Seriously?"

She grinned. "Seriously. You're worth every penny. Now get to work. You're going to be slammed over the next couple of weeks while we make my job easier."

He laughed. "Yes, ma'am." He saluted and walked out.

Excitement bubbled over. She reviewed her new schedule, which had scribbled notations all over it, and calculated how much extra time she would have in her day. She could spend a whole day programming if she wanted to. She laughed.

Getting sick was the best thing that could have happened to her.

***

The week at work was the best Carly had had in a long time. Though occasionally she got twitches that she was letting too much go, and she did attend one or two meetings just to make sure the handover was smooth, generally she had far less stress to deal with. To her surprise, her executives were all keen to take on different charities and business meetings, which left her with Casa Flanagan, which she supported with the Comunidad software and second-hand computers.

Hayden had run the two new position descriptions past her and she'd approved them, leaving the hiring of the admin assistant up to him. And the best news of all, she'd spent the equivalent of a day working on her app and had it close to the testing stage.

She'd spoken with Evan every night after work. He was busy painting, but they had arranged to spend the weekend together. She was driving to his place and then they were going somewhere – she wasn't sure where. It was quite thrilling to have a whole free weekend in front of her where she didn't know what was planned.

"I'm about to head off. Do you still want a ride?" Hayden stood at the entrance to her office.

"Yes, please." Her heart was a little giddy. She'd made an impulsive decision during the week and now she was going to pick up the results. Quickly, she packed up her computer and grabbed her overnight bag.

"How are you finding your new role?" she asked Hayden as they rode down in the elevator.

"It's great, Carly. Thank you for believing in me."

"I should be thanking you. This week has been the most relaxed I've had in a long time. Thank you for making the suggestion."

They got into his car and she gave him directions.

"Do you want to sit in on the interview for the admin assistant?" he asked.

"No. The person will be reporting to you, so he or she needs to be someone you can work with. If you want a second opinion, though, let me know." She spotted her destination and pointed. "Over there."

Hayden pulled up and looked at her. "A Mini dealership?"

She nodded, her smile wide. "I bought a car."

He shook his head. "I think the flu messed with your head. Either that, or Evan has changed something about you."

He was right. Evan had seen through her, given her the courage to do what she really wanted to do. "I've always wanted one."

"That's great. What are you going to do with the BMW?"

She shrugged. "I'm not sure." She got out of the car and grabbed her things. "Thanks for the lift."

He was smiling as he waved and drove away.

***

Half an hour later, Carly was behind the wheel of her brand new red Mini. She grinned as she navigated the traffic to Evan's house, stopping at a nearby supermarket to grab some things for dinner. When she pulled up at Evan's, she tooted her horn and he came out.

"What do you think?" she called as his face broke into a huge grin.

"You bought a Mini."

She nodded. "It's all mine. Want to go for a spin?"

"Absolutely."

He got in the passenger side and Carly drove onto the street.

"What made you buy a new car?" he asked.

"I was thinking about what you said the other day, about which car I would buy if I didn't care what people thought, and I decided it was time I did something for myself."

"Good for you," he said. "So is it as good as you'd hoped?"

"Better. I can't stop grinning. I feel free."

"That's great."

"How's your work going?" Carly asked him.

"Really good. I've only got a couple more pieces to do."

"What date is the exhibition again?"

"The fourth of December – it's three weeks away. I got the invitations this week. I'll give you yours when we get back."

Carly had a horrible feeling the date meant something, but she pushed it aside. With her new process of delegation, she could give whatever it was to someone else. She pulled up in front of Evan's house and turned off the engine. "What have you got planned for the weekend?"

"It's a surprise," he said, helping her carry her things inside. "What's all of this?"

"I said I'd cook dinner," she said.

"I didn't think you knew how to, what with the state of your fridge."

She rolled her eyes at him. "Mama would never allow any of her girls to go out in the world not knowing how to cook."

She put her bags on the bench and gave McClane a pat.

"What are you making?" Evan asked.

"*Salpicón.*"

"Do you want a hand?"

"No. If you've got more painting to do, go and do that. I'll call you when it's ready." She was quite looking forward to making dinner. On the few days a week she didn't have business dinners she'd never felt like cooking. It was hard to get enthusiastic about cooking for one.

"Are you sure?"

"Yes. I'll figure out where everything is."

He left and Carly got to work. There was a radio in the kitchen, so she switched it on, making sure it wasn't too loud, and began chopping what she needed.

***

When dinner was almost ready, Carly wandered into Evan's studio. He was standing in front of the easel, his eyes focused and his hand moving quickly across the canvas. She stood there watching him for a minute. His bangs were hanging over his eyes and he kept flicking them away. His shirt was the one she thought of as his painting outfit, because he wore it often. It must have been white once, but was now covered in splotches of different colored paints. He wore denim shorts and his feet were bare. It struck her that he was so comfortable in his skin. He wore what he liked, he cut his hair when it interfered with his work, and he didn't care what anyone thought of him.

It must be so liberating to be so confident, to not second-guess every decision and be happy with who you were.

She was learning a lot from the man she loved.

The only time she'd seen him doubtful was about his work. She hoped she could help him with that.

As she stepped into the room, he acknowledged her with a wave, his eyes not leaving his painting. "Almost done."

She waited where she was for a couple of minutes, not wanting to interrupt his process, when he put down the brush. "Done." He breathed out a big sigh and moved his neck from side to side, stretching it.

"Dinner's ready," she said.

"Great. I'm starving." He wiped his hands on a rag and cleaned his brushes.

"Can I have a look?"

He nodded.

As she walked over to the canvas, his eyes never left her. It was a little disconcerting.

She turned her attention to the painting. It was his back veranda. A woman was lying on the outdoor couch sleeping, and McClane was curled up next to her with one eye open as if he was checking out the painter. There was a protectiveness about the dog, but also contentedness as well. The woman's face was partially obscured by her hair, and she seemed peaceful. Carly recognized herself, but she'd never seen herself at peace. Is that how Evan saw her?

"You don't like it." The disappointment in his statement was clear.

She turned to him. "No, it's lovely. I've never seen myself so relaxed. Did you make it up?"

He shook his head. "It was the day you came for the movie night."

She examined the painting again. "You really are incredible, Evan." She slipped her arms around his waist.

He hugged her back. "Thank you."

"Let's have dinner and you can tell me more about your exhibition. When do you need to finish the paintings?"

"The gallery needs them about a week before the show, so I've got a couple of weeks to finish and frame them. I'm using the same framer as I did for the local exhibition, though he's a bit pricey."

They were the kinds of details she'd never considered. All of Evan's paintings had had frames at the exhibition, but not every artist had. "Can I help you pay?"

"No, I have enough savings."

She wanted to ask how much, wanted to help him, but she knew he wouldn't appreciate it. "Is the curator good?"

He nodded. "She's got a good eye and people respect what she shows."

Carly served the food and he took a seat.

"How's Hayden going with his new role?" he asked.

"He's enjoying it. So are the executives."

"I'm glad. Is it giving you enough time to do what you want?"

She nodded. "I have the whole weekend free."

"I'm glad. I've got a lot planned."

"Are you going to tell me what?"

"Nope. You can wait until tomorrow."

She didn't press him. She was quite looking forward to the surprise.

They finished dinner and stacked the dishes.

"Want to take McClane for a walk with me?" Evan asked. "He hasn't had much attention lately."

"Sure." She grabbed a light jacket from her bag. Winter was slowly approaching, and there was a pleasant coolness in the air.

Evan whistled to McClane and the three of them strolled outside. They walked down the back of the property while McClane darted this way and that, sniffing out different smells.

"What drew you to rent this place?" Carly asked.

"The quiet. I've spent most of my life in cities – New York, Boston, Milwaukee, Detroit. I was tired of being surrounded by people all the time. I needed my own space."

She understood completely.

"But people and places are so much a part of my work that I don't want to be too far away. I do like socializing, just not all the time. This place is perfect for the moment, until I get the urge to move on."

Carly's footsteps faltered for a second before continuing. *Move on?* "You don't like staying in one place?" she asked, hoping her voice was casual.

"There was never a reason to stay before," he said. "And so much of the world left to explore."

She was silent as the hurt sliced through her heart. He wasn't planning on staying. Did he think what they had was a nice distraction until he moved elsewhere? Because that's sure as hell not what she thought. She enjoyed talking to him every night on the phone and spending time with him. She'd learned a lot about herself being with him and she'd gained confidence to try more things.

She *loved* him.

But he obviously didn't feel the same way.

McClane trotted over to them and she let go of Evan's hand to pat him. She was an idiot. She shouldn't have gotten too involved, shouldn't have fallen in love with the first man who'd treated her like a woman. She should have known he wasn't after anything more. She was a foolish, naïve girl.

The dog saw something and dashed off. Carly stood, wrapping her arms around herself, trying to protect herself from the hurt.

"Are you cold?" Evan asked, wrapping an arm around her shoulders. "We can go back, if you like."

"No, I'm fine." She couldn't help leaning into his warmth. She should draw away, but she wanted to take advantage of every moment while it lasted. "So there wasn't anyone worth staying for?" she asked.

He shrugged. "Most women got fed up of me ignoring their phone calls or forgetting dates because I was painting. They didn't understand like you do." He squeezed her shoulders. "This is the longest relationship I've had since college."

The admission made her feel a little better.

They reached the border of the property and turned to walk along the fence line. "It must have taken your mother such a long time to do her garden," said Evan.

"It was only about a year," Carly told him. "When they moved in, she designed the garden and we got Barker Landscaping in to review the plans and do the hardscaping. She just needed to source the plants." It had been such a thrill to buy it all for her.

"She's done an amazing job. It's so peaceful."

It was. Carly enjoyed taking walks through the garden when she went for lunch. "She had many years without any land, so she's making up for lost time." It was so different from the apartment where they'd grown up. She'd shared a room with her mother, and her sisters had the other room. There was no garden, no green anywhere near the complex, but her mother had grown herbs on the kitchen windowsill.

"What was it like when you first arrived here?"

"Scary." It was the first time Carly had admitted that to anyone. "I'd promised Papa I would take care of the family and I couldn't understand everything people said. The American accent is so different from the Irish brogue of my father. It took me ages to figure out what people were saying." She'd been too scared to admit she didn't understand, and would nod her head at anything she was told.

"What about your mother?"

"Mama didn't learn English until we'd been living here at least a year. Papa had learned Spanish and taught us English, but Mama hadn't been interested. I made her learn when she was struggling to get a job."

Evan frowned. "How can a, what, nine year old, get her mother to do anything?"

"I borrowed a book from the library and I sat with her every day. I wouldn't do my homework until she'd done hers, and she wanted me to succeed." Carly had been adamant. She'd understood that they wouldn't go back to El Salvador, and the only way her mother was going to get on in Houston was to learn English. She'd begun to teach Zita as well, so by the time her younger sister went to school, she was speaking it like it was her native tongue. On the weekend, they spoke English one day and Spanish the next.

It had also given her mother something to argue about, something to interact with the girls about, because the first year after their father had died had been hard on them all.

"So you taught her English?" He seemed impressed.

"We all had to learn and improve. Communication is so important and Mama needed something to do."

"It took her a while to get a job?"

Carly nodded. "She grieved for over a year, but eventually she found her feet."

"What do you mean she grieved for over a year?"

She hated remembering that year. She'd been so scared all the time. Caring for her sisters, taking care of her mother, managing the money. "She was an empty shell after Papa died, going through the motions. She left most of the care of the girls to me. I picked up Bridget from school and we'd catch the bus home together, and then I'd make dinner and make sure everyone had showers and read them a story before bed."

Evan frowned. "What did Carmen do?"

"She cried a lot, or sat on the couch staring at nothing. There was a family in the apartment next to us who had a little girl the same age as Zita, and so I arranged for Zita to play there at least twice a week."

Evan looked appalled. "Geez, Carly. I can't imagine what it was like for you. You were only a kid."

She shrugged. "I had to look after everyone. I was the oldest, and besides, I used to care for the girls when we were on the farm. Mama and Papa worked long hours." It was the way things were in the country. "All the arguments about the English lessons eventually got through to Mama. She got better after that."

It had been such a huge relief. Carly had been at the end of her tether.

"And you've been looking after everyone since then. No wonder you didn't know how to take anything for yourself."

They arrived back at the house. Carly was tired of talking about herself, remembering the bad times. She wanted to live in the now, particularly if Evan was moving on. "Is it too early to go to bed?" She winked at him.

He grinned. "Never."

Chapter 17

Evan woke to an empty bed. Damn, he was supposed to have woken before Carly so he could make her breakfast in bed. He mustn't have set his alarm properly. He peered at the clock, it was only seven. He'd set his alarm for eight, hoping she'd sleep in. No such luck.

He slipped out of bed and pulled on some shorts, before following the coffee smells through to the kitchen. Carly was cooking.

"Good morning," she called, looking far too perky for this time of the morning.

"Morning. What are you doing up so early, Carly? Didn't we agree to sleep in?"

She smiled. "I did. I didn't get up until half past six. I thought you might like some breakfast."

He poured himself a coffee, took a sip to get his brain functioning and then hugged her from behind. "I was going to cook for you."

"Oh. Well, you're too late. Take a seat."

He did as she asked. She was rolling some dough on the bench and something brown and mushy was simmering in a fry pan behind her. "What are you making?"

"*Desayuno Salvadoreno,*" she answered. "Salvadoran breakfast."

He frowned. "Where did you get the ingredients?"

"I bought them when I bought the dinner things yesterday."

Carly flattened the balls of dough between two plates and he realized she was making tortillas. He'd always thought they came in a packet. "Can I help with anything?"

"You could feed McClane. He's been giving me sad eyes since I started cooking and I wasn't sure what to feed him."

Sure enough McClane's eyes were droopy sad and there was a bead of drool coming out of the corner of his mouth. Evan chuckled. "All right."

By the time he was done, Carly had three pans on the stove and various things were frying. He watched in fascination as she stirred one, flipped another, knowing exactly what she was doing. He'd not expected this side of her.

In no time at all, she was dishing up. She handed him the plate. "Fried egg with tomato, fried plantains, pureed black beans, tortillas and sour cream," she said, pointing out each item.

"Thanks, Carly." It did smell good even if the beans looked like miscellaneous sludge.

She sat down next to him and sighed happily. "I haven't had *Desayuno Salvadoreno* in years." She used the tortilla to scoop up the food, and Evan followed suit.

It was delicious. "This is fantastic. You should definitely make this more often." He grinned. "Particularly when I'm staying over."

She laughed at him. "So what are we doing today?"

"You'll have to wait and see." He was pretty excited about what he had planned and he hoped she liked it. He wanted to treat her.

After they cleaned up from breakfast and were ready for the day, they headed out to his car and McClane jumped onto the backseat. They were halfway down the drive when there was a knocking sound and the engine stopped. "That didn't sound good," Evan said. He turned the key again and nothing happened.

They both got out of the car and peered under the hood. He had no idea what he was looking for.

"Any idea?" she asked.

"None." His brother had received all the mechanical genes. "I'd better call a tow truck."

"Or we could leave it here for the weekend and take the Mini." She smiled at him. "It's not going anywhere."

"McClane will spread hair all over your new seats." He sighed. "Plus I'll need the car on Monday." He hated spoiling the weekend he had planned.

"So we'll put down a sheet and you can borrow my BMW next week if you need to."

The idea of being reliant on her was a little uncomfortable, but it was a good solution. "All right. Thanks." He transferred their bags into the small trunk and then made the backseat as McClane-proof as he could before they all got in.

"Where to?" Carly asked.

"I'll direct you," he told her, and smiled when she pouted.

An hour later Carly slowed the car. "We're going to Brenham," she said softly.

Evan nodded. "I'm told it's the home of your favorite antique shops." Zita had given him Bridget's number to get all of the details.

"It is, but I've never gone in person." She giggled. "This is going to be fun."

His heart squeezed. He loved the pure excitement in her voice, loved that he was able to do this for her. He directed her to the first shop and took McClane out of the car. He opened the door to the store for Carly.

"Is McClane allowed inside?" she asked, hesitating on the doorstep.

"Yeah, I checked." He'd rung to find out what time they opened and asked whether there was a park nearby he could take McClane. He *might* have mentioned Carly's name and was told McClane was welcome in the store.

Carly stood inside the shop, slowly looking around. Her eyes were wide and her lips turned up in a smile. She took a couple of steps forward and then glanced back at him.

"Go and explore," he said. "I'll find McClane some water." The shop assistant strode toward them with a determined look on her face. Evan smiled at her. "Are you Alice?"

The woman paused mid stride. "Evan?"

"That's right. If I can grab some water for my dog, He'll be happy out there on the pavement for a little while."

The woman seemed relieved. "Of course." She glanced at Carly, who was slowly walking around, running her hand over different pieces of furniture.

Evan figured they'd be there a while.

He took the bowl of water from Alice and led McClane outside where he set him up under a tree, with the water bowl in easy reach. He'd be perfectly fine out here while Carly looked at antiques.

Inside, Carly and Alice were discussing a clock. It was something Evan imagined on a mantelpiece, and probably needed winding every day. Not his kind of thing, but it looked nice. Carly was in her element, asking questions about the piece, so he left her to it and wandered around the store.

There were items that showed their age, despite the care that had been applied to them – a scratch here, a dent there – but each one told a story. He could picture that dressing table in an old southern mansion, or the chaise lounge in the Hamptons. Perhaps his next project would be interior landscapes. Imagine what stories the furniture could tell.

He wandered back to Carly, who was finalizing her purchases. She beamed with happiness. He was glad he'd brought her here. Bridget had said Carly would love it and she'd been right.

Outside, she hugged and kissed him. "Thank you! That was great!"

"You're welcome. Have you had enough, or do you want to continue?"

She raised both eyebrows. "What do you think?" She glanced around. "Where's the next one?"

He pointed down the road, collected McClane, and they strolled down the pavement to the next shop. By the time Carly was done, she'd bought half a dozen more items and she couldn't stop smiling.

Evan grinned. Seeing her so happy made him happy. This time the idea didn't scare him so much. He was a lucky man. He was doing a job he adored and had found a woman he loved with all of his heart.

He grinned. He couldn't decide when he should tell her how he felt. There was a tiny worry that maybe she didn't feel the same way about him that he tried to ignore. He was in no rush. If it was up to him, they'd have forever together.

They stopped for lunch at a cafe and then explored the town together, before Carly announced she was exhausted.

"Ready to head to our accommodation?" he asked.

"Yes, please."

They got into the car and he directed her back toward Houston. He winced as they took a dirt road to their destination. He'd thought they'd be taking his old station wagon, which could handle all the bumps and rattles the road dished out. As they pulled into the clearing, Carly breathed, "Oh." She stopped the car and stared, her eyes wide. "It's like the house."

He nodded. He'd searched all the accommodation websites until he'd found a place similar to the cottage in his painting that she'd bought.

"It's so quaint."

"Yes."

Carly got out of the car and he followed her up the steps of the cottage. He unlocked the front door and pushed it open so she could walk inside. McClane was already off exploring the trees.

The inside was a combination of modern and old-fashioned. The couches were large and soft, but the coffee table was sturdy and worn. There was a big television on one wall, and the kitchen across the room had all the mod cons. Carly wandered down the hallway to where there were a couple of bedrooms and a bathroom. "It's lovely." She turned to him. "Thank you for bringing me here."

He kissed her slowly. "No problem. Make yourself comfortable and I'll grab the things from the car."

He'd arranged a picnic dinner and food for breakfast, which he carried in and put away, before taking their overnight bags to the bedroom. Carly was lying on the double bed, her hands under her head, looking extremely contented.

Evan kicked the door shut with one foot. McClane would be fine on his own for a while.

He wanted to show this beautiful woman how much he loved her.

***

Carly felt like a pampered princess for the first time in her life. After Evan had shown her all the wonderful things he could do to her body, she'd reclined in bed while he'd brought in a picnic basket of food and they'd eaten naked. Now she was relaxing on the bed while Evan sketched her.

It surprised her that she wasn't bothered by the fact she was still naked. She was comfortable with him and she trusted him. She smiled.

"That's perfect," Evan said as his hand dashed across the page.

"What is?"

"Your smile."

She laughed. "Sorry, should I have frozen into position?"

"No. It's recorded in my mind."

Her heart squeezed. Did that mean she meant something to him? Could he care for her even half as much as she loved him? Carly watched him as he sketched. Sometimes he'd look at her a moment, his hand still, before concentrating on the paper with a slight furrow between his eyes, and other times he'd keep his eyes on her as his hand continued to move across the paper. She didn't understand how he did it. "You're a magician."

He looked up. "What?"

"It's like watching magic happen, seeing you paint and draw," she told him. "Your hand moves of its own accord. Sometimes you don't even look at the paper. It's amazing."

Evan shrugged. "I've never really thought about it. It's just what I do."

He was so casual about it, but there was a tiny smile on his lips when he looked back down at his drawing that made Carly think perhaps her words had pleased him.

"Why do you pretend not to like compliments?"

He frowned. "What do you mean?"

"You're always so offhand when people praise your work, as if the praise doesn't matter, as if what you do is just work, but it's not. It's art, and you are allowed to enjoy compliments."

He continued sketching as he said, "I learned not to need them."

She sighed. He was clearly uncomfortable with the conversation so she let it slide.

But she'd make sure she praised his work on a regular basis.

Chapter 18

"It's going to cost how much?" Evan stared at the mechanic across from him. The fantastic weekend he'd had with Carly was now a distant memory as the shock of the repairs blocked everything else from his mind.

"Three grand. Your timing belt snapped and bent the valves."

"The car's not worth that much."

The man shrugged.

Evan closed his eyes. He didn't need this now. He'd spent all of his savings on getting the paintings framed for the exhibition and didn't have enough to cover repairs or a new car.

"What do you want to do?"

"Give me a second." Evan walked out of the shop. He didn't have a lot of options. He needed a car to get around. Though he seriously hated asking Carly for help, he dialed her number.

"How's the car?" she asked.

"It's terminal." He sighed. "Would you mind if I borrowed your BMW for a couple of weeks?"

"Not at all. What's the problem?"

"The timing belt snapped and bent other parts. It'll cost more to repair than the car is worth, so I'll look at getting a new car after the exhibition." He'd hopefully have some more money by then.

"You can keep the BMW if you want. I was going to sell it

anyway."

His skin tightened. "No. You're not giving me your car."

"Why not? I've got no use for it now."

"No. I just need a loan until I get back from New York."

Carly sighed. "Sure. You can pick it up whenever you want."

"Thank you. I'll catch a cab in when I've dealt with the mechanic." He hung up. It was a relief to know he had wheels, but he wasn't going to accept such an expensive gift from Carly. It wasn't right.

He walked back into the shop. "How much to scrap it?"

***

Carly was getting used to her lightened workload. Work last week after going to Brenham had been fabulous and she'd just had another relaxing weekend with Evan. Their only disagreement had been over the BMW, which he wouldn't accept as a gift. She'd left a signed vehicle sales form in the car in case he changed his mind.

She strode into work on Monday morning with a smile on her face. Even faced with a calendar full of meetings — the last few things she needed to hand over to her respective managers — she was excited about the week ahead. Her plan was to get to the test phase of her app, spend some time in the indie hub, and work on the speech she was giving for the Refugee Symposium being held in Houston next month. Tonight she was meeting with the refugee advocate group to talk about it.

She was pretty nervous about the symposium. Some of the biggest refugee advocates were going to be speaking, and Carly had been invited to talk about her program at Casa Flanagan. She'd thought Zita or her mother would have been better candidates to speak, as they worked with the girls, but in the end, her reputation in the community was considered to hold more weight.

Suddenly, Carly had an uneasy thought. What date was the symposium? Checking her calendar, her stomach sank.

No, it couldn't be.

She checked again. December 4. The same day as Evan's exhibition.

Quickly she scrolled through her emails to check the time

she had been assigned. Two o'clock. She wouldn't be finished until three at the earliest. She opened an airline website and checked whether there was any way she could fly to New York in time for Evan's exhibition.

There was nothing.

Putting a hand to her nauseated stomach, she breathed in and out slowly. She couldn't possibly cancel her speaking engagement, it was too important. There had been talk about getting rid of detention centers for years, and Casa Flanagan was the shining case study of how this could work. If she could convince the powers that be that it was achievable, children wouldn't be forced to be incarcerated for long periods of time, facing such awful uncertainty as to their future.

But she felt dreadful.

The exhibition was so important to Evan. It was the next step in his career – the biggest step to date. And she was going to miss it. She really wanted to be there for him, to support him, but it wasn't possible. She sighed. Evan would understand how important the symposium was, she was sure of it.

***

Evan stared at the collection of paintings in front of him. Over the last week, doubts had entered his head, and he wasn't able to shake them loose. It didn't happen very often these days, but with the exhibition only weeks away, the voices in his head were getting louder and more insistent.

You're no good.

My six year old can paint better than you.

Who do you think you're kidding? You'll never be an artist.

The paintings were ready for shipping, but Evan could only see every flaw – the color wasn't quite right on that one, there was a brush stroke in the wrong spot there. Every painting just looked wrong to him.

He huffed out a breath, running his fingers through his hair, trying to release the tension that had gripped his chest and wouldn't let go. The exhibition would get a flurry of bad reviews and it would be canceled. And no one would offer to exhibit him again.

Evan walked away from the paintings. He had to get a grip.

He should go for a swim, clear his mind, before the anxiety overwhelmed him.

He headed out to the pool and when his phone rang, he grabbed it out of his pocket. He had to distract himself.

"Evan, it's Carly."

He breathed out a sigh of relief. She believed in him, she'd help calm him down. He paced along the pool.

"Hi. I thought you were busy all week."

She sighed. "I am, but I have to tell you something quickly."

He stopped walking. Her tone made his stomach squirm. "What is it?"

"I can't come to your exhibition."

Lead dropped into his gut. "What?" He hoped he'd misheard her.

"I'm *so* sorry, I feel really awful about this, but I can't make it to your exhibition. I've been invited to speak—"

He didn't let her get any further. All he heard was she had somewhere better to be. All his insecurities rushed at him at once, making him lash out. "I get it. There's something more important going on. Something more interesting than a bunch of paintings you've already seen. Don't worry about it." He turned to pace along the pool again and tripped. As he fought for balance, the phone slipped out of his hand. It hit the edge of the pool and slipped into the water. "Damn!" No. It didn't matter. He couldn't bear to hear Carly's excuse anyway. It hurt too much. She didn't really believe in him, she didn't think the biggest exhibition of his life was worth her time. *He* wasn't worth her time.

His throat burned and he blinked away the tears in his eyes. Carly knew how much the exhibition meant to him, but it didn't matter. She was just like his parents. She'd had a better offer.

He should have realized what she was like when she'd stood him up for their lunch date.

His laugh was bitter. To think he'd been about to tell her he loved her, had considered when it would be right to ask her to marry him.

He was a fool. He sunk down on the pavement and put his head in his hands.

And let his insecurities beat him.

***

"Evan?" Carly stared at the phone in her hand. He'd hung up on her. She quickly called him back.

No answer.

Her heart dropped. He hadn't let her explain. There was no way she would have missed his exhibition if it hadn't been for the symposium. If it had been virtually anything else she would have canceled, but this wasn't about her, this was about the lives of so many people. She had to make attendees realize that helping these people wasn't a burden on the government or society, it was for the betterment of everyone.

The nausea in her stomach swirled, making her feel ill.

She wanted to jump in her car and go to him, but her whole day was booked solid. And tonight she had the meeting with the refugee advocate group. It would be tomorrow before she could go to him; she'd just have to keep calling him in the meantime.

"Carly, your ten o'clock is here," Hayden said through the intercom.

She sighed. "Send him in."

***

It was almost dark by the time Evan roused himself. McClane came padding out to the pool looking for food, and shoved his big head into Evan's lap. He hugged his dog. "You understand me, don't you?"

McClane licked him and Evan grimaced. He pushed himself to his feet and stared at his phone on the bottom of the pool. It was bound to be ruined, but he slid into the cold water to retrieve it. The screen was black. He'd have to wait until he got paid to replace it. With a sigh, he got out, wrapped a towel around himself and trudged into the kitchen.

He fed McClane and switched on his laptop. There was an email from the estate agent telling him his lease here would expire in a month, and asking him if he would like to renew.

Did he?

Was there any point staying here if what he had with Carly wasn't going anywhere? If she didn't love him? No. He closed his eyes against the heartache. It was time to move on. He didn't belong here. He'd be in New York for a couple of weeks during his exhibition, so he could pack up his things beforehand, put them in storage, and then arrange for them to be moved when he decided where he was going next.

He replied to the estate agent and then turned on the video chat app so he could contact his brother, Karl.

"Hey, Evan. I got the invitation to your exhibition opening. Congratulations, man."

"Thanks." He couldn't work up any enthusiasm right now. "Actually, that's why I'm calling. I figured I might as well stay in New York after your engagement party. Have you got a spare bed for me and McClane for a couple of weeks?"

"Sure. There's always room for you. When are you coming?"

The sooner he left Houston behind, the better. He still had a bunch of packing boxes in his spare room from the last move, so he could start packing now, tonight.

"I've got a couple of things to arrange tomorrow," said Evan, "and I need to change my flight. I'll let you know the details."

"Great! Sarah or I should be able to pick you up from the airport."

He ended the call.

The sooner he left Houston behind, the better.

Chapter 19

Carly's phone rang. Her first thought was Evan, but one look at the phone left her disappointed. Zita.

She hadn't heard from Evan in three days. She'd tried to call him multiple times and on Tuesday she'd gone to his place but he hadn't been home. How was she going to make up for missing the exhibition? Maybe Zita could think of something. "What's up, little sister?"

"Is Evan moving in with you?"

Carly frowned. "No. Why would you think that?"

"His house has a big For Rent sign out the front. I peered through the windows and it's empty. I figured since he didn't mention it when I dropped him at the airport today, he might have wanted you to break the news."

"You took him to the airport?" Carly's mind was whirling.

"Yeah. His brother's engagement party is this weekend."

She'd forgotten about that. But why would he pack his things?

"If he's not moving in with you, where's all his stuff?"

"I don't know." She couldn't comprehend it. He hadn't mentioned moving.

"What happened with you two? I thought you were close."

"We had a fight Monday."

"So he's just left Houston?"

"I don't know," she repeated. "He was planning to stay in

New York while his exhibition is on." She was grasping at straws.

"He wouldn't have packed up everything if he was coming back."

Zita was right. Evan had left. He hadn't cared enough about her to even say goodbye.

Had she only been a distraction for him? He'd mentioned he liked to move around, and she'd ignored the warning.

Andrew had disappeared without a word as well.

She froze. Was that what this was? She'd given Evan her car and he was gone. Had he sold it, taken the money and run?

Had she been played again?

"You'll see him at the exhibition, won't you?" Zita asked. "You'll get answers then. He wouldn't leave if it wasn't important."

"I'm not going to the exhibition."

"What? Why not?"

"It's the same day as the refugee symposium."

"*Feck*. Really? I didn't notice the date. That means I can't go either. Is that what you fought about?"

"Yes." She didn't want to talk about it now. Not when her eyes were getting watery and her throat was closing over. "Sorry, I've got to go, Zita," she said, and hung up.

The computer screen in front of Carly blurred and she blinked to clear her eyes, but hot tears ran down her face.

"Carly, I'm heading off . . ." Hayden's eyes widened as he entered her office. "Shit, are you all right?" He closed the office door behind him and strode over.

She wiped her face, and tried to clear her throat to speak but it was impossible. The lump refused to move.

"What happened? Has someone died?" Hayden sat on the edge of her desk and took her hand.

Carly shook her head, heat rising to her cheeks at having him see her like this and being unable to control it. She grabbed a tissue from her desk and blotted her eyes, trying to stem the flood. She breathed in and out, in and out, and swallowed. "It's nothing."

"Don't lie, Carly." He was angry. "You don't have to tell me, but don't lie to me. I've never seen you this upset over anything."

She grabbed hold of his anger, and tried to channel her own. "I said it's nothing. Evan has left, but it doesn't matter because it obviously didn't mean anything." She pushed back her chair, determined to get out of there.

"I'm so sorry. I thought he was better than that."

The soft words dissolved her anger and the tears came again. Hayden opened his arms and Carly stepped forward into them.

He held her while her heart broke in two.

***

Carly didn't know how long she sobbed for, but eventually the tears stopped and the embarrassment set in. She drew away from Hayden. "I'm sorry."

"Don't be, Carly. This is what friends do."

Could she really count him as her friend?

"I know what you need – a night out to drown your sorrows. We can both lament lying, cheating men."

His tone had Carly looking up. "The guy in the bar didn't work out?"

"Caught him cheating on me," Hayden said with a shrug, but his eyes were hurt.

Carly didn't feel like drinking, she didn't ever get drunk, but Hayden seemed to need it. "All right. Let's go."

He blinked. "Really?"

She nodded, turning off her computer. "Tonight I want to forget about Evan and you want to forget about . . ."

"Travis."

"Travis," she agreed. "We'll find a nice bar and the drinks are on me."

"All right then." He held out his arm. "Let's go forget."

***

An hour later and two red wines down, Carly was pleasantly light-headed. She and Hayden had been chatting about past loves – well, he'd been talking about all the guys he'd dated, and she had made the appropriate comments.

"My round," Hayden said, getting to his feet. "What do you want, another red?"

Someone walked past holding a cocktail glass of some kind of frozen red concoction. "That," Carly said, pointing.

Hayden chuckled. "Frozen strawberry daiquiri it is."

She dug out some cash from her purse and handed it to him when he returned.

"What's this for?"

"The drinks."

"Don't be silly. It was my turn to pay."

She suspected the cocktail cost more than the wine. "Take it," she insisted.

"No, it's fine. My boss just gave me an incredible pay raise." He winked at her.

Carly laughed, surprised she was able to.

"So, do you want to tell me about what happened with Evan?"

His name sent a jolt of pain through her. How could he have just left like that? She took a breath. Hayden had been sharing all of his stories, it was only fair she told hers. "Zita called this afternoon to ask if I knew where Evan was. He lives next door to her, and apparently there's a For Rent sign out front."

"He didn't mention he was moving?"

She shook her head. "We had an argument on Monday. He's got this big exhibition in New York next month that means a lot to him and I can't make it. He was angry and he hung up on me."

"Why can't you go?"

"It's the same day as the symposium."

"Damn. Did you tell him?"

"He didn't give me the chance. I've tried calling, and I went around earlier this week, but he wasn't there." She took a long sip of her drink. "I gave him my BMW, and he moved out without saying a word."

"He took your car?"

She nodded. "It's like Andrew all over again."

"Who's Andrew?"

She was tipsy enough to want to confide in him, so she told him the whole sad story.

When she was finished, he whistled. "OK, so it looks bad, but don't give up hope yet. A guy doesn't spend a week nursing you if he's not smitten."

"He does if he's after your money." It wasn't much work for a car worth over sixty grand.

Hayden shook his head. "No. I didn't get that vibe from Evan at all. Is the exhibition a big deal? Could he be upset that you're not going?"

She pushed through her own hurt to think about it. Of course he was upset. She straightened her posture as the realization struck. He would have seen her response as a rejection of him and his work. "Yes. His parents always let him down." No wonder he'd ignored her calls. She let out a deep breath. "But there's still the car." She didn't want to get her hopes up.

"Are you sure he took it?"

"Zita would have mentioned if he'd left it behind."

"It's worth checking."

He was right. She dialed Zita's number. "Did you see my BMW at Evan's place?"

"No, I've got it here. Sorry, I forgot to tell you. I drove Evan and McClane to the airport and he told me you'd pick up the car at our next lunch."

"Thanks." She hung up, her mind working furiously. "He left it with Zita," she told Hayden.

"See, I told you! He'd got to be upset about you missing the exhibition."

"But why won't he answer my calls?"

"Maybe he needs time to cool off, or maybe his battery is dead, or maybe he's out of range."

"He's in New York."

"OK, so scrap that last one." Hayden smiled at her. "Is there any way you can get to New York after your speech?"

"I checked all the airlines. There's nothing after three o'clock that will get me there."

"What about a private jet?"

Carly stared at him, her brain not quite comprehending. "A jet?"

He rolled his eyes. "Yeah. Most billionaires use them all the time."

It had never occurred to her. Maybe she *could* hire a jet.

But did Evan want her there? He hadn't returned her calls, hadn't told her where he was going. But he'd been incredibly hurt as well.

She'd let him down. She downed the remainder of her drink and winced at the brain freeze. "I need to go."

"Where?"

"Back to the office. I need to find a plane."

"I'm coming with you. That's a job for a PA."

She didn't waste time arguing. They left the bar. Carly was a little unsteady on her feet, but Hayden kept close enough to support her.

"Geez, Carly. Can't you handle your liquor?"

"I can. It's the heels." She stepped into the elevator and kicked them off. Her balance was better already.

Hayden picked up her shoes and when the doors opened, he accompanied her to her office, helping her into a seat at her meeting desk.

"I need the computer."

"I got it," he said, sitting at her desk and switching it on. He started to type. "What's the budget?" he asked.

"Unlimited."

Hayden grinned and picked up the phone. In a very short period of time he organized a plane, plus helicopters either end to get her to and from the airport.

He put down the phone. "It's arranged."

Her stomach danced a jig of nerves. Was she doing the right thing? What if Evan didn't want her there?

Carly pushed aside her fears. No matter what, she needed to show him she was there for him. If he didn't want to see her, if this was his way of breaking up with her, then he could tell her face to face.

She deserved that at least.

***

The last thing Evan wanted to do was go to his younger brother's engagement party. Not when his heart was still so sore. But it would be selfish of him not to go when Karl wanted him there. Just because his heart had been broken, didn't mean that others couldn't be happy.

He just needed to tighten all of his defenses, be pleased for the couple, and be ready to face his parents.

It couldn't have come at a worse time.

He arrived in New York on Wednesday evening. It took him some time to find Karl at the airport as he hadn't replaced his phone yet.

"Evan!" His brother gave him a man-hug. "I'm so glad you could make it for Thanksgiving." Karl lifted his suitcase into the car.

Evan froze. He'd forgotten all about Thanksgiving. He forced a smile onto his face. "What do you have planned?" He opened the car door for McClane and helped him inside. The dog was a little subdued after flying for the first time.

"Not much. Mom and Dad are coming for lunch and then we'll watch the game."

Evan closed his eyes. He knew Karl meant well, but he didn't need their negativity right now.

They chatted about what Karl had been up to on the trip back to his brother's house in the suburbs. Karl had done well for himself. He'd bought a house, had a successful business, and was now marrying the woman he loved. Evan had met his brother's fiancée, Sarah, once before he'd moved to Houston, and she seemed down to earth and nice.

McClane barked in the backseat. It sounded like he'd recovered from his flight. Evan got out, unstrapped McClane, and together they followed Karl inside.

In the living room. Sarah was sitting at a table, putting paper lanterns together and swearing under her breath. She was originally from Jamaica and her dark hair was restrained by a red scarf. She looked up and smiled.

"Hey, Evan." She got to her feet and kissed his cheek.

"Hi. Thanks for letting me stay." It hadn't occurred to him until he was flying here that Karl might not want his older brother hanging around while he was newly engaged. Evan had made up his mind to see how things went, but he could always find somewhere else to stay if he was getting in the way. "What are you working on?" he asked Sarah.

"Decorations for the party. It completely slipped my mind

with all the other preparations."

"Need a hand?"

"Yes, please. The instructions make it sound simple, but they're tricky little things."

Pleased he could do something to help, he got to work.

***

The next day, Evan woke to the smell of turkey cooking in the oven. Thanksgiving. Briefly, he debated whether he could pretend to be sick and not leave his room, but he knew it wouldn't work.

He got dressed and found Sarah and Karl in the kitchen cooking. He smiled at the domestic scene. "Need any help?"

Sarah glanced over and smiled. "You could peel the sweet potatoes."

"Sure."

Karl glanced over from the pot he was stirring and said, "Mom was really happy when I told her you were coming."

Evan tensed. Mention of his parents was inevitable, but it didn't mean he had to like it. "That's a surprise."

Karl sighed. "They treated you badly, but it doesn't mean you can't have some kind of relationship with them."

"Why would I want to?" They hadn't believed in him at all.

"Because they're your parents. Because one day we're going to have kids, and it would be a hell of a lot more pleasant at family gatherings if I didn't have to stress about you fighting on what's supposed to be a happy occasion." Karl was agitated.

Evan had never considered that Karl might feel like he was caught between them. Was it worth holding on to his grudge, if it hurt his brother who had done nothing? It was hard. That shield had protected him for almost ten years. *Could* he let it go?

"I'll try."

"Good." Karl beamed at him. "You know, Thanksgiving has improved a lot since we were kids, but that's probably because I cook the meal."

His father had always grumbled about the cost, but instead of pointing it out he said, "That's not saying much. *Everyone's* a better cook than Mom."

Karl laughed. "Amen to that."

Evan smiled, pleased to see his brother happy. He would be on his best behavior when his parents arrived.

When the food was almost ready, the doorbell rang. Evan glanced at his brother. Karl's expression begged him to be nice. Was he ready for this? He had to be. He wasn't going to ruin the day for his baby brother, no matter what his own feelings on the situation were.

Sarah went to answer the door. Evan moved out of the small kitchen into the living room. He wanted space around him, wanted the opportunity to move if he needed to.

"Evan?" Karl wanted reassurance.

"I'll *try* to be good." He wasn't going to promise a miracle.

The voices in the hall came closer. Evan braced himself.

His parents stepped into the room. They were older; his father's hair had a generous sprinkling of gray and his mother's face was more lined than he remembered. He had a moment to study them before they noticed him, and all conversation ceased.

"Evan," his mother breathed. "You look well."

He nodded. "Mom. Dad." What the hell could he say? Nice to see you? That was a lie. "How are you?"

"We're both very well."

The child inside him wanted to say, look at me, see what I've done with myself, look at how much I've achieved on my own. Instead, he stayed silent.

"Helen, Powell, why don't you take a seat?" Sarah invited. "Lunch is ready."

Evan went into the kitchen to help Sarah carry out the food.

She gave him a sympathetic smile. "This really means a lot to Karl."

"I know. I wouldn't be here otherwise." He took the bowl of salad she handed him, and then followed her back to the dining room.

His parents were seated on one side of the table and Evan took a chair opposite. Karl and Sarah chatted with his parents while he concentrated on eating.

"So, Evan," said Powell, "Karl tells us you've got an exhibition in New York next week."

"That's right."

"Where's it at?" He laughed. "Or won't I have heard of it?"

"It's the Real Life gallery in Chelsea."

Both his parents raised their eyebrows.

"Didn't you used to talk about that gallery when you were younger?" Helen asked.

Evan blinked. He couldn't believe she'd remembered. He hadn't thought she'd listened when he'd come home from a day in the square and talked about the latest exhibition at Real Life. "I used to walk past on my way home from work," he said.

"That's right. You must be thrilled. I'm happy for you." She gave him a cautious smile.

"Thanks." He couldn't quite believe his ears. His mother was happy for him?

"So do people actually pay ridiculous sums for your paintings?" Powell asked.

Helen glared at her husband. Trust his father to bring it straight back to money.

"I earn enough."

"Not too much, I'd guess, if your brother had to pick you up from the airport."

Evan refused to rise to the bait.

"A cab wouldn't take McClane," Sarah said quickly and handed her future father-in-law a bowl. "More salad, Powell?"

"That's right." Evan smiled at Sarah. She was trying to keep things polite, but she needn't worry about his reaction. He wasn't going to spoil his brother's day. He would be civil.

"McClane? Who the hell is McClane?" Powell demanded.

Until now his dog had been sitting behind the sofa. At the sound of his name, he came trotting out.

"That's McClane." Evan nodded to his dog.

"Isn't he the cutest!" Helen exclaimed, leaning over to give him a pat.

Evan frowned. He never would have taken his mother for a dog person. They'd never been allowed any pets.

"Expensive creatures," Powell said, ignoring the dog entirely.

"Anyone for dessert?" Karl asked.

It was a very long afternoon. The conversation while they ate revolved around the engagement party, which avoided any further awkwardness. Then after lunch, they sat and watched football. Evan wasn't particularly interested, but he did what was expected of him and cheered for the same team as Karl and Powell. Finally, his parents left.

When they'd gone, Karl said, "Thanks, Evan."

Evan shrugged. "Don't sweat it." It hadn't been as bad as he'd feared, but he did have an urge for some fresh air. "I'm going to take McClane for a walk." He grabbed the leash, whistled for his dog, and headed out the door.

***

The engagement party was being held at a nearby bar. Evan wore his brown pinstriped suit and vowed to be on his best behavior. His parents hadn't embraced him warmly, but he hadn't wanted or expected that. His mother had been far more attentive than she'd ever been, and his father had barely changed.

He headed to the venue early with Karl and Sarah, so he could help them set up. As the guests filtered in, Evan was surprised how many people he recognized. Karl was still friends with almost all of his school friends and so there were guys Evan had known growing up. It was kind of surreal to see them all as adults. Then there were the family members – aunts, uncles, cousins, and his grandparents on both sides. He'd kept in touch with them a little over the years, though he'd never accepted any invitations where his parents were likely to attend. It was so great to catch up with the relatives, and they were all keenly interested in how he was doing. It was a nice change.

The party was quite a casual affair. After everyone had arrived, there were a few speeches and finger food was passed around. Toward the end of the night he was walking by his grandma and she grabbed his arm to stop him. She was talking to his parents.

"It's so lovely that Evan is here, isn't it, Helen?"

"It is." There was that cautious smile from his mother again.

"Why didn't you bring a date?" Grandma asked. "Are there no ladies in your life?"

His heart hurt. He'd made a concerted effort not to think

about Carly. It was too painful. "Not at the moment."

"That's a shame. I was sure you would have married before Karl."

"Who's going to want a man who can't provide for her?" Powell asked.

Evan's control slipped for a moment, but he grabbed hold of it again. It was Karl's night. His father's comments couldn't hurt him. It didn't matter what his parents thought of him, or his work. He'd been holding out for their praise for far too long and he might never get it. As long as he was happy, as long as he knew the work was the best he could do, that was all that mattered.

The epiphany chased all of the tension from his body.

"Powell, that's quite enough," Helen said. "Evan seems to be doing perfectly well and he's not once asked us for help. You need to let go of your resentment. Your son is doing what he loves." She stood with her hands on her hips, glaring at her husband.

Evan's jaw dropped. He'd never heard his mother speak so passionately.

She turned to him. "Ignore him, Evan. He's just jealous."

It was so ridiculous that his mother was defending him, that his father could be jealous, that Evan couldn't help himself. He burst out laughing.

"It's hardly funny," Helen said.

He didn't bother keeping the incredulity from his voice. "You told me to go and not to come back. There's no jealousy involved. But you're right. I am doing well for myself and I am enjoying life." He turned to go, but his mother grabbed his arm.

"I am truly sorry for the way we acted. We didn't want you living the hard life and we thought ultimatums would prevent that. We were wrong."

Evan had no words. He should say something, but nothing came out. His mother was apologizing to him.

"I'd . . . we'd like to come to your exhibition, if you'll let us."

His response was automatic. "It's open to the public." At the hurt on his mother's face he added, "But I might have a spare invitation for opening night." Karl was right. It was time he mended the fences, if only for the sake of his brother.

Helen positively beamed at him. "That would be lovely."

Not quite sure how to deal with this sudden change in their relationship, Evan excused himself.

He needed a drink.

Chapter 20

The Central American Refugee Symposium started at nine in the morning, and Carly was there with Carmen and Zita. She listened to the forums, taking in the latest research findings and was discouraged by the horrific standards of the detention centers. Why didn't those in charge understand that jailing these people wasn't the way to start a relationship with them?

At the lunch break, Carly called Hayden. She needed some positive news and she wanted to check the details of her flight to New York were confirmed.

"Sure is. The helicopter will be at the conference center at three. It will take you straight to the airport and your plane is scheduled to take off as soon as you arrive. There's a shower on board, so you can freshen up and change. You should land in New York just before the gallery opens."

Her stomach twitched. But did Evan want her there? She hoped so. "You've confirmed the transfer in New York as well?"

"Of course. There's a helipad on the building next door to the exhibition. You'll be there on time."

Carly hung up and breathed out. She hoped she wasn't about to make a fool of herself. She hoped Evan would be happy to see her. He hadn't called her in the week since he'd left. But there was no point worrying about it now. She needed to focus on why she was here. Her speech was straight after lunch.

She walked over to her mother and Zita.

"How do you think it's going?" Zita asked.

"I overheard a few government officials chatting during the morning break. It's definitely sparking debate."

The problem was, many of the presentations so far had dealt with statistics and costs. They needed to bring humanity into the picture. She had to talk about the girls' stories.

They went back into the auditorium and finally it was Carly's turn to speak. Her legs were wobbly as she walked on to the stage and looked out at the audience. There were thousands there to hear her talk. She swallowed. She had to connect with them. She had to drop her professional persona and speak to them as people. She had to be Carly, not Carolina.

All of her nerves melted away. She could be herself.

She explained her background, giving an overview of Casa Flanagan. Then she took a deep breath. "This situation is not about money, it's not about the legality of the refugees' actions, it's about humanity. My family started our charity because we were fortunate. Our refugee application was accepted before we arrived, but we paid the price to wait. My father was killed by the people we were fleeing from, the week before our application was approved."

There was a collective gasp from the crowd.

"It was difficult starting in a country so different from El Salvador, and in such a huge city, but we had each other to hold on to when things got tough, when US customs were confusing, and we were trying to figure out this new world. The unaccompanied children don't have that. They are far away from everything they know and everyone they love, but they have one thing in common. They want a better, safer life."

A few people nodded in the audience, but there were some who sat stony-faced.

"They've come from countries where gender inequality is at a peak, where they are treated like meat, and where violence is so bad that a father would give his own daughter to the gangs in order to ensure his own safety. They understand that fleeing their village or their city will not help because the issues are rife throughout the country." Carly told the stories of two of her foster sisters. "There is nowhere safe for them to go. And so they flee to the United States, the land of the free and the home of the brave, in hope of a better life."

A few people smiled.

"There is no one braver than they are, leaving their homes, risking their lives in search of freedom and hope. Now they are here, they don't sit around all day, living off handouts. No, they are some of the hardest workers I have ever met, practicing English, studying their lessons. They all have dreams of what they want to become: doctors, lawyers, teachers, and some dream of returning home and fighting to improve their country so they can stop the exodus of refugees. All they need is a little time, a little support, in order to be able to make a difference."

Carly swallowed the lump in her throat. "When I meet these children I always think, what if the situation were reversed? What if it was my sister fleeing the country, trying to find somewhere she wouldn't be raped and abused? Wouldn't I do everything in my power to help her? Wouldn't I want people to support her, to protect her, to give her the opportunities she wasn't able to get here?" She paused to let that sink in. "Of course I would. These refugees aren't faceless masses. They are people like you and me, they are mothers, daughters, sisters, brothers. They are your neighbors, your friends, your colleagues. They are people who deserve as much of a chance at a good life as you or I. So, please, stop thinking of them as numbers, as wasted dollars, and start thinking of them as people. Thank you."

The applause was loud and even the stony-faced people at the front clapped. Her heart lifted. She hoped it was enough to make a difference.

She went backstage and Hayden was standing there clapping.

"That was a sensational speech."

"What are you doing here?"

"I didn't want to miss your speech. Plus, I wanted to make sure you didn't get caught up with people wanting to talk to you and miss your helicopter."

She hesitated. Could she really race off now? Shouldn't she be around to talk, to answer questions, to cement what she'd said in her speech?

"What's wrong?" he asked.

"Am I doing the right thing?" she asked.

"Hell yes, Carly. You've done all you can here. I'll stay and represent Comunidad. Your mother and sister are here somewhere too, aren't they?"

At that moment Zita and Carmen came backstage.

"That was awesome, Carly." Zita hugged her and Carmen nodded, dabbing her eyes.

"She needs to get on a plane," Hayden told them both.

"What plane?" Zita asked.

"She's flying to New York tonight."

Zita grinned. "Evan's exhibition?"

Carly nodded.

"What time's your flight?"

"Now. I'm taking a private jet, so it'll wait."

"You should go, Carly. You've done all you can here." Zita said.

"What if people have questions?"

"They know where to find you, or they can ask us," Hayden said.

"Go, *niñita*," her mother urged. "Evan needs you."

She was right. Carly turned Hayden. "Where do I go?"

*

Evan had another couple of hours at least before he needed to get ready for the exhibition, but he couldn't sit still. He'd already taken McClane for the marathon of all walks, and his dog was recovering in a corner. Karl was still at work and Sarah was in her office working.

If he didn't find someone to talk to now, he was going to go mad.

He briefly considered calling Zita, but there was no knowing whether she'd talk to him. Breaking up with Carly meant he'd probably lost Zita's friendship as well. He sighed.

He walked past Sarah's door, hoping to catch her attention. She was on her computer, watching a video.

"Taking a break?" he asked, going in.

She turned to him. "No. This refugee symposium is work related. It's being live-streamed from Houston." Sarah worked for the Department of Homeland Security. "I'm really interested in the next speaker. She's been running a trial whereby unaccompanied child refugees are given housing in the community while awaiting the processing of their applications. People are totally against it because they fear the refugees will disappear and never be heard from again, but there has to be a better way than those detention centers. Her speech could change people's perceptions."

Wasn't it just his luck that his brother's fiancée was a big advocate for refugees like Carly?

He turned to go, not wanting to think about the woman who had broken his heart, when he heard the words, "Carolina Flanagan."

He froze. He'd forgotten all about the symposium. Slowly, he turned back to the computer as Carly walked onto the stage amid polite applause.

She looked good. So very good.

She held herself with such confidence, and as she spoke Carly shone through, not Carolina. She wasn't speaking as a billionaire philanthropist, she was talking as the woman who'd been a scared refugee and had grown from her experiences into someone who wanted to help those like herself.

As she spoke, Evan hung on to her every word, happy to hear her voice again. *This* was why she couldn't come to his exhibition. This was what was so important. This *was* more important than his exhibition. This was about improving people's lives. She spoke with passion, with determination, and as she spoke Evan couldn't understand why people could even question the legitimacy of refugees in the first place. He was one hundred percent behind her all the way.

When she finished her speech and walked off stage, he applauded along with Sarah.

"Isn't she amazing?" Sarah said. "She does fabulous things with the migrant community in Houston, and Comunidad is used all over the world."

"She is amazing."

Would she forgive him for his childish mistake? He'd been a fool. No, a jackass. He'd forgotten an important event in her life. He had to apologize. But what he needed to say shouldn't be said over the phone.

Evan ran his hand through his hair. He shouldn't have

jumped to conclusions. He'd let his insecurities rule him, and this was where it got him. He'd lost the one woman who had actually understood him.

He needed to get back to Houston. But he couldn't miss his exhibition opening. Heading for his computer, he checked the first available flight to Houston. It was tomorrow morning. He booked it and sat back.

He hoped she would forgive him.

***

Evan stared at his reflection in the mirror of the gallery's bathroom. He couldn't shake the nerves that had never affected him this badly before. Perhaps because he'd never had an exhibition this large. If the critics loved him, it could mean being able to concentrate on what he wanted to do, rather than having to grab every job that came his way. But the gallery had recommended ridiculous prices for his work. He didn't think anyone would pay that much – not for something he did.

His thoughts went to Carly and how she dealt with her nerves. Her speech had been streamed nationally, perhaps even internationally, and despite her fear of public speaking, she had been poised and in control. He needed to take a leaf out of her book.

"Evan, are you ready?" the curator, Georgia, called.

No. He wasn't, but it was already seven thirty. The gallery had been open for half an hour and now they would do the official opening. He was supposed to be out there, schmoozing with patrons, but his stomach hadn't been up to it. "Be right there," he called.

He washed his face, dried it with paper towel and stared into the mirror. "Don't mess this up."

He walked out and smiled at Georgia. "Are we ready to go?"

She gave him a sympathetic smile. "Don't worry. People have already been saying good things."

Evan followed her into the exhibition space. There was a crowd of people there, far more than he'd expected. As he joined Georgia on the stage, he noticed there wasn't a lot of standing space left. Hopefully it would create some buzz.

He scanned the crowd, and spotted his brother with Sarah

and their parents. Karl grinned at him and gave him the thumbs up. Evan smiled, some of the nerves calming.

Georgia began to speak and he turned his attention to her.

"I'm so pleased to be bringing you this exhibition. When my colleague told me about an artist he'd seen in Houston and showed me some of his work, I knew immediately I had to have him. His art draws you in, has you feeling the experience and touching part of you. He doesn't just capture a landscape, he captures its soul. I challenge you to look at his paintings and *not* feel something. Trust me when I say, you will want one of his works in your house. But enough from me. Let me introduce you to the man himself, Evan Hayes."

There was a round of applause and Evan stepped forward to the microphone. Georgia had told him to talk about one of his paintings and he'd chosen the one in the square. It was the only painting that didn't have some kind of connection to Carly.

"Thank you. I'm not sure I deserve those platitudes from Georgia, you'll have to make up your own minds." He gazed around the crowd and saw polite interest. "My painting 'The Square' is of somewhere you might recognize. It's in New York, not far from this gallery, and it was where I spent every weekend as a teenager. It's so familiar to me that I could paint it without a photo. I used to love watching people go by, and drawing them, and it didn't take long before people would stop, see what I was doing, and ask me to draw them."

Someone in the crowd gasped and murmured to the person next to her. Perhaps she remembered him.

"So I spent my weekends drawing and earning money doing what I loved."

There was movement at the back of the room as a latecomer arrived. The bright emerald green of her dress caught his attention. His breath caught.

Carly.

She was wearing her favorite color and her hair fell in riotous curls around her face. It was the first time she'd been out in public without straightening her hair. And she'd come to see him.

She gave him a small smile.

But she'd been in Houston. How had she gotten here?

Georgia cleared her throat, and Evan realized everyone was waiting for him to continue. His heart beat faster and he focused. "Thank you so much for coming and I hope you enjoy my work." He stepped back.

There was polite applause and the crowd split into smaller groups. Evan wanted to run over to Carly, but as he moved off the stage, he was stopped by a man.

"Evan, my name is Sergio Abate."

The name stopped him in his tracks. Sergio was the curator for one of the biggest galleries in New York. Evan shook his hand. "Pleased to meet you."

"I really love your work. You trained at the Rhode Island School of Design, didn't you?"

Amazed the man knew even that much about him, Evan nodded, glancing to see where Carly was. She was standing in front of the painting of her mother.

"Georgia has been raving about you, so I had to come. What other work have you done? What's your favorite medium?"

He had to focus. "I love oils, but I like experimenting with different media as well. I tend to do a lot of sketches before I do the painting."

Sergio raised an eyebrow. "And what do you do with the sketches?"

"They're in a folder at home."

"I'd love to see them." He handed Evan a card. "I won't take more of your time now, but call me during the week, and we can talk."

"Thank you." Sergio walked away and Evan clutched the card. Wow. Only in his wildest dreams had that conversation ever taken place. He couldn't get over his luck. He grinned and then saw the green out of the corner of his eye.

Carly.

He turned, but it wasn't her. It was another woman who wanted to talk to him. When he extricated himself from her, he spotted Carly and was halfway across the room when someone else stopped him. He met Carly's eyes and she nodded at him, encouraging him to talk with the people. She understood. Of course she did. This was her life. Not being able to do what she wanted to do.

He understood that now.

He finished talking to the man and finally strode across the room. He made it to her side.

"Carly." He didn't know what else to say. He'd been an idiot. He'd said hurtful things, been a complete ass.

"Congratulations, Evan. This is a great turnout."

He nodded.

"I'm sorry I was late. There was a delay with the helicopter."

"Helicopter?" What was she talking about?

She smiled. "Turns out if you have enough money, you can hire a private jet and a helicopter in order to make it to the opening night of the exhibition of the man you love."

His heart stopped. He was sure of it. "Love?"

"I love you, Evan." Her smile wavered a little, as if she was unsure of his reaction. She took a breath and continued. "When you left without saying goodbye, I realized how hurt you were. You only wanted one thing from me, my support. I wanted to come to the exhibition, but the symposium was so important to my mother, to Zita, and to all of those girls—"

"You don't need to explain," he assured her. "If I'd let you explain back then, I would have understood. I saw your speech." His fingers curled into her hair. "It was so amazing. You needed to be there." He had to tell her why he'd behaved the way he did, but it was too crowded here, too noisy. Taking her arm, he led her outside. "I was feeling so insecure before you called, so sure the exhibition was going to be a failure. I needed reassurance and it seemed like you were rejecting me." He sighed. "I reacted instinctively, defensively. I'm sorry. My heart was breaking, but I should have trusted what we have. For the first time, I'd found someone who understood me, someone I'd fallen in love with." His heart pounded as her smile widened. "I love you so much." He wrapped his arms around her and kissed her. "I'm so sorry for how I reacted, so sorry for leaving without saying goodbye."

"I understand, really I do. I'm sorry for not explaining right away."

It was his fault, but there was no reason to harp on about it. She'd forgiven him. "I like your hair."

She reached up to touch it. "Me too. I'm not sure anyone

recognizes me. No one has spoken to me."

That would be a nice change for her.

"Where are you living now?" Her question was hesitant.

"I'm staying with my brother until I figure out where I'll go next."

"There's always a place in Houston for you," she said. "I know you don't like the penthouse, but there's some acreage I was thinking of buying. I'm considering building my own cottage."

He grinned. "That's a great idea."

"So, what do you think?" she asked. "Could you handle living with me?"

His heart couldn't get any lighter. He paused for a moment, then shook his head. "No, your mother would never approve."

She gaped at him.

"But if you married me that would probably be OK."

She did a great impression of a goldfish. Grinning, he drew her closer to him. "Marry me, Carly," he murmured. "I don't want to be away from you ever again. I want us to be together, to ignore each other while we're working and come together when we're not. You're the only person who has really understood me."

"Yes," she whispered. "Yes, I'll marry you, yes, I'll live with you, and yes, I'll ignore you when I'm working." She laughed.

His heart sang as he kissed her again. His best friend was going to marry him.

"There you are," Georgia exclaimed, coming out of the gallery. "I'm sorry to interrupt," she said, "but Evan, you need to mingle a little more."

"Absolutely," he said. "Georgia, let me introduce you to my fiancée, Carly."

"Nice to meet you." Georgia gave Carly a brief smile. "I can understand you're both excited about the exhibition, but you need to let Evan meet people."

Evan almost swallowed his tongue. Georgia had no idea who she was talking to.

"Yes, ma'am," Carly said with a grin.

He shook his head. He loved this woman. She was amazing.

He slipped his hand into hers and walked back to the

entrance. He was ready for anything. He was where he belonged. "Let's see how this goes."

ACKNOWLEDGEMENTS

As always there are many people I need to thank for helping me with my research; Dave for talking to me about painting and the different processes that can be used, Karen for answering my questions about art galleries, Randy for information about indie game development, and Carmen for the Spanish translations and information about El Salvador.

I also want to thank Ida from Amygdala Designs for the gorgeous cover, Dianne Blacklock for editing and helping me to improve the story, and Brooklyn Ann from Grammar Smith Editing Services for proofreading the book.

About the Author

Claire Boston is the best-selling author of The Texan Quartet. In 2014 she was nominated for an Australian Romance Readers Award as Favorite New Romance Author.

Her debut contemporary romance novel, What Goes on Tour caught the attention of Momentum's Joel Naoum when her first scene was read aloud at the Romance Writers' of Australia (RWA) conference in 2013. This led to a four book contract for The Texan Quartet series.

Claire is proactive in organizing social gatherings and educational opportunities for local authors. She is an active volunteer for RWA, as a mentor for aspiring authors and the reader judge coordinator.

When Claire's not reading or writing she can be found in the garden attempting to grow vegetables, or racing around a vintage motocross track. If she can convince anyone to play with her, she also enjoys cards and board games.

Claire lives in Western Australia, just south of Perth, with her husband, who loves even her most annoying quirks, and her grubby but adorable Australian bulldog.

Claire loves to hear from her readers. You can find her at her website, www.claireboston.com, on Twitter, @clairebauthor, and on Facebook www.facebook.com/clairebostonauthor. You can also join her reader group at
http://eepurl.com/Z4-4z.

Break the Rules

The Flanagan Sisters # 1

Bridget Flanagan knows how to assess risks, but are the consequences of exposing her heart too dangerous?

Bridget has a passion for safety and in the world of oil refineries that makes her great at her job. So when her big promotion goes to someone else, she heads out on the town to forget her troubles. Jack Gibbs seems like the perfect man to distract her.

At least until Monday morning when she discovers Jack is her new boss. There's no way she's going to keep seeing him, no matter the connection between them. She's been burned before.

Jack can't understand why Bridget's so against their relationship. They positively sizzled during their one night together. He knows he has to be careful now she reports to him, but she tempts him in every way.

Can Jack convince Bridget to give him a chance, or is the risk too high?

http://www.claireboston.com/books/break-the-rules/

Blaze a Trail

The Flanagan Sisters # 3

They're from the opposite ends of town but they're worlds apart.

Zita Flanagan wants more. She wants to help more Central American refugees and make more of an impact. But her family comes first and fulfilling her own dreams seems impossible.

David Randall leads a privileged life and knows nothing about refugee issues. When he meets dynamic, sexy Zita, it seems like the perfect opportunity to learn. Zita's passion for helping those less fortunate and her selfless devotion to the girls her mother fosters brings David's life sharply into perspective.

Zita soon realizes that David is so much more than a rich boy. She begins to trust him with her foster sisters' stories, and her own hopes and dreams. But when David's father announces he's running for governor and the focus of his campaign is the 'refugee problem', Zita has grave concerns for her sisters' safety. Then David's betrayal exposes secrets, and it becomes a race against time to save lives.

Can David convince Zita to trust him again, or will his mistake put the life of the woman he loves in jeopardy?

http://www.claireboston.com/books/blaze-a-trail/